SOLOMON'S ARTIFICE

CRAIG CAUDILL

CHARACTERS

<u>Artist, Hazard, Kentucky</u>

Omar Cru

<u>Music Producers, Hazard, Kentucky</u>

Abner Giles, Owner

Sadie Kirkham, Engineer

Deianira Wathen, Business Manager

<u>Sutherland Tailoring, Harrodsburg, Kentucky</u>

Marcel Sutherland, CEO

Valerie Sutherland, Marcel's Wife

Brock Skinner, Investor

<u>Vigneron Winery, Hazard, Kentucky</u>

Maude Skinner, Proprietor and Brock's Wife

Truman, German Shepherd Guard Dog

<u>Private Citizen, Richmond, Kentucky</u>

Arlena Harring

<u>Slade University Professor, Lexington, Kentucky</u>

Saul Sardis

<u>Professional Musician, Lexington, Kentucky</u>

Titus Remington

<u>Master of the House, Lexington, Kentucky</u>

Solomon Pergamos

<u>Caterer, Lexington, Kentucky</u>

Ruby Lynch

<u>Python Deco, San Jose, California</u>

Carl Logano, AI Salesman

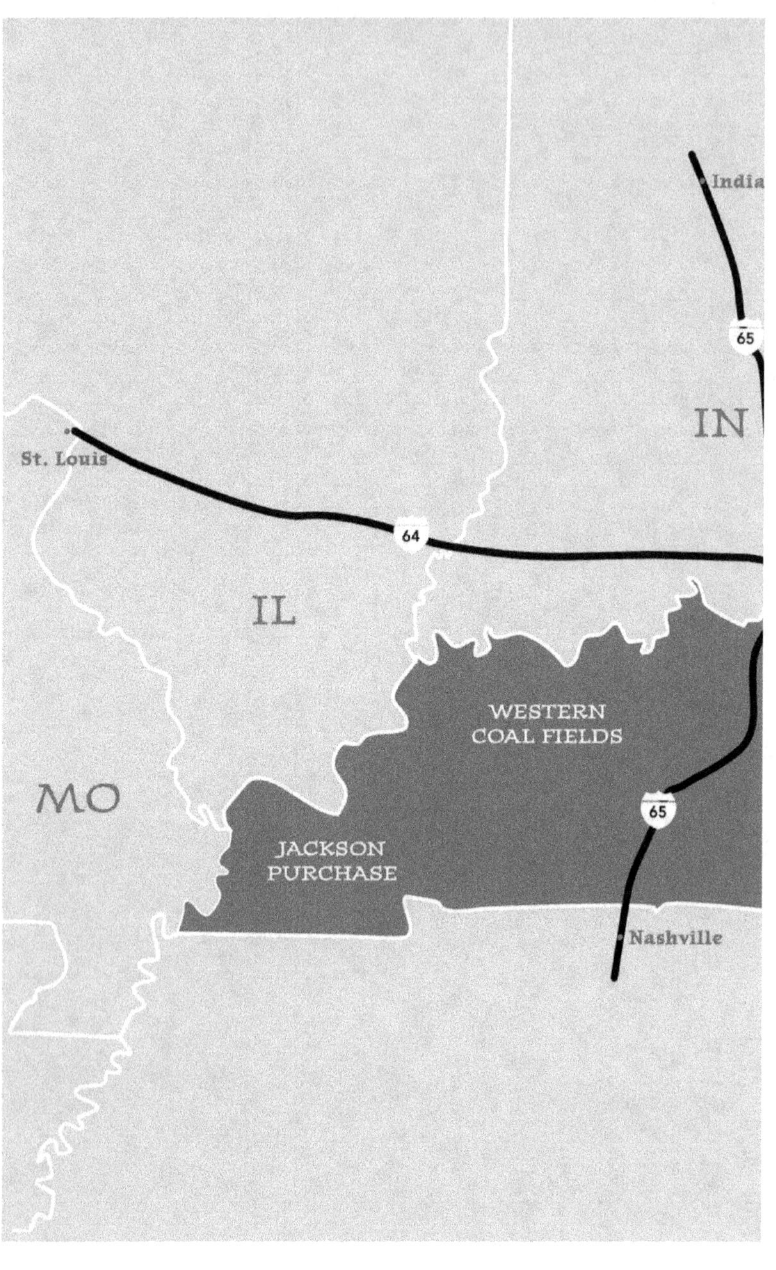

St. Louis
IL
MO
IN
India
65
64
65
WESTERN
COAL FIELDS
JACKSON
PURCHASE
Nashville

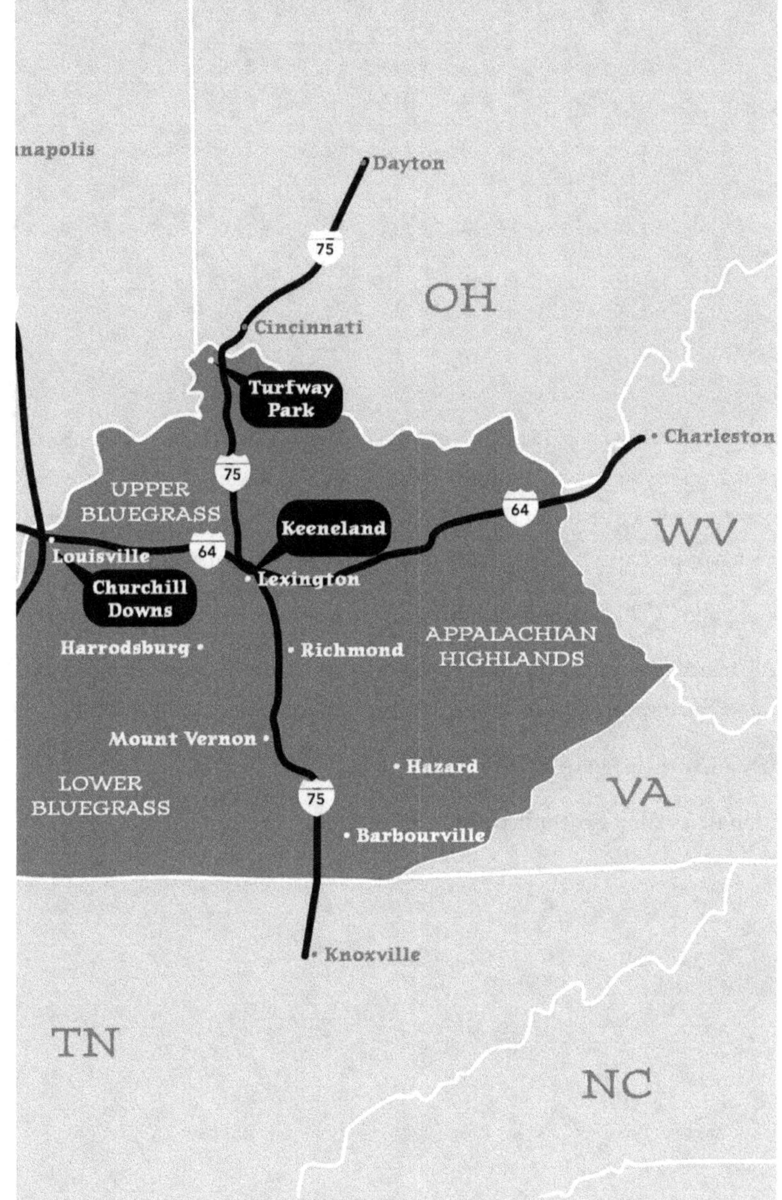
napolis
Dayton
75
OH
Cincinnati
Turfway
Park
75
UPPER
BLUEGRASS
Keeneland
64
Louisville
64
Churchill
Downs
Lexington
Harrodsburg
Richmond
APPALACHIAN
HIGHLANDS
WV
Charleston
Mount Vernon
Hazard
VA
LOWER
BLUEGRASS
75
Barbourville
Knoxville
TN
NC

For the wonderful times Jo and I had with our dance friends.

Chapter 1

The alluvial soil had been washed out down to the hardpan years ago, forming a runnel at the nadir of the pasture. Leggy sycamores lined one side of the creek, and a black rail fence across the way kept the valuable, injury-prone thoroughbreds from stumbling and getting hurt. Gliding along the fence row by shank's mare, Brock seemingly never arrived anywhere until the scene changed abruptly for no reason. He was now shadowing a brawny man wearing khakis and a yellow, nylon windbreaker. Reaching the top of the hill, the two of them were floating in front of a white, concrete-block barn that had six stalls and one horse in residence.

The empty pen to the right featured a tarnished brass plaque mounted at eye level that read: MAN O' WAR, THE GREATEST RACEHORSE–21 STARTS, 20 WINS. He barely lost one race because he carried fifteen pounds more than the colt who beat him. A plaque to the left read: SILKY SULLIVAN, THE GREATEST CLOSER–27 STARTS, 12 WINS. The stalker once made up forty-one lengths on the way to victory, running the last two panels in twenty-two seconds. Stall three proclaimed: SECRETARIAT, THE FASTEST RACEHORSE–21 STARTS, 16 WINS. He set the track record in each of his Triple Crown races.

The fourth cubicle, also horseless, extolled the virtue of JOHN HENRY, THE DURABLE RACEHORSE–83 STARTS, 39 WINS. Popular track announcer Dave Johnson once exclaimed, "And down the stretch they come! The old man, John Henry, takes command!" The fifth stall in the barn told the story of CIGAR, THE WIN-STREAK RACEHORSE–33 STARTS, 19 WINS. He finished first in sixteen straight races from October of 1994 to July of 1996, making him the top money winner of the century.

The man in yellow slipped his thick hand into his jacket pocket and pulled out a peppermint. He unwrapped it as he got near the Dutch door of the end stall. The plaque read: MR. PROSPECTOR, THE GREATEST STUD–14 STARTS, 7 WINS. He sired twelve hundred foals, often "covering" two mares a day. Over fifteen percent were listed as black-type thoroughbreds. All twenty horses in the 2018 Kentucky Derby claimed Mr. Prospector in their lineage.

Brock magically found himself in the stall beside the horse. A boogle of weasels were wrestling in the back corner, disheveling the ankle-deep straw. Mr. Prospector stepped toward the stable door to clamp onto the peppermint. His eyes were droopy and runny, and more pathetically, he was drooling uncontrollably because of his age. He crushed the candy with what teeth he had left and swung his head around to see who was next to him. The once-great stud's sad and lonely expression jarred Brock awake.

The Skinners would pull out at ten o'clock that late October Saturday and return by midnight, Lord willing. When Maude stepped into the kitchen wearing a dark, two-tone blue dress fit for a model, she asked her husband, "Have you been studying the racing form?"

Brock drank in her beauty, straightened the floppy bifold tabloid he was reading, and replied, "As we speak. You look gorgeous." He got up to refill his cup of coffee and prepare a cup for her the way she liked it. "I had a weird horse dream last night. I hope it's a good omen."

"Were you standing at the window cashing a big ticket?" She crossed her arms and hunched her shoulders.

"No. I was given a tour of the horse hall of fame. Maude, do you think artificial intelligence will be able to dream?"

She took the cup of coffee he offered, which was resting on his palm with the handle facing her. "I certainly hope not. Dreams happen when the brain is off duty. I don't think machines know how to play." She gave him a bumptious look.

———

Maude Skinner's Vigneron Winery, built from scratch a few years ago on a hillside overlooking downtown Hazard, Kentucky, had finally gained a reputation for producing tremendous wines. No one expected anything less. She and her husband, Brock, were loaded, and the place had been developed properly, without cutting corners or rushing the clock. If they couldn't make good wines, nobody in Appalachia could.

Maude's brother, Marcel Sutherland, started an online clothing business after graduating from college, and to get the company off the ground, Brock Skinner gave him some seed money he inherited from his grandparents in exchange for half interest in the clever enterprise. Both men became wealthy when sales shot through the roof. Marcel recently married Valerie Goddard, a sweet, unpretentious girl from New Mexico, and the Skinners and Sutherlands were joining forces for a big day at the track followed by dinner and dancing.

Brock glanced up at the sky as he pulled away from the log cabin that he and his wife lived in behind the grapevines of the winery. High, wispy clouds were being pushed along by a potent wind, not disruptive enough to dampen the afternoon activities at Keeneland, where people would walk around, drink bourbon, and bet on the ponies while folks seated indoors, dressed in monkey suits, would crane their necks to see the action on overhead TVs.

Decked out in a houndstooth jacket and yellow knit tie, Brock drove his Lamborghini up onto I-75 northbound. Maude said, "Oh, I forgot to tell you what happened right before we closed yesterday."

"What's that?"

"A raconteur driving an ostentatious, metallic-copper Bentley parked by the door and marched in like he owned the place."

Brock smiled. "I wonder what part of the world he came from?"

"Believe it or not, he just finished building a big place on a mountain ridge across the way from the winery."

"Did he tell you that?" Brock raised his elbows and gripped the steering wheel firmly.

"He led me out onto the veranda and pointed at it. I could barely see a far-off white building among the trees." She stuck her legs out, pressed the floorboard, and put her hands on her knees.

"Nobody with a Bentley builds a house overlooking Hazard," he said with a sour expression.

"Well, you're going to find out. He asked to have six cases of our best wines delivered there on Monday. I figured you'd drive them over."

"Just remember, if anything happens, you're the one who started it."

Maude put her left hand on the back of his neck and squeezed. "And you will not pack a pistol when you go."

"Why? Is it not permitted by the employee handbook?" He clutched his face with his left hand and kept his right hand on the steering wheel.

"It's not permitted by me." She shook his neck and pulled her hand back.

"Careful, you'll mess up my tie." Secretly, Brock couldn't wait to check the place out. "Did this cat give his name?"

"Yes. Abner Giles."

Brock punched a button on the steering wheel to place a call to his brother-in-law, Marcel. "Hey, when are you guys leaving?"

"A little less than an hour." Marcel, from experience, knew something off the wall was coming.

Brock quietly asked his wife, "How old is this guy?"

"Late forties."

"Marcel, see if you can find anything on an Abner Giles before you leave. Late forties. He just built a house not far from the winery. Drives a Bentley. I smell a rat."

Marcel's company, Sutherland Tailoring, had the most sophisticated computers in the world. They could hack into almost any database out there. "You always smell a rat. What's his claim to fame?"

"He breezed in yesterday and asked Maude to send over the best wines she has."

"Okay. I'll see what I can find. We'll catch you at noon."

"I'm counting on you to pick the winners," Brock remarked before he hung up.

———————

Their table on the third floor, overlooking the paddock, was primo for checking out the horses parading in a circle before a race and watching people flouncing around, taking in all the action while slowly getting drunk. A panoply of colors made the elegant facility special: jockeys' silks, numbered saddle cloths on the thoroughbreds, and the vibrant clothing upwardly mobile racegoers dared to wear. Dark green trim on the smoky stone buildings, green infield grass, and brown track dirt were the perfect backdrop for the bright splashes of color seen all around.

Marcel's wife, Valerie, had something else on her mind. She fixed her eyes on Brock and said, "Do you think horseracing is dying?"

He didn't respond at first, gathering his thoughts. "Dying implies it will cease to be."

Valerie had on a purple, ruffled lamé dress that was holographic. It looked spectacular on her. "That's what I meant. With the publicized deaths in the sport, it would seem the end is near."

Maude and Marcel were listening but offered nothing. The server came and introduced himself. Horses for the first race had reached the paddock area, and the jockeys were getting a leg up. Brock said, "There will always be horseracing somewhere in the world. It doesn't require fancy betting machines to handle the action. After all, the sport was borne out of gambling."

"Beyond the death of the horses, I thought some other factors might spell doom for the sport," Valerie added.

"And what would those be?" her husband asked.

"Other things vying for the betting dollar, and the fact that people don't seem to want to get dressed up and go out anymore."

"You're on to something there," Maude said as she nodded her head rapidly.

The four of them went to the window by their table to watch the nine horses in the first race go through the tunnel out to the track. It was twelve minutes until post time. Marcel announced, "I'm betting a three-over-five exacta."

Brock handed him a twenty-dollar bill. "Bet the same for me." He addressed Valerie: "There are fifty thousand people killed on the roads every year. What if there was an Amber alert every ten minutes showing the crash scene of each death? Would we stop driving cars?"

"Probably not, but something to reduce the deaths would likely be done," she replied.

"And that's probably the way it'll go in horseracing."

"I'd hate to see the beautiful horse farms in this area lose their luster," Maude lamented.

Marcel offered, "Would be a big blow to Kentucky if horseracing took a dive."

Brock sat back down and said, "I don't know. Seventy years ago, tobacco was grown all over the place. Now you rarely see it. The state has adapted."

Maude returned to the table and said summarily, "Nonetheless, thoroughbreds are powerful, majestic animals. I'd sure miss coming out to see them compete."

The server took their lunch orders. At post time, the foursome moved out to the grandstand rail to watch the race live. The first and second finishers, 3–5, matched the tickets they held. A twenty-dollar bet paid $319.43.

As the afternoon wore on, the two couples gave back some of their winnings until the fifth race, when the table hauled in a thousand dollars. Maude said to Valerie, "I say we go down to the art tent and see what we can find."

After the girls were out of earshot, Brock asked Marcel, "Did you spade up anything on this Abner Giles character?"

"I only had twenty minutes. Found quite a bit though."

"Why are you keeping me in suspense?" Brock trifled.

"He seemed boring until I looked at his 1040 from last year. Abner lived the first forty-five years of his life on Radcliff Drive in Brentwood, Tennessee, a southern suburb of Nashville. He studied music at nearby Ensworth High School and went on to take classes at the Dark Horse Institute to learn sound engineering. He worked at Bluebird Studio for a few years before he quit there and started living off his equity interests in several companies."

"Equity interests?" Brock sat up and frowned.

"Yeah. He has stock in fourteen LLCs that threw off various amounts of money last year, which added up to over a million dollars."

"What do these corporations do?"

Marcel tilted his head and looked grimly at the ceiling. "Hell, I don't know. What do you expect in twenty minutes?"

"Sorry." Brock threw down the program he was holding and popped the clutch in his head.

It took Maude and Valerie several minutes to get into the art tent because of its popularity and narrow footpath. Once inside, they casually perused the mediocre equestrian art on both sides of the aisle. On the end wall, an interesting painting caught Maude's eye. She stepped in closer to see if she could figure out how it was made. "Look, Valerie, that's gouache on wood."

"In the style of Klee and Kandinsky," she replied.

"With a little Klimt thrown in." The painting, 38" X 46," had a red, wooden frame. The two main elements were a horse and big tree, straight out of Brock's dream. Other objects were sprinkled around, not to mention every color imaginable. "It's an original by, from the signature, a chap named Omar Cru."

"Proud of his work. He's asking eighty-five hundred for it," Valerie said derisively.

"Cheap at that price, don't you think?" Maude voiced her contradictory opinion.

A prim beanpole of a woman wearing a khaki dress faintly reminiscent of a girl scout uniform moved in behind Maude and commented, "If you're interested in that, you better buy it now. I'm surprised it's still here."

Maude grinned her off and said, "What a salesperson you are. I believe I *will* take it, provided you have the papers to prove its authenticity and provenance."

"But of course. Are you not familiar with Omar Cru?"

"No. Fill me in."

"He's all the rage. This is his sixteenth Kentucky piece, and the last that'll go for under twenty grand," the woman remarked with confidence.

Valerie wove her arms and thrust her head forward. "I need to bone up on my art."

"Where does Mr. Cru come from?" Maude asked.

"Someone told me he has a studio in the mountains near Hazard."

Maude snapped her head in the direction of the slight woman and declared, "You don't say."

CHAPTER 2

The treacherous gravel road up the craggy hillside, when first cut in, was patently unsafe. After Omar Cru sold the other end of the ridge to Abner Giles, Giles widened and paved the steep driveway to haul materials up to a construction site, where he built a palooza of a home. That occurrence had been a boon for Omar since snow marooned him above Hazard during the two winters he lived there before Giles upgraded the two-house neighborhood by fixing the road and running electricity, gas, and water lines.

Omar's place to the left at the top of the mountain, technically an art studio—best characterized as a high-class Appalachian shack—was far enough away from whatever it was Giles built to the right to not reflect poorly on his neighbor's creation, now up and running, with a wrought-iron gate blocking anyone from approaching unannounced.

Omar Cru was well on his way to the big time and, so far, had only made sixteen of his paintings available to the public. One hundred seventy-seven more were queued up, waiting to be moved at the right time. He figured his works would sell for a quarter of a million apiece within a year, and by that time, he'd upgrade his domicile to make it more attractive to female acquaintances, along with the handsome nature of his bank account.

Before Giles came around, Cru put in a cistern, septic tank, propane gas tank, and generator. He built his cabin with the belief that having public utilities, like the townsfolk had, was not in the cards until he became rich. Thanks to Giles, however, his studio gained access to the modern conveniences of city life quicker than expected, which allowed him to accelerate his timetable.

A satellite dish anchored to the roof of the shack powered a big-screen TV tuned to the racing channel covering Keeneland. Omar checked to see how many minutes to post before the sixth race. If it was about to go off, he'd stand there and watch it, and then head out back to find birds to photograph among the deciduous trees that had changed colors and evergreens offering stark contrast. The horses stood in the gate and soon were off. He quit watching when the number four horse cleared the field by ten lengths in the homestretch.

The baguette-shaped mountain ridge dropped off sharply a hundred yards behind Cru's cabin. The soil up there was sparse, mainly found in fissures of rock. To his delight, Omar came upon a male yellow finch clutching a branch of a dwarf maple tree that had turned deep red for the fall, surrounded by scruffy Virginia junipers. Finches were usually gone by that time of year. The wind had calmed, and the light was right. Distinctive barbules on the bird's feathers added texture to the little animal and would translate well in a painting.

Once back inside, Omar's cell phone rang. "Hello," he answered soberly.

"Is this Mr. Cru?"

"Yes." He glanced at the TV. The featured eighth race would be running in ten minutes.

"This is Connie from the art shop at Keeneland. I wanted to tell you we've sold your painting for eighty-five hundred dollars."

"Ah. I'm guessing you're calling to see if I'll replace it with another one."

"Naturally, that would be a good way for you to get more exposure," she replied smoothly.

"I agree. The piece I have for you this time is priced considerably higher than the one you just sold. It's larger and has more detail."

"Oh, I predicted that. Have you thought about putting your works up for auction with us so we can learn their true market value? Our bidders have lots of money," she said solicitously.

"All in due time, Connie. Did you get the name and address of the buyer?"

"Yes. Her name is Maude Skinner. Oddly enough, she lives in Hazard."

Omar padded to the short front window of the shack, squinted his eyes, and crouched to find Vigneron Winery on the hillside across town. He spotted it and said, "I've heard of her."

Connie remarked, "She's a tall, beautiful woman. Had on a three-thousand-dollar dress."

"Not surprising. I've been told her wines are the best in the area." Omar heard a car pulling up. "I trust you'll be sending my check?"

"It'll go out Monday. Good day, Mr. Cru."

Omar waited patiently to be summoned by the visitor. When he opened the door, there stood Abner Giles. He wasn't Colonel Parker but was a slant on the genus at 6 feet 2 inches and 240 pounds. He wore brown ostrich cowboy boots, creased blue jeans, and a caramel-colored crepe shirt that called attention to his ostrich belt. His bare pate revealed a case of alopecia, with a few strands of sandy-colored hair standing up like rampikes in a burnt-down forest. A matching ten-gallon hat would fix that, Omar surmised. "Hello, Abner. What can I do for you?"

"May I come in?" Abner's eyes sparkled as he stepped over the threshold without permission.

"Certainly. I'm getting ready to watch the feature race at Keeneland. I drew one of the horses entered."

"You mean like in a betting pool?" Giles asked.

Omar, with a humorous expression, turned to face Abner. "No, I mean I did a painting of him."

"Oh. Do you still have the painting?"

"I do." He pointed at the TV and said, "They're in the starting gate."

Giles crossed his arms and leaned back on his heels. "What number is the horse?"

"Two." The nine thoroughbreds sprang free. "Come on, two!" Omar belted.

The horse rated easily with the speed on the backstretch and fired in the homestretch to win by three lengths. Abner commented cheerfully, "I guess your painting just increased in value. What's his name, anyway?"

"Chuzzing," Omar replied as he strolled over to his studio in the back corner of the main room. An easel in front of a worn-smooth leather stool had on it a painting in progress. Brushes of various sizes were in a Ball Mason jar next to tubes of pigment.

"Huh?" Giles uttered.

"The name's a portmanteau. It means the process of backward chaining using fuzzy math." He kept up his search for the horse picture.

"You know something about artificial intelligence I take it."

"I worked for a software company until four years ago when I quit to follow my dream of being a successful artist. That's when I bought this land and built this studio."

Giles stood next to the unfinished work on the easel. He peered at it critically for a time. "What style of art is this?"

"Expressionism, symbolism, abstraction." Omar lifted the horse painting from a rack, spinning it around for Giles to see.

"That could be any horse. This picture you're doing here doesn't look like oil on canvas." He ran his fingers down the edge of the board on the easel.

Omar announced, "It's gouache."

"What's that?"

"Water-based paint with gum Arabic as a binder. It's watercolor with a load of pigment, not as finely ground. The colors are opaque and more vibrant. I apply them on wood instead of cloth canvas. It tends to give the content more texture." He picked up a tube of pigment and waved it around.

Giles inspected the horse painting carefully. "The more I look at it, the better I like it. You want to sell it?"

"Abner, let me tell you that in a couple of years, I expect my art to skyrocket in value, so if you buy it, somebody will be calling you wanting to pay ten times what you'll pay me for it now."

"You sound like a huckster, but I'll bite." Giles retreated to the sitting room by the front door. "How much do you want for it?"

"Twenty-five thousand." Omar didn't care if Giles bought it or not.

"Will cash be acceptable? I'll run to the house and get it."

"Yes, sir." Omar carried the painting over to the door and leaned it on the wall. "Here, take it with you. Better yet, I'll bring it to your house. You've never shown me around inside. I'd like to see it."

Giles replied seriously, "That's for a reason. My place is a confidential location for an event that will be happening soon. Afterward, I'll invite you over for a fancy dinner."

"It'll be hard to keep the event secret from me. There's only one way up here," Omar reminded him.

Giles took the painting and walked out. He said over his shoulder, "I'll be back with your cash in a few minutes."

Omar waited for Abner's car to disappear before he went to the wall behind his studio. He took a set of keys out of his pocket to open a brown steel door. The cabin had been built around a fireproof room. A computer, printer, all but a few of Omar's completed paintings, and several in progress were inside to keep them safe. He downloaded the finch pictures, picking out the best one to be printed on large paper. Satisfied with the quality, he set the print on a side table and locked the room when he left it.

Abner came back and handed over the money, saying, "I've found the perfect place to hang it. I think you'll approve." When he started to swing his leg back into the Bentley, he said, "If you've got any more paintings you want to part with, trot them out and I'll run and get more cash."

"I've got a better idea. Why don't you pick a subject matter and I'll paint five in a series for you." Cru walked closer to the Bentley in a gesture of eagerness.

"Hey, that's a great idea. Could they be musicians playing their instruments?" Abner propped one arm on the roof of the car and the other on the top of the door.

"Sure. They'll be abstract. I'll have to work from good photographs."

"How long would it take you?"

"I can crank one out every two or three days." Omar smiled and put his hands on his hips. "How does eighty thousand for the set sound?"

Giles scratched his head and looked at the sky. "I'm going to have to trust they'll be good. I guess I can go for that."

"Tell you what. If you don't want them, I'll sell them to someone else." Omar seemed slighted.

"Okay, let me run back over to the house again and grab pictures of the guys." He didn't knock when he returned. Omar got up from the couch to see what Giles had brought. The photos were high-quality shots of five men playing their instruments: a drummer, organist, two guitar players, and a bassist who was singing.

"I can make these work. I take it you're going to hang them in your house. If so, how big do you want them to be?"

"Three feet by four feet. Can you make them that big?" Giles asked, fearing rejection.

"I can and will. Who are these guys?"

"Musician friends of mine. Four live in Nashville. What makes them special is they can mimic any style and sight-read any score without practicing it."

"What's this guy's name?" Omar pointed at the picture of the bass player.

"Titus Remington. He goes by Remy. His friends call him T Rem."

"Maybe he should buy Chuzzing. They'd make a fine pair." The men broke out in laughter.

Abner added, "You should hear him sing. He sounds like Tom Jones."

"And how is that?"

"He's a robust baritone with the dramatic agility of a tenor. You would need to know something about music to understand what I'm talking about," Abner replied almost apologetically.

Omar took the slicks of the musicians and laid them on the leather stool. "I'll take your word for it. Maybe someday when I hear him, I'll get the picture. That was a pun. Did you get it?"

"What do you take me for?" Giles threw his arms to the side and widened his eyes. "Of course, I got it."

Omar barked, "Why don't you get out of here so I can get started on your project."

"When you've finished the first one, come over and buzz me on the gate speaker." Giles waited for a reply.

Cru gave him one: "I will."

———————

The last race of the day at Keeneland was a sideshow because of the mass exodus of the crowd. Maude said to her husband, "The painting I bought is down by the car park. Are we ready?"

"Yes. I took care of the bill. This has been a delightful time, and we won a little money," Brock reported in the happiest tone he could muster.

Marcel asked his sister, "Who did you say the artist was?"

"His name is Omar Cru. His studio's in Hazard."

Marcel looked at his brother-in-law. Keeping his hands low, bouncing them in a tamping action, Marcel said dramatically, "I know. You want me to find out about this dude, and what the Sam Hill he's doing in Perry County."

Brock's happy tone left him faster than an exorcised demon. "In a single day, I learn that two peculiar characters have dropped anchor near the winery. I'm not going to think the worst yet. One of them is driving a Bentley, and the other is an artist my wife likes."

Valerie pushed back: "You drive a Lamborghini. What's the difference?"

"I'm an upstanding citizen. Everybody knows that."

Maude said, "Everybody? Really?"

Marcel was madly tapping his cell phone with his finger. "What's the name of this place we're going?"

Maude answered, "The Silk Cravat. Do you have the address?"

"I do." Marcel's red Mercedes was brought up before the Lamborghini. The parking attendant opened and closed the passenger door for Valerie, and then scurried around to the driver's side to buck for a tip. "I don't remember ever going there."

Brock said comically, "It's a big boot scoot barn for redneck men and desperate women. We're overdressed."

"Stop it." Maude gave her husband a dirty look. She yelled out, "You'll be impressed."

Marcel was just about to get into his car when he stopped abruptly, paused, and held his phone high in the air. "Brock, I'm not sure if I should tell you this now, or when we get there."

"What? You might as well tell me." He saw the Lamborghini approaching, as did the rest of the people waiting.

"Omar Cru, artist in residence, lives next door to Abner Giles."

"For crying out loud!"

Maude loaded her purchase in the trunk of the car while her husband was acting childishly.

The two vehicles worked their way over to the interstate, headed for the Silk Cravat.

Chapter 3

Sixty miles south of Lexington, the little town of Mount Vernon, west of I-75, got its name from General George Washington's farm. Settled in 1790, things picked up when the L&N Railroad put a spur there for the train from Louisville to Knoxville. Among the three thousand people now living in the area, all were white. Diversity hit town when the Silk Cravat held a dinner dance featuring a live band. Ideally situated between the Skinner and Sutherland residences, the ride home was less than an hour for each couple.

"The Cravat," as it was referred to, occupied an old, two-story, brick building. The storefront had been converted into a white tablecloth eatery, and the floor upstairs with its raised bandstand was primed for action. The front two-thirds of the downstairs had twenty-five tables for four. The kitchen across the back was run like a banquet operation, trotting out beef and fish along with vegetables favored by Kentuckians. Events, once announced, sold out in twenty-four hours.

A small slice of America still practiced ballroom dancing, mostly retired people in their seventies who intended to go out swinging. Some were kooks, some lonely, many were socialites, but all loved to pop out there, break the calcium loose, and get a little exercise. Showboats looking to bolster their egos came around as well. They had something to prove, but the live-and-let-live hoofers paid no attention to them.

Fewer young people were dancing these days. That thought came to Brock when he and his wife were fifteen minutes north of Mount Vernon. "What Valerie said about horseracing got me thinking about ballroom dancing. Should we put a death watch on it too?"

"Honey, your mind runs to the suspicious and negative occasionally. Why would you ponder the fate of ballroom dancing right before we're set to have a bang-up time out on the tiles? The future is just an illusion. There is only the here and now. It isn't dead, so hold that discussion until we're at the winery doing jobs we don't particularly enjoy."

"Let me rephrase what I meant to say: I hope ballroom dancing is still going when we're in our seventies because I love dancing with you. Heck, I just love you, period."

She put her hand on her forehead and said, "And I love you. You *are* a piece of work."

An asphalt lot next to the venue held a dozen cars. The other twenty would have to park on the street. Brock took a spot beyond the front door that had an open space behind it for Marcel. A local farmer in a rusty, red truck rubbernecked as he went by, wondering what had attracted all that expensive rolling stock to town.

As they were walking in, Maude piped up, "Doesn't that dress look fabulous on Valerie?"

Marcel jumped in. "Not only does she look fabulous, she *is* fabulous." Valerie gazed skyward and shook her head.

Brock ran around in front of her and said, "No, it's true, Val. I say, without fear of contradiction, that you are the second most fabulous woman in the whole wide world."

Valerie stopped, turned around, and asked Maude, "Do you think Mount Vernon runs taxis?" The four of them tittered in unison. The two parking spots by the front door had traffic cones to reserve the spaces for VIPs.

Couples dressed to the nines were streaming in now. Two-thirds arrived in German cars. Marcel got the attention of the dapper host and gave him a name for the reservation. Most seats were filled, and they were given a table in the middle of the room. Sconces on the windowless side walls began to cozy up the atmosphere inside as darkness set in outside.

"Marcel, did you notice how many people drive Mercedes?" Brock asked.

"There's a reason." He looked over his shoulder, afraid someone might hear him. "It's the best car on the road."

"I beg to differ. It's the best affordable car on the road," Brock corrected him, looking earnestly at his wife and sister-in-law. "Valerie, a little birdy told me you taught ballroom dancing in your spare time when you lived in New Mexico."

"I did. I was trying to meet men but soon found that to be a bad idea. I won't bore you with the details."

Brock sat up and said, "Okay. Bore us then with the details of ballroom dancing."

Valerie shrugged. "I'm not sure I know what I'm talking about. I've drawn my own conclusions, and some of them might be wrong." She took a breath and started in: "While England, Portugal, and Spain were trying to take over the world during the 1600s, Vienna became the epicenter of classical music and ballroom dancing."

Maude asked, "Should I be taking notes?"

Valerie ignored the question and prattled on: "Piano key patterns were standardized, and music time signatures had been formalized by then. The waltz, first seen in Paris, was introduced with a step pattern of one-two-three, four-five-six. When the tempo increased, the dance morphed into the Viennese waltz. In the beginning, all dances traveled counterclockwise around the room."

"Then what happened?" Marcel baited.

"Well, the peasants out in the country wanted to dance too. The music sped up even more and two/four cut time had to be used for the step pattern of one-and-two, three-and-four, which became the polka. This rapid-fire step caught on, and the use of syncopation would be incorporated in future music and dances."

Brock put his arms on the table and leaned forward. "What then?"

"The samba. It adopted the one-and-two, three-and-four syncopated timing of the polka and looked like a jazzed-up waltz. The problem was that Latin dance clubs didn't approve of traveling dances. They wanted them to be done on a spot, so the samba, done in place, developed into a step pattern like a person jumping back and forth over a mud puddle in the street.

"Next came the foxtrot based on four/four common time: slow-slow-quick-quick, slow-quick-quick, and quick-quick-quick-quick. The waltz, polka, samba, and foxtrot became the most prevalent traveling dances on the ballroom circuit. There are a few others like the tango and quickstep, but those, in my opinion, aren't worth the effort to learn."

"It seems there are several other spot dances these days," Maude reported.

"Right, like the swing, the most popular dance of all. It was initially based on an eight count, one-and-two-three-four-five-and-six-seven-eight. This is now called Lindy timing. Early dance teachers found that step pattern too hard to learn, so they dumbed it down to a six count, one-two-three-and-four-five-and-six. That means every other repeating pattern does not start on the down beat in four/four time. No one particularly cares. The faster tempo swing is known as East Coast, and the slower version, West Coast."

Marcel asked, "But what about the other Latin spot dances?"

"All are based on medium tempo common time. The rumba is slow-quick-quick, and when the music slows, it turns into the bolero. The mambo is two-three-four, six-seven-eight. The salsa is quick-quick-slow, and the cha-cha adds syncopation at the end of each four beats as one-two-three-four-and-five-six-seven-eight-and.

"Finally, there is the disco dance known as the hustle. New dancers should start there. The step pattern is rock-step-march-march, or the syncopated version is one-and-two-three-and-four. Is that enough for now?"

Brock said, "If I heard you right, a person, at a minimum, should know the waltz, foxtrot, swing, rumba, cha-cha, and hustle to have fun at a ballroom dance."

"That's fair. One more thing: you were talking about German cars earlier. They, and ballroom dancing, are linked to the Aryan race. When we studied extraterrestrial beings in Roswell, my colleagues considered Aryans to be from outer space."

"Ooh, that's not good," Marcel uttered.

Couples began drifting upstairs as they finished eating. Maude pointed to a table she thought would be a good home base. Dancers were putting on their dance shoes.

Ten six-tops with black plastic tablecloths were perpendicular to both mirrored side walls. The brown plank floor, redolent of pine, creaked and sank when stepped on. The bandstand across the back had instruments on it, ready to be played, but there wasn't a musician in sight. When the full cast of dancers had moved upstairs, they began congregating on the floor.

At 8:08 p.m., five middle-aged men came out from behind the stage wearing silver paisley blazers, black collared shirts, and black jeans. They took up their instruments, and the keyboard player spoke into a mike: "On the Beat is our name. We hope you enjoy our dance music." When the crowd recognized the song as a swing, everyone jumped into action.

The Skinners stayed on the floor for the first five numbers: swing, foxtrot, salsa, waltz, and cha-cha. Valerie and Marcel bailed out one dance earlier. When Brock sat down next to Valerie, she leaned over to his ear and said, "Something strange is going on."

"What do you mean?"

"Every player in this band is a professional. The music is the tightest I've ever heard. Each guy up there wouldn't consider a gig for less than three grand. Do the math."

Brock thought she was starting to sound like him. "Okay. A hundred people are here at two hundred per head. The take is twenty thousand. Feeding everyone costs four thousand, and with a thousand in overhead, which would leave fifteen thousand. You're saying this bunch wants at least that much to get out of bed?"

"Precisely."

Brock glanced at the band and grabbed his chin. "I can think of two possibilities: they're taking less for a reason, or someone else is paying the difference."

Maude, sitting across the table, said to her husband, "Do a mambo with Valerie while I dance with Marcel."

Valerie kept up the conversation out on the floor. "And have you noticed every guy up there is sight-reading sheet music, even the drummer? What kind of a dance band does that?"

"A damn good one."

The band took a break promptly at nine o'clock. Dancers stood around and mingled with one another near their tables. Maude said to Brock, "I've noticed two women over there who are here together without dance partners." She pointed at them discreetly. "I want you to ask them to dance."

Brock swiveled his head and replied, "They don't look like stalkers, so I guess there's no harm in it."

"Take Marcel with you for protection if you want."

Marcel heard his name. "What did I do?"

"It's not what you did, it's what you're going to do. Your sister is volunteering us to dance with those two fine ladies over there." Brock nodded in their direction.

Valerie added, "That's so us fine ladies over here can dance with other men."

"Ah, I should have known."

After the ten-minute break, the band got right back at it. The rumba number they were playing made conversation easy between partners. The girl Brock asked to dance said familiarly, "My name's Arlena Harring. What's yours?"

"Brock Skinner."

"I happened to notice the lady you're with. Is she your wife?"

"Indeed."

Arlena didn't act the least bit disappointed. "She's attractive, and a good dancer. You're lucky to have such a wonderful partner."

"How about you? Yours couldn't make it this evening?"

"No. He doesn't dance. Where are you folks from?"

"Hazard. My wife owns and runs Vigneron Winery there."

"Oh, that's interesting." She flashed a cryptic smile.

Arlena was a marvelous dancer, able to follow Brock's every lead. "Where are you from?"

"Richmond. I work for a big art supply store."

He kept the happy chatter going, asking, "Are you an artist yourself?"

"No, my boyfriend is."

"He's the one who doesn't dance." Brock smiled congenially.

"Right." The music ended. They thanked each other and separated.

Back at the table, Valerie said, "I was watching you. Those girls can dance." The four of them sat around and made small talk for a couple of numbers, and then cut the rug again until the ten o'clock break.

At 10:10 p.m., the start of the last set, the band broke into a bluesy West Coast. The guy playing base guitar next to the drummer in the back sang the lead vocal. It was the first time he'd opened his mouth. The crowd pressed up to the stage like at a rock concert. When the singer finished the number, everyone clapped. It had become obvious that this band was more than just a hack outfit working for meal money.

Brock said to Marcel, "I'm going to run down to the street and get the license numbers of the cars parked by the door."

"What cars?"

"I'm sure the band members pulled up at 8:05 in two cars, and at 11:01, they'll be out of here again. I want to know who they are."

When Brock got to the street, he saw a black limo and copper Bentley. After he returned to the table, Maude asked, "Where'd you go?"

"Out front. Guess what's parked by the door?"

"What?"

"A Bentley."

She leaned back in her chair and exhaled. "There aren't many of those around." She panned the crowd, looking for Abner Giles.

"Marcel, I think I know what those fourteen LLCs Giles owns part of are into—music."

"And you think this is one of his bands?" his brother-in-law supposed.

"Something like that. Come on, let's switch partners and ask those girls to dance again."

At eleven o'clock, the organist thanked the crowd, and the band members disappeared from the stage. Brock thought about following the cars but knew it would anger his wife. They'd had a great time all day and ending it on a high note would be the smart thing to do.

As they were walking out, Marcel said to Brock, "What'd you think of Arlena Harring?"

"Seemed like a nice gal to me. Why?"

"Did you ask who her boyfriend was?"

"No. She only told me she worked at an art supply store in Richmond."

Marcel halted and grabbed Brock's sleeve. "I asked her. His name is Omar Cru. Sound familiar?"

Maude heard what he said. She peered at her husband, pleading, "Don't make anything of it, Brock."

"What's to make?"

CHAPTER 4

Truman stirred at six o'clock on Sunday morning. He wanted to go out but decided not to wake his "mom and dad." They had gotten in right at midnight, and he figured they wouldn't rise until daylight. The dog stood next to the back door when Brock appeared. "Here you go, buddy." He pulled open the slider. A dense fog blocked the sight of the grapevines beyond the backyard. Truman's tracks on the dew made a pattern Brock had seen often.

Maude, bright-eyed and bushy-tailed, came into the kitchen a few minutes later and said, "Let's go to early church and Bible study. You up for that?"

"Sounds good."

Most leaders of Bible classes like to hear themselves talk. At Perry County Christian Church, the layperson who led the study was quite the opposite. Ben Hicks asked questions to stimulate conversation and would make comments when things that were said needed to be clarified or corrected. The Skinners entered the study room as soon after the church service as possible, to keep a low profile. That didn't last long.

"I see that Mr. and Mrs. Skinner have joined us this morning. Since they haven't been here in a few weeks, it might be good for us to provide them with a synopsis of what we learned studying Ecclesiastes. But first, let's see what they may already know. Brock, what can you tell us about Solomon?"

"Ben, my memory's rusty. I'm getting old, you know." He had an "aw-shucks" look that didn't fool Hicks.

"Is that so. I'm guessing you're not even forty yet."

"And I can see you're not going to let me off the hook, are you, Ben?" The two dozen people in the class chuckled. "He was the son of David and Bathsheba, the second and last king of unified Israel, around 950 BC. He built the first temple in Jerusalem."

"That's a good start. What was he most famous for?"

"His wisdom," Brock answered instantly, like he knew the question was coming.

"How did he get it?" Ben intended to set the hook.

"Solomon prayed for wisdom, to rule Israel wisely, instead of for selfish things like a long life, great wealth, or death to his enemies. God was impressed and granted it."

Ben panned the room and asked, "How's he doing so far?" A few "goods" were uttered. "What can you tell us about the book of Ecclesiastes?"

"You're putting me on the spot now, Ben. I don't want to be wrong in what I say."

"Come now, Brock, give us something to bat around."

He clamped his hands on the edge of the table. "How about this? That prayer for wisdom might have been an artifice in the end."

"Artifice? How so?"

"He might not have used his wisdom solely for good. He amassed two trillion in gold by today's standards, had a thousand wives and concubines, and built a few temples to idols worshipped by some of those wives of his."

"I see. How does that relate to Ecclesiastes?" Ben couldn't keep the smile off his face.

Brock glanced at Maude and said, "Kick me if I should shut up." She turned her head away. Laughter in the room bubbled up again. "Well, writing as an old man, he said flatly that pursuits in this life are vane and meaningless."

"Okay, class, now we're getting somewhere. So, what you're saying is that he recognized in the long run that things of this world do not mean much or don't lead to contentment."

An old lady sitting alone offered, "At the end of the book, Solomon says to fear God and keep his commandments."

Ben used the teaching moment to say, "Which suggests he knew intellectually that following God was the only thing of value in this life, but the human condition caused him to use his wisdom for things of value *and* things that were meaningless. After all, Solomon did a lot of good for the nation of Israel and is known as one of the great kings in all of history. Can anyone think of a parallel conundrum voiced in the New Testament?"

A young man sitting on the other side of Maude spoke up: "In Romans chapter seven, Paul says that he does not do the things he wants to do but instead does the things he hates because he sees another law at work—that of sin."

Ben put his hands in the air. "Bravo! What does he say after that in chapter eight?"

The young man replied, "There is no condemnation for those in Christ Jesus."

"And that is the only solution for the sin problem. Brock, thank you for having the courage to speak up." Brock nodded contritely. Ben posed another question: "Can anyone think of how this relates to something going on in society today?"

A burly man near Hicks hit the mark. "Certainly. Artificial intelligence. It can be used for either good or bad, and people are beginning to believe that the bad side of AI will destroy life on this earth as we know it."

Ben primed the pump with one last benign admonition: "On that not-so-positive note, who else thinks they've got this doomsday scenario figured out?" People in the class began to loosen up, and opinions flew around for the next forty-five minutes. The Skinners eased out of the room while the commotion continued.

On the way home, Maude said, "I'm glad he called on you instead of me." Fog had lifted by late morning. The air was still and cool, and the sun bright. She knew the crowd at the winery would be huge after lunch.

"No matter the circumstances, it's good to be in the Bible. It smacks you right in the face."

Maude, consumed by her own thoughts, stared out the window. "Yes, I suppose you're right. It takes a lifetime to understand it."

"You can say that again. What are you planning for the rest of the day?"

"I'd like to take the picture I bought and put it somewhere inside the winery where it can't be stolen. But first, let's check out Skyline Drive and see if we can find out how to get up to where Giles and Cru live."

Brock, enthused by the idea, U-turned and hit the gas. "Did Giles give you an address?"

"Nine ten."

Houses on Skyline Drive were intermittent after the turnoff. The farther up the road they drove, the elevation increased, as did the spacing between the properties. A few places near the end had spectacular views of Mother Nature's fall color masterpiece, which was changing by the hour. At the very end of the road, black iron numbers sticking up out of the ground like giant lollipops reminded Maude of the carnival. "This must be it." She thrust her hand upward in a diagonal direction. The asphalt access road had a galvanized guardrail along the cliff edge.

Brock turned in and started up the hill. There weren't any switchbacks, and at the very top, the road split. Massive wrought-iron gates appeared on the right. One gate leaf had an A on it, and the other, a G. The chrome card reader and speaker box mounted on a gooseneck post were accessible from a car window. Brock pointed left and said, "Cru must live up that way."

"Drive over there. We might as well see if he's home."

Brock cautioned, "I hope he's not the jealous type."

"Or philandering type," Maude hurled back.

Once through the gap in the trees, they saw a small cabin made of wood. The rocky hillside had been cleared to supply a view of downtown Hazard and hilltops across the way—one featuring Vigneron Winery.

Omar opened the front door before they were able to get out of the Lamborghini. He stood on the threshold wearing a tattersall flannel shirt with his legs wide apart, arms crossed. When the uninvited visitors approached on foot, he said, "Can I help you folks?"

"Not really. We're just being nosey," Maude replied demurely.

"About what?"

"I'm Maude Skinner. This is my husband, Brock. We visited Keeneland yesterday. I bought a painting of yours. I was curious to know if there were any more for sale anywhere."

"I see. Connie from the art shop did call and tell me that you had bought it. How did you know I live up here?"

Brock was worried his wife wouldn't have an honest answer to the question, but she did. "I saw the address of your studio on the authentication paperwork that came with the painting."

"Please come in."

Once inside, Brock went to the front window to see if he could find the winery. Maude directed a comment at Omar: "By way of full disclosure, I should tell you that my husband here danced with a lady friend of yours last night. What was her name, honey?"

Brock pivoted to read Cru's reaction and answered, "Arlena Harring."

"Where was that?" he asked.

"At the Silk Cravat in Mount Vernon. It's a supper club and dance hall. Arlena's a great dancer. Maude and I went there with some relatives."

Maude steered the conversation away from dancing, saying, "Your artwork is nothing short of spectacular. It won't be long before everybody knows who you are."

"Well, thank you for the compliment. You asked if there was anything else out there for sale. I'm afraid there isn't."

With a stiff upper lip, Maude replied, "That's too bad. I'm going to keep the one I bought at the winery. Thousands of people stream through there every year. You'll be a household name in no time."

The artist, looking sheepish, remarked, "Wait here." He walked around his studio and through the door behind it, and not long after, came out holding a small abstract landscape. "Would you be interested in this?"

Maude surreptitiously studied the painting and the work area where he must have painted it, then smiled. "It's marvelous. How much do you want for it?"

"You can have it. If I do become a household name, your winery would be a good place to offer some of my work for sale. Could be good for both our businesses."

"Indeed. Thank you. I'll hang it this afternoon." She moved toward the front door. "We'll be off now. It was nice meeting you. Please do visit us at the winery and bring Arlena along. I'd like to meet her."

"I'll do that."

Brock shook Omar's hand and nodded on the way out. As they were descending the hill, Maude said, "Something's not right."

Brock looked at her sideways and bantered back, "What?"

"I can't put my finger on it. His studio is too clean. His eyes are not those of an artist. Why did he come to Hazard and build a shack on top of a mountain?"

"Maude, I can't believe I'm hearing this. Has my suspicious and negative nature, as you called it last night, infected you? If so, I'm sorry."

"Don't be." She patted his leg.

Brock added, "He seems on the level to me. It's Abner Giles I'm suspicious of. I can see an artist working out of a studio on a mountain in Appalachia, but I have a hard time understanding why a rich fat cat would spend a lot of money on an estate overlooking Hazard."

"We did the same thing when we built the winery."

"That's different," Brock argued.

"Why, because it's a business? Maybe what he's doing is a business too," she posited.

"You may have a point there." Brock raised his eyebrows and stuck out his chin.

Maude examined the landscape painting she was holding and said, "Let's have lunch and then find good places to hang Mr. Cru's masterpieces."

A decorative mezzanine had been added inside the winery above the main entrance so people would notice whatever Maude wanted them to see as they were leaving. Sometimes it was the announcement for an upcoming event or recently received awards. She told her husband to get the ladder and place the bigger Omar Cru on the short-legged easel right over the door. That took him all of two minutes as he worked around the people who were going in and out. While he did that, she hung the landscape in the alcove behind the tasting bar.

Brock scratched his head. "I've been noodling on why Cru came to town. One explanation is that the real artist lives nearby, and Cru is his stand-in."

"That would make sense."

The crowd exploded over the next hour. Brock stood by the warehouse door and watched to see how many folks noticed the painting on the way out. Virtually all did. Many stopped and studied it for a few seconds. When Maude walked over by him, he said, "Why exactly do you think that piece of art is so good?"

"Composition, brushwork, use of color, and the feeling you get when you look at it. On a larger scale, the expressionistic and abstract nature of the work is reminiscent of earlier great artists of the genre."

"Such as?"

"Klimt, Kandinsky, Klee."

Brock grinned. "Those names all begin with the same letter. I think we should start calling Cru *Special K.*"

"Ha. Ha. You know that's the nickname for ketamine."

"I wasn't aware of that. I'm not on social media. Let's go in your office and see if you have an unobstructed view of his studio,"

Brock prodded. When they skirted the desk and peered out the window, a branch from a tree was blocking the line of sight. "That'll have to go."

"Why is it you need a clear view of his place?"

"Because I'm going to borrow Marcel's high-powered scope. It's got a tripod we can set it on to see what's going on over there. You said it best: something's not right."

Maude closed her eyes and muttered, "Oh, no. Down the rabbit hole we go again."

Brock conjured up a defense. "Remember what I said when you told me about Abner Giles?"

"Yeah. If anything happens, I'd be the one who started it."

Brock got out his phone and called his brother-in-law. "Marcel, have you begun looking into Omar Cru yet?" He listened for a minute. "Okay, call me when you find out anything. Also, I want to borrow your land-viewing scope. I'll come and get it as soon as I can." He cut the line and went outside to saw off that tree branch.

CHAPTER 5

The lacquered heartwood lecture hall at Slade University in Lexington featured coffered frames around the sinewy human and animal caricatures lifted from murals of Thomas Hart Benton, most notably the figures in *Achelous and Hercules*. Per the wont of the university, a local artist was hired for an exorbitant fee to design something kitschy while paying little attention to copyright and trademark laws. Either the Benton estate wasn't aware of the copies, or the artist had secretly bought the rights to the images, which was unlikely. None of the students sitting there waiting to hear a mordant lecture that Monday morning knew or cared about the origins of the unusual art. They would soon be reflecting on the purported origins of something more interesting.

The door to the hall creaked open in the back, and Saul Sardis strolled in with the aplomb of a card-carrying member of Mensa International. His springy gait would have drawn disdain from an Appalachian coal miner but impressed the future tech company programmers in the class. He serenely worked his way up to the lectern, advertised a disingenuous smile, and kicked off his spiel with a recondite question: "What will artificial intelligence be like in a hundred years?"

A male student with no discernable direction in life, thoroughly disinterested in the curriculum, answered insouciantly, "It'll have its hobnail boot on our necks." The rest of the class tee-heed rudely.

Sardis brushed off the belittlement. "What about in a thousand years?"

A cute young girl with mesmerizing cobalt-blue eyes suggested, "I suppose it will have figured out the mysteries of the universe."

"Very good. What might it have done with such knowledge?" Sardis walked around to the side of the lectern and propped an arm on it.

"Maybe travel beyond the speed of light, back in time, or into the future," she replied without a hint of sarcasm.

Saul hadn't expected a ball to be teed up that fast for the outlandish supposition he intended to reveal that day, so he used the driver in his head to whack it into outer space. "I believe that somewhere there's a civilization at least a thousand years ahead of us, which by your reckoning has conquered the spectra of time and space."

The blue-eyed girl wagged her head uncertainly and replied, "I guess that's a possibility."

The possessed professor straightened his arms as though a power surge had jolted his body. He proclaimed loudly, "And I submit to you that's precisely what happened."

Two dozen students in the class looked at each other, sat up, and thought to themselves that the lecture on this day wouldn't be as lackluster as those in the past. A girl sitting next to Blue Eyes took the bait. "That would explain the documented UFOs in recent years."

Sardis couldn't believe how yet again another girl had set the table for him. "Let me tell you a story about artificial intelligence and how it has already affected life on this earth. A civilization ahead of ours traveled back in time some six thousand years. They put Adam and Eve between the Tigris and Euphrates. That's the only explanation that fits the scientific evidence."

A gangly science nerd sitting under the Benton art stood and said, "What seems more workable to me is that they were ten thousand years ahead of us and didn't have to travel back in time six thousand years."

"Plausible for sure. It doesn't change the fact that humankind was brought here by aliens in the form of Adam and Eve. The extraterrestrials returned three thousand years later and saw how much the Egyptians had advanced and are here again to see how far along we are on artificial intelligence."

The nerd took issue. "I'm not sure I buy that, sir. What about the flood, Moses and the burning bush, and most importantly, the death and resurrection of Jesus Christ?"

"They manipulated those events to make humankind believe a powerful and omnipotent God created everything, hoping that a society of people who rejected science would never reach the point of developing artificial intelligence."

A third female student asked fearfully, "Are you saying the Bible is a lie?"

Here came the fastball up in the zone. Sardis swung hard and drove it over the center field wall. "Seems self-evident, don't you think? If aliens brought Adam and Eve here, the God of the Bible did not create them." The flummoxed girl who asked the question gathered her belongings in a hurry and marched out.

The disinterested young man took the opportunity to swipe at the professor one last time. "That means AI is an evil thing. Why the hell are we studying it?"

Sardis came around to the front of the lectern and asked, "What's your name, boy?"

Before "the boy" got up and walked out, he said, "I'm the guy who's going to get you fired."

Saul Sardis was born and raised in Menlo Park, California, one of the best places to be from on God's green earth. He attended Stanford University, fifteen minutes down the road from his house, where he studied computer science during the flurry of start-ups popping up in Silicon Valley, and then joined a fledgling software company in San Jose when he graduated, which in recent years had been focusing on the Wild West of artificial intelligence. An unusual client whom he attracted to the company was from Lexington, Kentucky, and when he made his first trip to that part of the world, Saul resolved to move there someday. His IQ got him promoted to president of the West Coast operation, but he only stayed in the position for a year before going out on his own five years ago and moving to the Bluegrass State. Once settled in, he caught the horseracing bug. As smart as he was, Sardis could've made a good living from the pari-mutuel windows at Keeneland but had something else in mind.

The dean at Slade University pointed to the chair across from his desk when Sardis entered his office. Sardis sat and waited patiently for the dean to start in. "Saul, I received complaints from several students right before lunch about the content of your lecture." The dean propped his elbows on the chair arms, leaned back, and made a tent with his hands.

The professor rolled to one side and crossed his leg. "Because I said the Bible isn't true?"

"Yes."

"What's the problem?"

"This institution was started by, and is still affiliated with, a sect of the Christian Church. They are not in favor of teaching that aliens brought Adam and Eve here." The dean indicted Sardis with his eyes.

"You trying to tell me I can't discuss ideas that conflict with a Christian worldview?"

The dean grabbed the chair arms with both hands, flared out his elbows, leaned forward, and growled, "Damn right I'm telling you that."

"I'll teach my students whatever I want, and if you don't like it, I'll sue this university."

"Oh, will you? Better read the fine print in your employment contract. It explicitly says that the university has the right to tell you what to teach and how to teach it. I'm letting you know that if you push the idea that Adam and Eve were brought here by aliens, I'll fire you on the spot."

Saul smiled to confound the dean. "Is that a threat?"

"Threat? No, it's just a descendant of Adam and Eve disproving your satanic theory."

"I never mentioned Satan." Sardis feigned being hurt.

The dean pulled open the middle drawer of his desk and removed a small cassette tape from it. "One of your students gave this to me. It's a copy of your lecture. I could fire you based on this alone." He put his arms out to the edge of the desk and swayed forward. "Now, I want you to teach what artificial intelligence is, not where it came from. Not another word about the origins of humankind."

Sardis showed no fear and a frightening amount of resolve. "I refuse. You might as well fire me now, and when you do, I'll go right to the media and expose this university for what it is: a place that indoctrinates students with religious claptrap."

The dean stood and said steadily, "Come on, I'll follow you to your office. I want you to gather your personal belongings and I'll escort you out. You no longer work at Slade University."

The professor emeritus got up, smiled again, and said in a singsong voice, "You'll be sorry."

Saul continued dabbling in artificial intelligence when he arrived in Lexington five years ago. He bought a nondescript home in Westmoreland Estates, a housing development near Keeneland, and reinforced the floor to handle the weight of the computer hardware installed there. He continued scraping and using latent diffusion to develop products with commercial significance. It took him the better part of a year to make progress on his AI projects and find a companion whom he could trust. He took his résumé to Slade University three years back and secured a teaching position, kept his nose clean, and was highly regarded for his knowledge and style. That had all seemingly come to an end.

As Sardis was stepping from the garage into his house, he called the local paper. The woman who answered the phone said, "This is the *Herald-Leader*. How can I help you?"

"I want to report a news story. Is there an email address where I can send a Word file of info?"

The woman replied, "Yes, this is it." She recited the address slowly and repeated it to make sure he got it right.

Saul's phone rang shortly after he hung up with the paper. He recognized the caller's voice on the burner phone. "Good morning." He listened to what was said. His reply was rather pinched. "After these last few that you have, I want to pause for a while. I got fired temporarily from my teaching job this morning. I'll meet you in an hour at our usual place."

Brock was sitting at a table in the warehouse breakroom at the winery finishing his lunch when Maude came in and gave him labels with the names of the wines and number of bottles of each to put in the six cases to be delivered to the Giles house. He said, "Is this going to be COD, or do we trust his credit?"

"If he offers to pay on the spot, take it. If not, I'll mail the bill. If he tries to stiff me, I'll send you over there to collect."

"Can I take my pistol with me then?"

"No." Maude spun around and left the warehouse.

Brock filled the cases and stuck labels on the boxes before loading them into the pickup truck. When he climbed in to leave, Marcel's number popped up on his phone. "What's new, chief?"

"Your buddy, Omar Cru."

"Is he a grifter as Maude suspects?" He put the truck in gear and eased onto the county road.

"The guy was a hard one to run down."

"Why's that?"

"Because his name isn't Omar Cru, it's Nomar Crugleac. His parents are Moldovan. He dropped the *N* on his first name and the ending of his last name. His tax returns are in his real name."

"Why is it we cross paths with these shadowy characters? What else did you learn about him?"

"He was born in Seattle thirty-seven years ago. He worked for software companies for ten years after college and started painting in his late twenties, selling a dozen pieces for chump change. The odd thing is his paintings are all a variation on Mark Rothko. He used the name Omar Cru on that art, yet no one he worked with in the Seattle area knew he was painter."

Brock tapped the brakes as he coasted down the hill, moving away from the winery. "So, he wasn't a good artist when he lived in Seattle and became a great one when he moved here."

"Apparently. He bought that land he built on a little over four years ago. I can't find anything on how he found it, or why he decided to move there. He put in a road to the top of the mountain and had someone construct a cabin for him. Another odd thing: the plan he gave the city to get the building permit shows a fireproof concrete room in the center of the cabin. Now, why in the world would he need something like that?"

"I suppose he wanted a place to store his art so it wouldn't burn up in a fire."

"Makes sense. The room is only ten by ten. I'm guessing he's got a laptop and printer in there and racks to store his paintings on."

"I didn't tell you this, but Maude and I were in his cabin yesterday. We went up the mountain to make sure I knew where to deliver wine to Abner Giles. We knocked on Cru's door to introduce ourselves. He went in that room you're talking about to get a small painting to give to us."

"What'd you do, just walk up and knock on the door?"

"Yep. He seemed normal to me." Brock turned onto the highway toward town. "Your sister thinks he's a fraud. Says he doesn't have the eyes of an artist, and his studio is too clean, like it's staged or something."

Marcel didn't reply at once, and when he did, he suggested a couple of possibilities: "Either the real painter has a secret way to get the art to him, or he's producing it with AI, maybe from a computer in the fireproof room."

Brock said, "That room wouldn't be big enough for an AI printer that produced art. What if one is off-site somewhere?"

Marcel replied, "I like that idea. We should try to find out where it is."

"If I were him, I wouldn't send any electronic versions of content by email to avoid ever being traced or found out."

"So, he might have an intermediary whom he works with in person," Marcel concluded.

"Uh-oh. That could be Arlena Harring. Better find out where she lives." Brock motored through town and turned onto Skyline Drive.

"She must go to his cabin to pick things up and drop them off, or he comes to her place, or they meet somewhere else that's private."

"That won't take long to discover. I'll tail them. I wonder if Abner Giles knew Omar Cru before he bought the other end of mountaintop and built his Taj Mahal?" Brock asked.

"Well, if he didn't, how would he have found that land? As far as I can tell, Cru wasn't looking to sell it to anybody."

"I'm heading up to Giles's place right now. I'll ask if I'm introduced to him."

"When are you going to come by and pick up the scope?" Marcel asked.

"Not sure. Soon." Brock ended the call as he turned onto the billy goat driveway that led up the hill to the AG iron gates. He stopped at the speaker box to announce his arrival.

A syrupy woman's voice asked, "What's your business?"

"I'm from Vigneron Winery. Here to deliver six cases of wine ordered by Abner Giles."

The woman said nothing more as the gates began to part.

CHAPTER 6

The mountaintop had been shaped into a flat deck by a perimeter of concrete that flared down the hill on all sides except at the keyhole where vehicles drove through. Sturdy fence posts, set in the concrete every twenty feet, supported woven steel cables, one inch thick, a foot apart, strung taut, post-to-post. Brock looked around and found the green electrical cabinet that supplied the juice for the fence. A massive two-story structure of white stucco, done in a bland pueblo style, had been erected in the center of the mesa. A row of arborvitae blocked the first-floor view of downtown Hazard. The way in had champagne-hued corrugated metal panels in the alcove that matched the color of the metal roof. Brock punched the chime by the entrance.

The woman who came to the door blurted, "Hey, handsome, will you be the delivery boy every time we order wine from your fine establishment?" Based on her voice, she was the one who had opened the gate. Her blonde hair was natural, and her purple blouse unbuttoned too low.

"Probably. My name's Brock Skinner. What's yours?"

She moved into his personal space. "Deianira Wathen, business manager. People call me Dee."

"Your mother must have been well educated to name you that."

"Not quite. She didn't know her ass from a hole in the ground." Dee scrunched her nose.

"Shall I bring the wine in?" He pointed over his shoulder while gazing into her hazel eyes.

"That's what you're here for, isn't it?" She hooked her arm through his and led him back to the truck.

"Is Abner Giles here?"

"No. He's out. If you know what's good for you, you'll run things through me."

"Or what? You'll do what Deianira did to Hercules?" Brock cowered and raised his eyebrows. She didn't react.

"I can see you're a bit of a smartass. I like that in you, though, as well as other things I see."

"Is this where I tell you how good-looking you are?" Brock figured he better get in like Flynn or end up on the wrong side of history.

Dee planted her hands on her curvy hips. "What do you take me for? A louche woman?"

"Not now, I don't. Where do you want me to put these?"

"In the kitchen. Follow me." She led the way in a huff.

Expensive appliances were against the wall. A kidney-shaped granite island had cooking utensils hanging overhead. Brock set the first case of wine on the edge of the island near the stove. He made five more runs and confirmed, "That's the lot. Do you live here?"

"I do, with Sadie and Abner." She took the white wines out of the boxes and started putting them in the fridge. Fresh meats and vegetables were piled on the glass shelves.

"Awfully big place for three people. You've got enough food in there to feed an army."

"And I'm the cook. You're mighty nosey." She paused and then continued, "House sleeps nine. We often have visitors. This place is a recording studio."

"Really? Kind of off the beaten path, wouldn't you say? Now I know why you need all this wine. Is Sadie Abner's wife?" Brock figured he might as well drain the well dry.

"Are you kidding me? She's serious as a heart attack. No, she's the sound engineer and music producer. Her interest in men is down the scale from mine."

"Any chance I could meet her? I'd like to make my own assessment."

Dee pursed her lips and asked, "Why, so you can pass me up and jump her bones?"

"No. I'm married to the best woman in Appalachia, and I'm not a chaser," he revealed.

"Okay. Come on." She walked through the main living area to the back of the building where there was a windowless, bright-lit room with everything needed to record music. An attractive girl sat behind the sound board. "Sadie, the wine delivery boy wants to meet you. He's married, and I presume he's harmless."

Brock approached the girl and said, "Hi."

She stood and said somberly, "Hello, I'm Sadie Kirkham. And you are?"

"Brock Skinner. My wife runs the winery you can see on a hill across the valley."

"Pleased to me you." Sadie had a smart, pretty face. There was a healthy shine to her brown hair. She was wearing blue jeans and a white blouse with the sleeves rolled up.

"Are you planning on recording music anytime soon?"

"That's confidential. We don't publicize who our clients are and when they visit us. In fact, we prefer that no one knows what we do. I presume you'll honor that request and be discreet?"

"Of course. It's been nice meeting both of you. I'm sure I'll see you again when you run out of wine." He nodded and began retracing his steps to find the front door.

Sadie asked, "Does your wife's winery serve lunch?"

Brock stopped and turned toward her. "They do. You should run over for a visit sometime."

"We may do that. Our guests like to leave the grounds occasionally for a little variety."

Dee went out to the truck with Brock to see him off. She said, "You'll send me a bill, I'm sure. I hope you've got better wheels than this in your personal life."

He grinned. "We will and I do. A Lamborghini. Everybody in town knows who I am."

"Well, aren't you special. Get out of here." She turned away and headed inside.

When Brock passed through the keyhole, coasting toward the gates, he saw a car pulling away from Cru's cabin, so he hit the brakes. Cru was driving, and he didn't turn his head. Brock waited a minute before debouching from the gate and shooting straight across the way. A set of tools were in the glove box of the truck for picking locks. He used them to enter Cru's cabin. There was nothing interesting in the kitchen, bedroom, and bathroom. It took him eleven minutes to defeat the lock in the door behind the studio.

As predicted, a laptop and standard printer were on a table in the corner. The rest of the room had racks of paintings, close to two hundred, Brock surmised. A section of the shelving was dedicated to several works of art that were unfinished. Browsing through the completed paintings, he noticed there was a finished version of each partially done piece. Brock decided to do what his wife would not approve of—steal one.

He locked up, put the painting in the passenger seat of the truck, and began easing down the hill. The best place to hide what he'd pilfered was in the cabinet next to his Lamborghini.

Maude saw her husband eventually return to the winery, and when he came into the tasting room, she asked him how it went. He took twenty minutes to explain everything he saw and what was said. He left out the part about stealing one of the pictures.

Maude concluded, "He probably sets those unfinished works out to fool visitors if he needs to."

"That's what I think. The printer must spit out unfinished and finished versions of paintings."

"Marcel just called me. He and Valerie are on their way here. He said he's got the scope and thought you would need help setting it up. He also said he found some information on Arlena Harring."

"I presume they're going to stay the night?"

"Yes."

"Excellent. We can play a few hands of bridge," Brock suggested.

The weather had drifted into a colorless malaise by closing time. The Sutherlands had already brought their bags into the house before the Skinners got home. Valerie was standing in the kitchen. She said, "Long time, no see, since Saturday night."

Brock remarked, "Val, there's only one thing more enjoyable than seeing your lovely face, and that's seeing your husband's sister's angelic smile."

Valerie peered at Maude. "He must want something, or he's done something bad."

Marcel reported, "Absolutely he's done something bad. He always does something bad. It's up to us to find out what that is."

Maude said, "Well, he hasn't been out of my sight except for when he ran over to deliver wine to the Abner Giles house. Wait a minute. He told me he broke into Cru's house and saw a whole bunch of art locked in a fireproof room."

"That's it!" Marcel stuck a finger in the air. "I bet he stole one of the paintings and didn't tell you."

Brock grabbed the top of his head and squeezed his scalp. "I was going to tell her over dinner."

"No, you weren't," Valerie rebuffed.

"Where is it?" Maude asked.

Brock stiffened his arms, put his hands in his pockets, and examined the floor. "In the cabinet in front of the Lamborghini."

"Go get it." He did, and when he brought it into the house, he set it by the fireplace. "It's another horse picture," Maude said flatly.

Valerie asked, "How would a machine be able to produce something like that?"

Her husband said, "I suppose the computer starts with a scanned image, like a photograph, and distorts it based upon the style of the artist or group of artists being emulated."

"That would make sense," Brock affirmed. "A new image would be created and sent to a printer capable of applying actual paint to the chosen substrate. In this case, wood." He pointed at the Cru painting.

"That's not the hard part," Marcel said. "Engineering a printer that could apply paint to look hand drawn would require some very advanced artificial intelligence."

Maude theorized, "I can't see Arlena Harring being the brains, but she could be the mule."

"Speaking of her, she has a place in Richmond off the main highway about a mile, on a narrow road that runs through the woods," Marcel revealed. "Google Earth shows it as a rectangular ranch house with a gray roof."

Brock said, "She works at an art supply store. If the printer is at her house, she could easily get the paints needed to keep it running. Marcel, do you think you could find her credit card or art store orders? We could see how much supplies she's bought in the last couple of years."

"That might be doable."

"But who's the brains?" Valerie queried.

Maude answered, "Whomever it is, you can bet he or she has taken every precaution to conceal their identity. And just for the record, Brock, I'm not happy with you stealing that painting."

Her husband treaded lightly, saying, "Can I get you a glass of white wine?"

"Might as well. We're having baked chicken for dinner."

After they finished eating, Marcel used Brock's computer to get into the Sutherland Tailoring system. He couldn't find a credit card for Arlena Harring but did find the art store invoices. Harring had consistently bought gouache paints, and paid cash every time.

Brock told his wife, "Marcel and I are going over to your office to set up the scope."

"Isn't it too dark to do that?"

Marcel explained, "The scope has a day lens and thermal one for night. They rotate on and off. Once we find Cru's house, we'll calibrate it to record activities around the clock."

"How exactly does the scope work?" Valerie asked.

"It has high-magnification lenses. Once we pinpoint the target, we'll set it to capture the field of view we want. The attached camera sends pictures of movement to a phone."

"That's handy," Maude chirped.

The men got back to the house at 8:10. Brock reported, "All set. That thing is sophisticated. It must be the latest in military technology. Let's deal the cards."

The women played the men in bridge and beat them soundly. When they were done, Brock's phone pinged. A picture came in from the camera, a silhouette of a girl leaving Cru's house.

Valerie glanced at the phone and said in blasé fashion, "*Cherchez la femme?*"

———

Since the scope was trained on Omar Cru's cabin and not the gates into the Giles estate, the copper Bentley passing through did so unnoticed by Brock and Marcel. Giles pulled the car into the garage. When he ran into Dee in the kitchen, he asked her where Sadie was.

"She's in the theater room watching something."

Abner politely asked Sadie to pause the movie when he found her. "Sorry to interrupt. I wanted you to know the band will arrive tomorrow afternoon and evening. We'll rehearse each tune separately and then record it as soon as they're ready. There'll be twelve songs on the album."

Sadie asked, "What kind of music is it?"

"Dance numbers."

"No, I mean what kind of sound does the band have?"

"Well, the drummer will play like John Bonham, organist like Mac Rebennack, rhythm guitarist like Malcolm Young, lead guitarist like Stevie Ray Vaughan, and the bass player like John Entwistle. And he's the lead singer, in the voice of a young Tom Jones."

Sadie paused in thought, then said, "How do you know they play in the style of those famous rock musicians?"

"Because the music they'll get is written that way," Abner retorted.

"So, they're following a score written for each instrument, for each song?"

"Now you're catching on."

"Very few rock musicians can sight-read and play in another style," she said.

"These guys can. They're pros, and they want to make a lot of money."

Sadie got up from her seat and asked, "Are they wild men or gentlemen?"

"Choir boys," Abner assured her.

"Good. You said the songs are dance music?" Sadie tried to read the expression on his face, but it was too dim in the room to do so.

"Yes. A foxtrot, waltz, samba, rumba, cha-cha, hustle, salsa, bolero, mambo, West Coast swing, East Coast swing, and tango."

"What a circus this will be," Sadie whined. She approached recording sessions with the notion something would go wrong, or the musicians would grow weary of getting the song right.

Abner moved closer and gave her a warm smile. "This'll be the finest music you'll ever engineer and record. Remember, you get a percentage of the corporation, and if this music is as good as I think it is, you're going to be a very happy lady."

"I certainly hope so." Sadie returned a not-so-sincere smile and resumed watching the movie.

Chapter 7

Marcel and Brock stepped through the aluminum door of the gym in downtown Hazard at six o'clock Tuesday morning, the last day of October. They jumped rope, punched the bag for an hour, and ran outside for twenty minutes. Maude and Valerie were returning from a brisk walk when the men got back to the log cabin. Brock said, "Let's whip up a hearty breakfast."

Everyone showered, dressed for the day, and then congregated in the kitchen at eight thirty. Valerie cooked four rashers of microwave bacon. Maude put together ramekins of shirred eggs with butter, cream, and Parmesan cheese. Marcel placed a small dollop of Greek yogurt with fruit on each plate, and as usual, Brock ended up with the easiest job—making toast with jam.

A newscaster on television reported the fate of a Slade University professor as they sat around the breakfast table. "Saul Sardis was relieved of his duties yesterday as the artificial intelligence instructor at Slade, and according to him, he was fired for suggesting that Adam and Eve could have been brought here by an advanced civilization somewhere in the universe. He contends there is no freedom of speech at the school because it is dominated by a Christian worldview. Sardis claimed that would be acceptable if the institution didn't take any taxpayer money. The university had no comment. In other news..."

Brock spoke to his brother-in-law in a raspy voice, "See if you can find any evidence of that character being acquainted with Arlena Harring or Omar Cru."

Maude asked, "You think he could be the mastermind behind the painting scam?"

"Got any other suspects?" her husband asked in reply.

"No."

"We have to start somewhere."

Maude and Valerie drove to the winery at nine o'clock, leaving their husbands to clean up the kitchen. Marcel got on Brock's computer as soon as he could and began unpacking the life of one Saul Sardis.

Marcel shared his findings after an hour of digging. "Arlena Harring worked at Keeneland four or five years ago, but Saul Sardis never had her as a waiter that I can see. She quit there and began working at the art store in Richmond. Omar Cru has been hanging around the track as long as he's lived in Kentucky. I can't find where he was ever with Sardis either."

"Okay. I'm going to drive up to Richmond to see if I can pin the tail on the donkey."

"What donkey?"

"Arlena Harring. I need her address." Brock's phone pinged. "Look. Cru's leaving his house. Get in your car and see if you can follow him from a distance. Let's try to find out what he's up to."

Brock swapped out the Lamborghini for the winery truck and arrived at the turnoff to Arlena's house in Richmond in seventy minutes. He assumed she was at work. If not, he'd be sunk if she came to the door. He knocked three times and waited a bit before he picked the lock.

The house was plain outside, but the inside was decorated like a Manhattan penthouse. The room where the recessed TV was hanging had a floor made of huge gray sheets of slate. White-and-olive sandstone tiles covered three walls. Brown leather furniture was trimmed out with curved cherry legs. A gigantic, tasseled rug had been woven using red, orange, and yellow rope. The small pictures on the walls were by Omar Cru.

The room that had computer equipment in it featured a cheap, pedestrian printer, not of the AI pedigree. Brock searched for the door to the basement. It was hidden in the kitchen pantry on the end wall between the shelves. He couldn't figure out how to turn the lights on, so he got a big flashlight out of the truck. Nothing was down there except a parquet dance floor and mirrors. There were no doors to other rooms visible.

Brock closed the front door and pulled out. When he got on the highway, Marcel called to report what was going on. "Your boy, Omar, is walking into Circle of Blue sandwich shop on Richmond Road in Lexington."

"I know where that is."

"Arlena Harring got out of her car to join him when he arrived."

"I wonder why she isn't at work?"

"Probably taking a long lunch break," Marcel said.

"Do you think you can go in there and not be recognized by her?"

"I do."

Circle of Blue, a Greek establishment, had blue-circle wallpaper in the eating area. Cold chrome chairs screamed, "Eat your food and get out of here." A dozen or so people, who had placed their orders at the counter and picked up their food, were doing just that.

Saul Sardis and the dean took their sandwich baskets and sat at a two-top against the wall. The dean, overdressed in his thousand-dollar suit, didn't like the position he was in and hoped he could wriggle out of the mess unscathed. He said diffidently, "Saul, what do we need to do to work this out?"

"You mean unring the bell? It's too late for that." Sardis redirected the congenial dialogue with his sharp reply.

"Does money solve the problem?" The dean squinted his eyes.

"No. I want to be reinstated and receive an apology from the president."

The smug comment rattled the dean. He twisted in his seat and took a clipped bite of his Greek sandwich. "That your final position?"

Omar Cru, sitting across the room with Arlena Harring, for some unknown reason answered a question that wasn't intended for him. "Yes." Suddenly, he shot to his feet and bellowed, "What's happening to me?" Saul Sardis also stood with a start, terror in his eyes. He looked at the dean and then surveyed his own clothes before parroting what Cru had just said. The two men met in the middle of the room, and Cru said viciously, "What are you doing in my body?"

"And you in mine. What's happened to us?" They stood there dazed for a few seconds. Sardis stepped around Cru and shuffled over to sit across from Arlena. He uttered with a tremorous voice, "It's me, Omar, honey. I don't know what's going on, but I'm now in this guy's body."

"I don't believe you. My friend's name is Omar Cru. He's over there," Arlena rebuked.

Cru said, "I can't explain what's going on either." He kept rotating his arms as though someone had spilled acid on them.

The dean was as confused as everybody else but quick on his feet. He decided to quiz Sardis, who claimed to be in Cru's body. "I'm going to ask you a series of questions to confirm that you are Saul Sardis, even though you look like someone else." He did. The man who looked like Cru answered every one of them correctly, and the questions were about things that only Sardis could have known the answers to. The befuddled dean came to the only conclusion he could reach: the event was supernatural.

Marcel was in the corner sipping a bowl of soup, watching everything that was going down.

Sardis, sitting across from Arlena, wobbled and jiggled his head. He looked at her and said, "For a few minutes there, I was in his body." He shot a finger in Cru's direction. The two men were in their own bodies again. They went back to their seats and began recovering from whatever had gone on. Saul, looking remorseful, said to the dean, "I . . . I was wrong."

"What do you mean?"

"Before I left that man's body, I heard a voice that said: 'Saul, why are you persecuting me?'"

"Whose voice?"

"God's, you imbecile. Don't you know your Bible? Saul of Tarsus was blinded temporarily and knocked from his horse. After that, he was on fire for Jesus Christ."

The dumbfounded dean asked, "Does that mean you are now?"

Sardis got to his feet again and crowed loudly, "Yes! I'm changing my name to Paul." He leaned on the table with straight arms and added, "It'll be me who makes an apology. Some advanced civilization did not bring Adam and Eve here; they were created by the God of the Bible." He ran out, leaving his sandwich uneaten. The dean shook his head and watched Sardis drive away.

————————

"That's ridiculous," Brock asserted when his brother-in-law gave him a full report of the events after he got into his Mercedes and started back to Hazard.

"It sure looked real to me."

"Come on, Marcel, what you saw was heresy."

"How's that?"

"God doesn't swap brains, and for Professor Sardis to claim that was gold-plated blasphemy."

Marcel looked at his GPS to see when he'd arrive at the Skinner house. "Then how did he pull off a stunt like that?"

Brock had returned to the winery from his foray at Arlena's house and was standing in Maude's office looking out the window. "AI. Cru must have been wearing an earpiece."

"What good would that do?"

"I figure Sardis has built a robot in his computer with his personality and memory, essentially him in the form of AI," Brock supposed.

"Say what?" Marcel squeaked.

"The human version of Sardis must have spent hundreds of hours describing everything in his past and is loading new memories in the machine daily."

"What good is that?"

"Cru had a microphone and earpieces on him so the bot could hear the question and quickly provide an answer to make it look like Cru had become Sardis."

"But why?"

"To increase the lore around Omar Cru and give the newfound Paul Sardis the opportunity to become a Christian conman. If I'm right, Sardis, Cru, and Harring are planning to make a lot of money from their fame." Brock crouched to look through the camera aimed at Cru's house.

"Where do you think Sardis has his AI machine?"

"It'll be in a locked room in his house."

Marcel concluded, "There doesn't seem to be any doubt that the three of them are in league. What can we do to expose them?"

"Why should we do that? Their grifting isn't hurting us. Maude's paintings will grow in value."

"I thought you fought evil and were always on the side of good." Marcel smiled at his phone.

Brock told his brother-in-law to come to the winery when he got back to Hazard. Maude walked into her office as her husband ended the call. She asked, "What have you found out?" Brock explained what had happened, and she responded, saying, "All of this is just conjecture on your part, am I right?"

"It is." Brock put his hands on her waist.

"Can we mind our own business now?" she asked.

"Absolutely not. We must prove my theory is right." He let his arms drop.

"How do you propose we do that?"

"Find the link between Arlena Harring and Saul Sardis."

Marcel arrived at the winery shortly thereafter and took a seat by the indoor lunch area. Valerie saw him from where she was standing at the tasting bar. She went and sat beside him. He took a half an hour to report what had gone on and how Brock saw things. The Skinners and Sutherlands met up in Maude's office to make plans for the evening.

Brock's phone pinged again. He peered through the camera. The arrival of the two cars at Cru's cabin tripped several pictures. Arlena and Omar began unloading large paintings from the trunk of her car. "Check this out." Brock backed away and let the other three see.

Cru closed the front door of his cabin after Arlena brought the last of the five pictures in. She said, "I dried them with fans overnight. They should be okay to deliver."

Cru inspected each painting carefully. "They look fantastic. I don't plan to take the first one over to Giles until tomorrow. I must stretch out the deliveries to make him think I hand-painted them."

Arlena changed the subject. "How do you feel it went at lunch?"

"It seemed to fool the dean, which is all we really needed to do. Let's put these in the safe."

They carried the artwork of the five musicians to the fireproof door behind his studio. Omar went in to pick the places to rack them. He noticed the picture of the horse that was supposed to be at the end of the middle row was no longer there. "Arlena, someone has stolen one of the paintings."

"How do you know?"

"Because I put it there."

"Who could have done that?" she asked.

Cru thought it through and said, "Either our neighbor, Abner Giles, or the husband of the lady who owns the winery across town. She bought a painting of ours at Keeneland on Saturday."

"Well, whoever did it, do you think they're on to us?"

"I doubt it," he replied as he moved the five frames into the fireproof room. "I think I'll just lean these up against the wall since they'll be out of here so quickly."

"Why would they risk getting caught breaking in?"

"Because the paintings are valuable. I said as much to Abner Giles, and the woman who owns the winery commented that I'll be famous soon, ergo my works will increase in value rapidly."

"It's now up to Saul to get the word out. As soon as he does, what's your plan?"

"I'll call the Lexington art shop and offer them most of the paintings for several million dollars. I believe they have the money and courage to do that kind of deal. They'll probably advertise some of the pieces right away and hold back a batch to auction later, after the prices escalate." Avarice and greed welled up in his eyes.

"So, Saul and I will get big cuts right away?"

"A couple of million for each of you."

"Unless we get found out. Then we might end up in prison," she reminded him.

"That's not true. It's legal to sell a machine-made product for any price you want. We're better off if no one knows how they were produced though." He closed the door and went over to the window at the front of the house. "Would you like to get a pizza and eat it here?"

"First, I want to visit the winery of the woman who bought your painting. I think I danced with her husband on Saturday night. I'm guessing he's a lot smarter than he looks," she warned.

"They visited me on Sunday looking to buy more paintings. She told me her husband met you."

CHAPTER 8

Movement outside Cru's cabin registered on Brock's phone. He looked through the scope and saw Omar and Arlena getting into her car. Brock voiced the alarm he felt to his family. "It's a sure thing; those two are coming this way." He showed his wife the photo.

Maude said, "If they ask me if you stole a painting, I'm not going to lie about it."

Valerie suggested, "Brock, why don't you go back over there before they show up here and put it back. That way Maude, if asked, can truthfully say you didn't."

"A technicality," Marcel said, "But probably the best way out of this mess."

"I'll run by the house, load it in the truck, and head that way. Call me if you see them pull in."

Arlena entered Vigneron Winery ahead of Omar. She eyeballed the place, stepping aside when a heavy-set, countrified couple with a carrier full of wine approached the exit. The man stopped, looked above the door, and said, "That's a neat painting."

Omar arced around to see his horse art overhead. Arlena spotted Maude behind the tasting bar where she was pouring samples for a dozen people lined up like birds on a wire. Arlena raised her hand and came forward as if she was serving a search warrant. "Do you remember me?"

"Of course. You danced with my husband and my brother on Saturday night. You're quite the dancer." She glanced at Omar. "Brock and I met Mr. Cru on Sunday at his house. He gave me this beautiful little piece." She swept her hand in the direction of the inset in the wall behind her. "I feel guilty not paying for it. I'm going to send over some of our wines as a thank you."

With the countenance of an obsequious waiter, Cru said, "Please, it's Omar. I love how you've displayed the horse. Have you received any compliments?"

"If I had hung a price tag on it when I put it there, it would have been gone six times by now."

Marcel texted Brock to alert him of the couple's arrival at the winery, and then he and his wife walked out of Maude's office, over to the crowd at the tasting bar. Maude said to Arlena, "This is my brother, Marcel, and his wife, Valerie."

"Nice to see you again. Arlena, is it?" Marcel asked politely.

"Yes, and this is my friend, Omar Cru."

Maude jumped in: "He's the artist who painted the picture over the front door. You remember, I bought it when we were at Keeneland last Saturday."

"It's very impressive," Valerie remarked perceptively.

Arlena asked, "Where is your husband?"

"He's running an errand. He should be back shortly." Maude braced herself for the question she didn't want to answer. To sidetrack them, she asked, "How did you find the property on the hill where you built your cabin?"

"Funny you should mention Keeneland. Four and a half years ago, I went to the spring meet and met Arlena. She was working there. I told her about my dream of being a successful artist. She gave me the idea to look for an inexpensive place to build a barebones studio I could afford. I bought the mountaintop across town for a song."

Maude stood up straight and put her hands on the edge of the bar. "That sounds familiar. I did something similar. Years ago, I dreamed of running my own winery. I got a deal on this property as well, and Marcel lent me the money to build the place."

"And from what I can see, you've made a marvelous success of it."

"We have. Brock was a friend of Marcel's in college. He came to visit three years ago and talked me into marrying him. We live in a log cabin beyond the grapevines, on the other side of the mountain."

Omar added, "And I noticed your husband drives a Lamborghini. Rather notoriously, I'd say."

"For sure. Speaking of notorious, we didn't tell you this when we visited you on Sunday, but the reason we were up the hill by your house was to find out where to deliver some wine to a guy who came in here driving a Bentley."

"Yes, that would be my neighbor, Abner Giles. He knocked on my door a couple of years ago and said he wanted to buy the other end of the mountaintop, where he could put in a big house and paved driveway. When he told me he'd run utilities I could tie in to, I asked where to sign."

Brock pulled as close to Cru's cabin as he could. He carefully removed the painting from the truck and set it on the porch while he picked the lock. It took him less time to get into the fireproof room than on his first visit. He used a handkerchief to wipe any fingerprints off the frame of the picture before placing it back on the rack.

As he was getting ready to lock up and leave, Brock noticed the paintings leaning on the wall by the door. He gingerly fanned through them. They were distorted expressions of five musicians. The portrait on top was the guy who sang the bluesy number at the dance party. Therefore, the other four compositions must be the rest of the band. Cru had to have some sort of connection to Abner Giles, Brock surmised.

A small box truck was coming up the hill as Brock made his way down. Arlena and Omar were getting ready to leave when he got back to the winery. "Fancy meeting you here," Brock said after he came in from the warehouse.

Arlena spoke up, "Brock, now that you're here, I want to ask you and Marcel when I might get a chance to dance with you gentlemen again. I thought it best to ask in front of your wives. Good dance partners are hard to come by."

"I've got an idea," Maude interjected, pointing a finger upward. "If you'll let Valerie here teach Omar a few moves, the six of us can go out together sometime. Valerie was a dance instructor when she lived in Roswell."

Omar turned cautious. "Roswell? Isn't that where UFOs have been seen?"

Valerie replied, "Why, yes. I'm an alien myself." Everyone laughed.

Omar twitched and twisted his neck. "That's not so funny. I had the strangest thing happen to me at lunch today. For a few minutes, my brain jumped into the body of a man across the room whom I've never met. Something otherworldly happened. The guy whose brain went into my body proved who he was by answering questions only he knew the answers to."

Arlena said, "I saw the whole thing. Pretty spooky."

Valerie decided to float a scenario of her own. "There's nothing unusual about that. When I was in New Mexico, we heard those kinds of stories often."

"How could something like that happen?" Marcel asked.

Valerie crossed her arms, tilted her head back, and smiled wryly. "The God of the universe or an advanced form of artificial intelligence did it. Take your pick."

Brock used Valerie's theory as a cudgel. "Or there's a third explanation: someone played a trick on you."

"How could that be? I know what I felt. On another subject, Brock, you didn't happen to steal a painting of mine, did you?"

"No."

"Just thought I'd check. One's missing. I need to find out what happened to it," Omar remarked in an untrusting manner.

Maude circled back. "Well, Omar, do you want Valerie to teach you how to dance or not?"

Arlena arbitrated a plan. "Why don't the four of you come to my house on Saturday night. I have a dance floor in the basement. We can teach the artist here a few steps. What do you say to that, Omar?"

"I don't know," he said painfully.

"What time shall we be there?" Brock asked.

"Five o'clock. Do you have something I can write my address and phone number on? I'll have sandwiches for us." Maude gave her a pen and pad, though Brock had already been there.

When they were gone, Marcel warned, "She doesn't trust you. We better watch our step. She might try to lock us in the basement and kill us with poisonous gas."

"Or she could put poison in the sandwiches. My kind of party," Brock said absentmindedly.

———————

Passing through town on the way to the pizza shop, Cru asked, "Why are we getting involved with those people?"

"Because they're on to us. We must do something about it."

"How do you know that?"

"Brock said someone could have played a trick on you. He didn't ask whose body you jumped into, which means he already knows."

"How?" Omar whined.

"Because when I saw Marcel again, I remembered him. He came into the Circle of Blue when we were there. He slinked inconspicuously to a seat in the corner and kept to himself."

"What are we going to do?"

"Try to make a deal with them, I suppose. They're too high profile to kill and dispose of."

A chill ran up Omar Cru's spine.

———

Sadie Kirkham introduced herself to the slender drummer sporting a buzz cut and announced, "Let's get your kit into the studio and do a sound check before dinner."

When he got set up, he asked, "What sound are we going for?"

"Well, I've been told we're doing dance music in the rock genre, and that you'll be playing like John Bonham. I believe his technique was heavy—on the back of the beat. Play like him for me." The drummer began pounding away. "Okay, stop. I've got to bring your drums forward and take away the echo. The music needs to have a street feel." She pushed the rolling booth back and added insulation to the three sides and roof. "This time, play something that uses everything in the kit. You can play the triplets, I take it?"

He did four minutes' worth, including the triplets, without cracking a smile.

"Good. I've heard you can sight-read. See if you can play this." She put the score on a computer screen in front of him. While he was playing it, she donned headphones and adjusted several knobs on the sound board. When the song was finished, she said, "You're one hell of a talent. I'm surprised you're not with a top-tier band."

"Don't want to be. I'm a nine-to-five kind of guy. I like to take care of myself and read *The Wall Street Journal* and *The New York Times*. I'm sure I could have gotten filthy rich, but I do all right." He got up from the stool behind the drums and gave Sadie that smile she'd been waiting for.

"Come on, let's go down to the kitchen and sample some of the stuff we had delivered from a winery across town."

"When are Abner and the rest of the guys showing up?"

"In time for dinner, I expect." She peeked at her watch. "Which is in about two hours."

Dee Wathen entered the kitchen and began flirting with the drummer. He took a shine to her as she began preparing the evening meal. Sadie left him there and went back to the studio.

———————

The night air was crisp and breezy, foreshadowing worse weather for the weeks ahead. The Skinners and Sutherlands decided to play gin at the log cabin before putting a beef Wellington in the oven to bake for a half hour. Maude seemed worried. She voiced her concern, saying, "I'm not sure I trust those people."

"You shouldn't. They're crooks," Brock shared.

"We should get away from them then," Marcel said.

"It's too late for that. We've been made. They know we know what grift they're running. I'm betting Arlena recalled that you were in Circle of Blue when they put on their little show. She figures we must be on to them. Otherwise, how would you just happen to be in that lunch place when they were?"

"So, what do you think their play is going to be?" Valerie asked.

"They'll try to bribe us to keep quiet."

"That means he'll offer us a couple of his paintings," Maude continued.

Brock said, "Before we get too far into this charade of learning how to dance, I'm going to go up there and make a deal with Cru. What we really need to do is find a connection between Sardis and those two."

"Cru said Abner Giles knocked on his door and offered to buy the other end of the mountain. Who steered him there?" Maude asked.

"We don't know yet," Brock answered. "There's something mighty strange about Giles building a recording studio here in Hazard. Why would he do that?"

"Lots of recording studios are out in the country, all over the world. The musicians concentrate better when there are fewer distractions," Marcel argued.

"It's the two women who live there that's confusing me. One is prim and proper, and the other is itching to get raped. What the hell kind of operation is Giles running?"

Marcel suggested, "It would seem to me that one of them produces the product, and the other keeps the artists interested and engaged. Giles records the music and sets up a corporation for the benefit of those involved in writing and playing it. He's done it fourteen times before this."

"Yes, you're probably right. I've got a feeling Giles expects his next recording session to be a masterpiece. If it's that spectacular band we saw on Saturday night, I wonder who wrote all the new music?" Brock put his hand on his forehead.

Valerie had an opinion: "Remember the guy who sang that West Coast swing at the dance? It was the only time he opened his mouth, and the song was original. The rest of those men in the band are phenomenal studio musicians. The singer must have approached Giles with a demo. Giles knew it was good music, so he offered to put together the best band possible and record the songs."

"But he could have done that in Nashville where he's from," Marcel said.

"We need to find out why he came Hazard," Brock implored.

The men won the gin tournament by the skin of their teeth. The beef Wellington was cooked to perfection. After the meal, and when everyone got settled, Truman came into the family room to flop down in front of the fireplace before the humans began watching a mystery movie.

Maude whispered to her husband, "I hope you can find out how Sardis fits into this."

After the movie, the Sutherlands reported they'd be going home first thing in the morning.

Chapter 9

Since it was cold and drizzly outside on Wednesday morning, the musicians at Abner's house were inclined to sleep in until it was light enough to shame them out of bed. Most were down in the kitchen perusing the coffee and tea choices by eight thirty. Dee had laid out a buffet of sausage, fruit, croissants, and quiche. She barked, "I expect this food to be eaten while it's hot. Dig in." Four of the players stopped chatting and formed a line.

Sadie Kirkham appeared in the open arch near the breakfast table. "Good morning, gentlemen. I trust you slept well. We've got a busy day ahead of us."

The rhythm guitarist asked farcically, "We gonna rake leaves?"

The organist put in his two cents: "You wouldn't know which end of a rake to hold." The other two stifled chuckles with varying degrees of success.

"So, this is how it's going to be," the lead guitar player tossed out. He noticed the last spokes in the wheel were right behind Sadie. "And here's T Rem, with his Svengali, Abner Giles." The rest of the bandmates clapped mockingly.

Titus Remington bowed with style and grace. He looked something like David Beckam, but his face was rounder and hair a lot thicker, along the lines of Claude Akins. His sonorous, stentorian voice had a tincture of Kentucky twang in it, not enough to brand him as a country singer, but totally legit for his form of musical expression. He remarked in jest, "I guess you're wondering why I called you all here today."

"We know why you did: to make some kickass music," said the rhythm guitarist.

Abner broke in: "At least we have one bright bulb on the string. Seriously, we are putting the band back together because you all are the best musicians on the planet. We've got some tunes for you that will make us all rich."

The drummer offered, "Listen to him. He's already got stars in his eyes. Let us be the judge of that. Sadie said it's dance music."

"That's right."

The organist blathered, "I don't want to do any more of that infantile crap. I feel so cheap when I play on those sessions."

"You won't feel that way with these tunes," Abner scolded. "First of all, there'll be no revisions to the finished product using artificial intelligence. We won't overdub anything either. We'll lay tracks down separately, but nothing will be added over and above what the five of you will be able to play live."

Remy waded into the particulars. "There'll be twelve cuts, each a different dance rhythm. I've written the arrangements for everyone. You'll sound like a supergroup of famous musicians."

"I've been told I'll be playing like John Bonham. Who are the rest of the artists being copied?" the drummer asked.

"Malcolm Young, Dr. John, Stevie Ray Vaughan, and John Entwistle."

"Good Lord, Remy, all those people are dead. Rather macabre, don't you think?"

"Not really. You're going to bring them back to life, in a eulogy of sorts," Remington argued. He nodded at the rococo highboy against the wall and said, "Sadie, hand those computer tablets to our esteemed guests."

She read the names and distributed them accordingly. "I spent this morning placing big screens at your workstations. Everyone will practice the songs alone before we start layering the tracks together."

The lead guitarist remarked amazingly, "I wish every session I played on was this organized. I've never seen so much detail. You write all these parts, Remy?"

"I did," he remarked indignantly.

"Well, you're damn good."

"See what I'm saying?" Abner posed rhetorically.

In drill-sergeant fashion, Sadie said, "Okay, meet me in the studio in a half hour. We'll spend an hour balancing out the sound of all five instruments. Each of you can take twenty minutes to run through your part a few times. We'll start recording after that."

"Hold on a second, Sadie." The rhythm guitarist raised his hand and furrowed his brow. "Abner, tell us about the money."

"Usually, the musicians get forty percent and the songwriter thirty. Since you men are so good, Remy has changed the ratio to fifty twenty. The studio will get fifteen, the producer ten, and business agent five."

The drummer thought about it for five seconds and recapped the numbers aloud. "Remy will receive thirty percent, you will own fifteen, the other four of us and Sadie will each get ten percent, and Dee ends up with five percent. Is that correct?"

"Yes. The corporation will use accrual accounting, and I'll lend cash to it at five percent interest to cover the expenses that must be paid before we start making money."

Dee piped up, "I've got all the paperwork in my office. I'll let you read it and sign on the dotted line whenever you're ready."

"I'm ready to make music. Let's do it," Remy urged, delivered with the spark of a locker-room speech.

"One more thing," said the organist. "What's the name of the album?"

"Songs for Dancing Lovers," Abner replied as though he was revealing an important secret.

"A reference to Garner and Sinatra from the fifties," the rhythm guitarist remembered.

Giles said with a smile, "I told you he was a bright bulb on the string."

————

Students were on the edges of their seats waiting to see who the replacement instructor would be for their artificial intelligence class. They were befuddled when Saul Sardis entered as usual through the back door of the lecture hall. He stopped short of the lectern to address the crowd, saying, "I suppose you're surprised to see me again. I believe you deserve an explanation." He moved to where he normally spoke from and said, "On Monday, I shared the possibility that Adam and Eve were brought here by aliens. Even though it may be a possibility, I know for sure that the God of the universe put them here. You see, we can't have it both ways: it was either supernatural intelligence or artificial intelligence. Evidence in favor of supernatural intelligence is found in God's love, justice, and moral code. Artificial intelligence, as portended by Elon Musk, is merely 'summoning the demon.' AI can sin freely without fear of punishment. That, students, is its fatal flaw. Now, let's begin reviewing the reading material for the week."

The boy who thought he'd brought the professor down wasn't big on love and justice. He read his watch, quit listening to the lesson, and stared aimlessly at the artwork on the walls.

Sardis went home for lunch after teaching class. He fixed a corned beef sandwich and ate it in his office while studying the pictures of the five musicians he mutated and had printed for Cru. He stuck the pictures in the shredder by his feet one at a time to get rid of the evidence. Light rain kept dropping out of the low clouds and pinging on the gutters, causing Sardis to fall into a mild depression. He opened the manuscript of the book he had sent off to a publisher entitled *When I Met God.* That cheered him up.

Omar had been patiently waiting for the rain to stop. It did so a little after three. He carefully loaded the painting of Titus Remington in the trunk of his car and drove a few yards to the intercom by the gates of the Giles estate. Dee came on and asked, "Who are you?"

"I'm your neighbor next door. Abner asked me to do some paintings for him. I have one ready. I want to deliver it."

"Oh, like the one he brought in the other day and hung over the fireplace?"

"I suppose. He said he'd found a good place for it." Cru inspected the formidable concrete wall past the gate and the keyhole to gain entry to the estate.

"Let me go find out if he has time to see you." Dee went to the recording studio and waved Giles over while the musicians were playing. "Your artist friend across the way says he's got a painting for you. He's at the gate in his car."

Giles shook his head. "It's a bad time. See if he'll bring it in and leave it if you let him through."

Dee's voice came on the box again. "Abner says he can't meet with you right now, but he would like you to leave the painting here if it's okay with you."

"Works for me." The gates began to open.

Dee was standing in the driveway when Omar stopped his car next to her. When he got out, she introduced herself. "I'm Deianira Wathen. People call me Dee. Your name's Omar Cru I believe. I suppose the picture is in the trunk."

Cru took a chance. "I wish I had met you sooner. You're easy on the eyes."

She gave him a clunky stare. "Are you trying to come on to me?"

"That's a little harsh. I was just speaking my mind. Did I offend you?" he asked sweetly.

"Hell no. I've got plenty of suitors, but you might be able to work your way up the list with good manners."

"So, you're telling me there's a chance?"

"You stole that line from *Dumb and Dumber*." She was used to busting people's chops.

"Everybody steals everything from something or somebody," he remarked, holding his ground.

"I guess that means if I took up with you, I'd be stealing you from some other woman."

"You're getting personal now. I'd better get the painting out of the trunk and ferry it inside." When he went through the front door, he saw the fireplace across the room with his picture of Chuzzing above it. "That looks good there." He could hear music coming from somewhere.

Dee studied the piece Cru brought in the house. "Is this a cartoon version of Remy?"

"I'm not sure. I'll be doing the rest of the band over the next few days."

She ogled him and said, "You're as talented as you are good-looking."

"Where's the music coming from?"

"The recording studio. The band is here making an album."

Omar replied, "You weren't supposed to tell me that. Abner was keeping it a secret from me. I won't rat you out."

She wore ersatz aggravation on her face. "That's big of you. You'd better get along now. If you give me a good reason, I might pay you a visit at your little shack over there."

"How would you like to model for me in the nude? Or if that's a little much, just give me a nude picture and I'll do a nice painting of you."

"Don't you wish." She pointed at the front door, gesturing for him to leave.

———————

The band members and Abner Giles were carrying on three lighthearted conversations when they entered the kitchen in search of refreshments and a pupu platter of meats and cheeses. The recording session was finished for the day. Playing right through lunch, the band spent six hours grinding out an East Coast swing.

Remy asked, "How'd you like the song we did today?"

"Pure genius," the lead guitarist affirmed.

The organist said, "The damn thing sounds like a number one hit. Remy, your voice fit that tune to a T."

"The cowbell and triplets were tricky to play, but I think I got them at the end," the drummer remarked.

Abner reported, "Sadie will bring the tape up here in a few minutes so we can hear the finished product. We've got some nice red and white wines. Help yourself. I picked them up from a winery across town that makes pretty good juice. The woman who owns it is quite a looker."

"What time do they close?" the drummer asked.

Sadie appeared. "Six o'clock," she answered.

The drummer looked at his watch. "It's only a little after five. Shall we run over there?"

"If you don't mind, I'd like for us to wait and have lunch there tomorrow. I'd prefer that you do not drink when we go. It'll give us a chance to get out for a nice break midday."

"You want us to go to a winery and not have a glass of wine? Are you running a concentration camp here or something?" the rhythm guitarist questioned half in jest.

Sadie loaded the tape into the player and struck a pose. "Maybe this will convince you to stay sober as a judge until five o'clock tomorrow." She hit play. The song they'd laid down began piping through the speakers in the kitchen. She turned up the volume.

No one spoke but everyone smiled before the tune was over. The lead guitarist enthusiastically said, "Abner, you need to release that tomorrow. It will rock the music world."

"I'm with you. The other eleven songs are just as good. This thing's going to make a Steely Dan or Fleetwood Mac album sound flat. Sadie, you're doing a masterful job. Keep it up."

Dee came through the back entrance to the kitchen carrying a half dozen raw filet mignons. She told Abner, "You need to take the crew out to the living room and show them the painting your artist friend next door did of Titus. It's impressive."

"Let's go." Everyone turned and fell in behind Giles.

Remy was the first to see it. "Look at that. Incredible."

Abner informed the men, "He's doing all five of you. Says he'll have them done quickly."

"How much did you have to pay for them?"

Abner, looking embarrassed, told the band, "Eighty thousand, sixteen thousand a piece. But before you commit me to the loony bin, you should understand that his art is skyrocketing in value. I want to hang them in the formal dining room. I'll put Remy between the windows and the other four of you from the corners to the windows. Another idea came to me as well. I'd like to use them for the album cover art."

"Like Santana did on *Abraxas*," the organist reflected.

"What are we going to tackle tomorrow, Remy?" asked the rhythm guitarist.

"A tango."

"Rock bands don't play tangos," the drummer said officiously.

"Think of it like the transition Jonny Lang made from the first to second song on *Lie to Me.*"

"Huh. Lang became a Christian in 2000. Said he hated Christians before he had a supernatural encounter with the Holy Ghost," the lead guitarist noted.

"More power to him," Giles added. "Let's have another encounter with that pupu platter."

Chapter 10

Saul Sardis entered the dean's office early on Thursday morning to close the loop on the events of the week and discuss his changing plans. The sun, beaming through the window, brightened the atmosphere in the narrow room, and the dean could read every nuance on the mercurial professor's face. Saul said pleasantly, "What a week this has been."

"It has indeed. I'm still dumbfounded by what happened at Circle of Blue. Are you sure you weren't playing some sort of trick on me?"

"You heard what I said. I was in the body of that guy, Omar Cru. I've never met him before. I understand he's a gifted artist. When you asked me what my ranking in high school was when you interviewed me over dinner and I answered it correctly, that should have clinched it. Omar Cru would've never known the answer to that. I'm telling you, I was in that man's body."

"No, what clinched it was when I asked you what I had for dinner. When you said Nashville hot chicken without hesitation, I knew it was you in there." The dean redirected the conversation. "What is it you wanted to see me about?"

"I thought it best to let you know I plan to quit teaching after this semester. I'm going to publish a book about my experience and travel the country to share my testimony."

The dean tilted his head to the side and grinned. "Can't say that I blame you. All I ask is that you say good things about our university and mention us in your bio. We can use all the publicity we can get. So, you say that God spoke to you. Aren't you worried about being called a nut?"

"Certainly not. There is no higher calling than sharing the truth about our creator. That's what I'm going to do," Sardis responded.

"Just don't go overboard with that stuff during the last five weeks of the semester. I don't want the students complaining that you've swung too far the other way."

"I'll conduct myself professionally. You don't have to worry."

The dean pushed back his chair and stood. "Well, Saul, I suppose I'll have to authenticate your supernatural experience sometime down the line. I believe something very strange happened, and I have no reason to disbelieve your account."

"Thank you, sir. Remember, it's Paul now, like the conversion Saul of Tarsus experienced."

"All right, Paul."

November weather can occasionally be spectacular in Appalachia. It can also be colder than a well digger's knees in the Klondike. The temperature had clawed its way up to seventy degrees by noon, and with no wind, the sun made it pleasant enough to eat outside on the veranda at the winery. The entourage arrived in two cars. High-stepping Abner Giles led the way through the main entrance, followed by the five bandmembers, Sadie, and Dee.

When Abner saw Maude, he asked, "Can we have two tables for four outside for lunch?"

"Why, certainly. Are you going to introduce me to your friends? I'm Maude Skinner, by the way. I have the pleasure of making wine here at this outpost."

"And, as we can attest, damn fine wine it is. I'm Abner Giles, you may remember. This is Sadie Kirkham and Dee Wathen. These other gentlemen are musician friends of mine who've come to visit me. We're recording a few new songs. I have a little studio in the house." Maude offered her hand, and everyone gave their names when they shook hers.

"Follow me."

As they were going back out, Abner saw the Cru above the door. "Hey, that was painted by my neighbor. He sold me one like it, only more elaborate. He's talented, don't you think?"

"Extremely. I bought that last Saturday at Keeneland," Maude reported. The tables she gave them on the veranda were in a spot where the Giles mansion was visible. She jerked a thumb at it and confirmed, "There's your hacienda over there. Pretty swanky for these parts."

The organist appended, "Mighty swanky for anywhere."

"I must ask: why in the world did you build such a nice place overlooking Hazard?"

Abner was ready with his answer. "Not far off I-75, affordable, secure, beautiful country, far enough away from Nashville and the paparazzi, but close enough to get back there, and most importantly, Remy here, who lives in Lexington, suggested it."

Maude asked, "How'd you know you could get that particular mountaintop?"

Remy replied, "Dumb luck, I guess. Abner and I found Skyline Drive, which had some nice views. We went to the end of it and saw a gravel road up the hill. Omar Cru came to the door of the cabin up there. Abner made a deal with him on the spot."

Dee broke in, addressing Maude: "Where's your husband?"

Brock came around the corner and said, "I'm right here. Nice to see you again, Dee. And you as well, Sadie. Looks like you brought along some friends."

Abner introduced the bandmembers, then said, "The guys are not all that happy. We've asked them not to drink any wine because we're busy in the studio."

Brock suggested, "They'll forget all about it when Maude brings out what she's got on the lunch menu: beet and apple salad to go with a Monte Cristo sandwich."

Abner clapped his hands. "Hot damn. Bring it on." Maude retreated to fetch the food.

Brock, not hearing the earlier conversation, asked Remy, "Where do you live?"

"As we were telling your wife, I live in Lexington. Born and raised there. I went to Henry Clay High School."

"I did too. I was probably a couple of years ahead of you," Brock reported. "We know you're all professional musicians because Maude and I danced to your music on Saturday night in Mount Vernon. It didn't take a genius to see that you folks are gifted. We were wondering why a band of your quality took such a small-time gig."

The drummer answered, saying, "Abner flew us over from Nashville in a private jet, and on the way to the gig on Saturday night, he sprang on us that he wanted us to play on a recording session here in Hazard. So, here we are."

Giles said politely, "If you don't mind, Brock, we're trying to keep this music business quiet until we're done recording and can get the album out."

"How long's that going to take?"

Abner deferred to Sadie. She said, "We're shooting for a week from Sunday."

"If that happens, the album should be available by Black Friday after Thanksgiving," Dee said. "We'll do a fair amount of marketing as soon as the date is a sure thing."

"I take it you think the music is pretty good."

The lead guitarist asserted, "It's not pretty good, it's unbelievably good."

"I hope it sells like hot cakes; I'll be sure to get a copy. Thanks for stopping by, and enjoy your lunch," Brock said as he was heading inside to help deliver the food. When he saw Maude in the kitchen, she told him, "Titus Remington steered Giles up the hill. How does he figure in this?"

———

At four o'clock that afternoon, Brock informed his wife that he was going to run up to Cru's place. She warned, "Don't get those people after us. There's money involved. They might do irrational things."

"If he tries to bribe me with a painting, I'm going to refuse it. Otherwise, we could get caught in the crossfire if the shooting starts."

"Just come back with a peace treaty," she said with finality.

Brock parked his winery truck behind the vehicle in front of the cabin at the top of the hill to keep Cru from driving out. Omar seemed friendlier than he should have been when he came to the door. "All of a sudden, I'm getting lots of visitors up here."

"There's going to be even more when the story about you and Saul Sardis hits the news."

"What is it I can do for you, Brock?"

"Nothing per se. I just wanted you to know where we stand."

"How do you mean?" Cru stepped aside to let Skinner in the house.

"From what I can tell, you and Arlena Harring intend to sell a lot of your art. The paintings are excellent. I don't think anyone will be able to prove you've had a little help. In fact, I'm positive everything is on the up and up. You need to know that we're not in the business of tearing down other people's enterprises, as long as they're legal."

Cru sat on the cloth couch and Brock took the leather side chair. "You're implying there's some illegal path that might present itself?"

"If you affirm what happened in Circle of Blue and it turns out to be hoax, the police might put you in jail. Before you say anything, I don't want to know what happened at that lunch place. I've got my own opinion about that. I'm just recommending you not swear on a stack of Bibles that the brain of Saul Sardis jumped into your body and God spoke to him. If I were you, I'd make myself scarce to the press, and if you're backed into a corner, I'd decline commenting on what happened."

"Are you a lawyer or something?"

"No. You don't need one yet," Brock presumed out loud.

"I get the feeling you're looking for something from me. What is it?" Cru scooted to the front edge of the couch and put his arms on his thighs.

"I'm not looking for a bribe to keep quiet. Quite the contrary. We bought one of your paintings, and when it goes up in value, that will be okay with us. I'm trying to learn how you found this property, and how Giles knew to try to buy the other end of the ridge up here."

"I can't speak for Giles. He just showed up here one day with another guy. Wait a minute, now that I think back to that visit, the other guy might have been Titus Remington. He had shorter hair then. I just did a painting of him for Abner. I'm doing the other four musicians now."

Brock said, "All that tells me is that Giles and Remington knew each other. What about finding this spot in the first place?"

"I took up with Arlena Harring four years ago. She told me she'd driven past the sign posting this hillside for sale. She pushed me to see about it and offered to lend me the money to buy it. I didn't need it. I had enough to buy the land and build this cabin."

"She's not from Hazard. Why would she be driving around out here?"

"Brock, I can't tell you. Why is it that important?"

"Someone must have tipped her off. I wonder who it was?"

"I have no idea," Cru fired back.

"Let's talk about Saul Sardis. What do you know about him?" Brock sensed he was cornering Cru. "Does Arlena know him?"

"Taking your advice, I'd rather not comment. I can't tell you where I heard it, but I understand he's planning to write a book about his experience."

Brock jumped up and said, "That's it. It explains why he built his own AI personality for several years. He'll have it write a book about his life and how he had a supernatural encounter with God. He'll get rich off the book, and you'll be mentioned in it, which means your artwork will become extremely valuable. I see the play now. Ingenious, I must say."

"Well, if it works out that way, it won't hurt my feelings," Omar affirmed.

"Is Arlena Harring your business partner or lover or both?" Brock was squeezing him hard and fast now.

"We see each other."

"When the two of you become wealthy, will you go your separate ways?" Brock asked.

Cru got to his feet and went to the front window. "If she leaves me, I'll put some money into this place and attract another nice girl, one who appreciates what I have to offer." He turned to face Brock, expecting another barrage of questions.

"I think I know where you're going with this. Arlena may prefer Saul's money over yours."

"You never know with women. I just met Dee from next door. She's an interesting character."

"I've met her as well. What do you know about what's going on over there?"

Cru reported, "I don't know much about Abner. I learned yesterday that he's got a recording studio in that mansion. He seems like a nice enough guy. Apparently, a band is making music over there right now. He told me Titus Remington was a tremendous singer."

"He's right about that. The band played at our dance party last Saturday night. Remington sang one song and knocked it out of the park," Brock shared. "Look, Omar, let me cut to the chase. If Harring and Sardis get the last two chairs when the music stops, you may be in danger."

"What do you mean?"

"You are the only person, besides Arlena, who could expose Sardis as a fraud."

"What's the big deal about that?"

Brock sat again and leaned back in the chair. He looked away as he spoke. "They may kill you."

"What? That's ridiculous." Omar flashed back to when Arlena suggested Brock was too high profile to kill and dispose of. Doubt began creeping into his mind.

"I have a funny feeling that in a few months, Abner Giles is going to make you an offer for your half of the mountain. One you can't refuse."

"Why would he want to do that?"

"Because he's got some use for your cabin here," Brock conjectured. "Why did you decide to put in the fireproof concrete room when you built the place?"

"Arlena suggested the idea."

Brock got up to leave. "I recommend you let her know I came by and told you I hope your art increases in value, and that Maude and I wish the best for you and her."

"What will that accomplish?"

"You need to get her to believe that we don't care what the two of you do."

Cru opened the cabin door and went out onto the front porch. He asked, "Is that true?"

"In a sense, yes. You do need to follow through on one thing: taking a few dance lessons from my sister-in-law on Saturday night."

"What if Arlena doesn't believe your story?"

"Let us worry about that. We can sell her on the fact that we're innocent bystanders." Brock stepped off the porch toward the truck.

"Okay, I'll do it," Omar acquiesced.

"Who knows? You might like dancing. Then the six of us can go out and have some fun." Brock got in the truck and backed out cautiously. He waved to Cru as he descended the hill.

Cru went back inside after a minute and peered across the valley at Maude's winery.

CHAPTER 11

Maude was preparing to close when Brock returned from his visit with Omar. There were two well-to-do couples playing kissy faces, wasting time at the tasting bar. The Skinners would head for home when the four of them cleared out. Brock called Marcel and asked, "Can you hack into the Perry County records and find out whom Omar Cru bought his land from?"

"Hang on, I might be able to pierce that veil quickly. What's the address again?"

"Nine ten Skyline Drive."

"Here it is. Cru bought a little over thirty acres in late October four years ago. The seller was the estate of Garrison Lynch. The parcel was subdivided in December two years back. Abner Giles bought the fifteen acres to the west."

"How much did Cru pay for it?"

"Fifteen hundred dollars an acre."

"How much did Giles pay for his fifteen acres?"

Marcel replied, "Three thousand an acre."

"So, Cru ended up with his land for free. Try to find out if Lynch had any heirs and then let me know."

On the way home, Brock filled Maude in on his visit with Cru. She said, "If he tells Arlena that you suggested his life might be in danger, she'll put two and two together."

"He won't tell her. She'll eventually come to that conclusion herself," Brock replied confidently.

Brock took Truman out for a two-mile run-walk while Maude whipped up a spectacular version of chawanmushi. Marcel called back before Brock had cleaned up the kitchen. "Garrison died in May four and a half years ago. He inherited the thirty acres from his folks and left it to his only child, a woman by the name of Ruby Lynch. She never married. Garrison lived in Lexington his whole life, and Ruby moved back into the house where she was raised after he got tossed into a casket. Her address is 9839 Bowman Mill."

"Marcel, you're a miracle worker. I'll see if she comes to the door when I knock."

"Bowman Mill is beautiful horse country. The Lynch house looks to be modest compared to the places nearby owned by the gentry."

"You don't say," Brock said, preoccupied with his own thoughts.

"Are you interested in who lives in the big house next door to her?"

"Should I be?"

"Probably. His name is Titus Remington."

———————

Remy and the band were engaged in the cut and thrust of the tango they'd mastered that day. It, too, was a phenomenal track. Everyone at the table felt good about the arrangement except the drummer. His glum appearance caused Remy to ask, "Is something bothering you?"

"I don't know. You've done such an incredible job on the music scores; I hate to even suggest what I'm thinking."

"Spit it out, man," Remy said sternly. The conversation stopped.

"I don't think Bonham's style is the right one for the tango."

"Is that so. Whose style should I have emulated?"

"Ginger Baker's would have been better," the drummer reported. "Here's the thing: I know that if we all start tinkering with your arrangements, this session will turn into a free-for-all. I don't want that to happen. At least I feel better now that I've shared my opinion."

Remy stood, walked around behind the high-back chair he'd been sitting in, and put his arms on it. "You're right. It would be a mess. This wouldn't be the first time that's happened. Billy May tinkered with Nelson Riddle's arrangements, and Sinatra had to make a call occasionally." Remy looked at the other musicians one at a time. "Do you all think I should change the drum part?"

The lead guitarist spoke up: "We'll play whatever you tell us to. Why don't you rewrite his part and use it on a second version of the song, and then we can see if he's right."

No one else, including a disinterested Abner Giles, said anything for at least a minute. "All right. I'll run home tonight and bring Ginger Baker back in the morning," Remy said.

The rhythm guitarist added a little humor: "One good thing: he's dead like all the others."

———

Brock left the house in his Lamborghini at six o'clock on Friday morning. The wind had picked up and was gusting in all directions. He stopped south of Lexington to get a cup of coffee once the light of day was coming on. At nine, he pulled into the driveway of Ruby Lynch and parked on the right side, away from the direct path to the garage. The ranch home looked to be seventy years old. The outside had been spruced up recently. Brock figured

Ruby still had money she'd gotten from her dead dad and had used some in a meager attempt to keep up with the Joneses.

Brock expected a downtrodden hussy to open the door, and much to his surprise, a stunning woman of forty stood there. Her hair and clothes suggested she was a groupie, and it was one fine look on her. He asked politely, "Are you Ruby Lynch?"

"I am. What can I do for you?" She gave him a smile that signaled she wasn't unhappy he was there.

"I'm Brock Skinner. My wife and I live in Hazard, and we just met the gentleman who bought a piece of property from you four years ago. He's an artist. His works are going up in value. We've been trying to learn why he built his art studio there, which is such an out-of-the-way place."

"Why do you want to know that?" She peered at Brock's car and concluded he wasn't a rube.

"We own a winery nearby. We're trying to figure out if he's going to stay there as he becomes more famous, or whether he might move out. You see, if he stays, we're going to ask him if he'll let us sell his works at our shop. We were wondering if he has some special attachment to the place or if it's just a location he might readily abandon."

"The only person who ever had any attachment to that property was my father. I urged him to sell that worthless mountain while he was alive. He refused. After he died, it was going to come to me, and I was thrilled to get a touch over forty-five thousand for it."

"So, Omar Cru, the fellow who bought it, has no connection to you or your family?"

"No. The lawyers for my father's estate put a sign up by the road in early October, and to my surprise, they found a buyer in a couple of weeks."

"Well, that's what my wife and I were afraid of. It probably won't be long before he sells out."

"The winery business must be pretty good if you can afford a car like that."

Brock couldn't tell if she was jerking his chain or being serious. "I'm also part owner in an online clothing company by the name of Sutherland Tailoring. You should look it up. There are outfits on there that an attractive woman such as yourself might find appealing." Brock began backing away slowly. "By the way, how did your father die?"

"He used to go hiking on that mountain. When he went missing for a few days, I sent the police to look for him. He apparently fell and hit his head. He was dead." She acted as though it was considered the predictable outcome of his risky behavior.

"Was there any sign of foul play?"

She shifted her weight to the other leg. "I was wondering when you were going to get down to business. That poppycock about selling an artist's paintings didn't hang together very well for me. You're trying to figure out who killed my father and why, aren't you?"

"I might already know who. I just don't know why, and I'm a long way from proving it. Your neighbor, Titus Remington, didn't kill him. How well do you know Titus?"

"Funny you should bring that up. I've never met him. He goes out of his way to avoid me."

"Anyone who avoids you has bad eyesight or a good reason to stay away. I'm betting it's the latter. I'll make you a deal: when I figure out what happened to your father, I'll come see you again and lay it all out."

"Fair enough. What's the name of your winery? I might run up and visit you before it gets too cold."

"Vigneron. My wife, Maude Skinner, is the owner and proprietor. We'd love to have you come by." Brock climbed into his car and backed out of the driveway. He drove slowly past Remy's house to see if any creatures were stirring. From what he could see, not even a mouse.

———————

Remy got back to the Giles estate at nine thirty on Friday. He handed the memory stick to Sadie when he reached the recording studio. She downloaded the arrangement and brought it up on the screen in front of the drummer, who was ready to pound away. He wore headphones that piped in the song without the drum track. It took him seven takes to get it right, and boy, was it right. When the rest of the band came in at ten o'clock to start learning the third song, Sadie played the tango with the second drum track. Remy admitted, "It's better than the first version. I say we keep it." The rest of the players agreed.

———————

Brock called Marcel and got the address of Saul Sardis. His house was less than five miles from the homes of Ruby Lynch and Titus Remington. Marcel said, "He's not there. His class at Slade is from ten o'clock to eleven thirty on Monday, Wednesday, and Friday."

"All the better. I can snoop around a bit."

"I'd be careful. He probably has cameras everywhere."

Brock pulled into Westmoreland Estates, which was only a short distance beyond Keeneland. "Yeah. I just want to get the lay of the land. Marcel, look to see where Sardis was and who he worked for before he came here."

"Will do. What did you get from Ruby Lynch?"

"Her father fell and hit his head while hiking on the property in Hazard."

"I'm afraid to ask. Do you think someone killed him?"

"Certainly. I'm parked in front of the house of the man who did it, but I'm sure he's too smart to get caught. I wonder why he wanted him dead?"

Brock finished the call and hoofed it up to the house. It was a brick affair, one where the mason had left the mortar in place that had oozed out of the joints, and the top of every feature had a pronounced arch over it, including the wall that ran in front of the entrance. Trees and bushes were all over the place, many leafless now, left untrimmed for the season. As Brock placed one foot on the porch, a voice came through a flush-mounted speaker overhead. "This is private property. Please leave."

"I'm a reporter for a Louisville newspaper. I'm following up on a life-changing event involving Saul Sardis. Is he available?"

"No."

"Whom am I speaking with?" Brock asked.

"My name is Solomon, master of the house."

"When will Mr. Sardis be available?"

"He does not receive guests or grant interviews." The cadence of the voice had changed.

"Who is it, Solomon?" A different person came on.

"It's a newspaper reporter. I asked him to leave."

The second voice inquired, "What does he want?"

"To ask you questions, I presume."

Brock interrupted, "Is that you, Mr. Sardis?"

"Yes."

"Our newspaper wants to run a story about your encounter with God. Would you be willing to answer a few of my questions and tell me just how it happened?"

"That's a waste of time. A book is coming out chronicling what I experienced. You can pull out what you need from that."

Brock turned his back on the door and said, "If you give me something to publish, I'm sure the publicity will jumpstart your book sales."

"I won't be needing that. The book will do fine on its own."

———————

The girl with the stark blues eyes in the artificial intelligence class at Slade University raised her hand meekly after the lecture was over. When called upon by Professor Sardis, she probed a point. "You told us during the last class that the downfall of AI will be rooted in the fact that it has no conscience. Could you expound on that idea?"

"Well, let's start with the premise that AI has no soul. There is no sense of justice, no penalty for wrongdoing or deviating from the truth. People who have that same mentality do not fear the possibility of being punished for harming others. What keeps a religious person from doing evil things? I suggest to you that a moral code authored by a supernatural force, also known as the law, sets up the concept of good and evil, which can only be reconciled by justice."

She responded to his explanation by commenting, "Then you are saying that AI will gravitate to doing only evil things because it cannot rationalize truth and justice."

"Not exactly. It will gravitate to selfishness, doing things that are considered accomplishments for its own purposes at the expense of everyone and everything it meets."

"But how can that be? Isn't it possible to program a moral code that drives only good behavior and restricts bad?"

The professor tapped his toes and looked down. "Of course, that's possible. You're missing one important point: AI systems programmed for evil will have the power to devour those built to do good. Nothing can stop predatory systems from being developed."

Blue Eyes leaned to the side and gazed at the Benton art on the wall. "I think I understand what you mean."

"Let's examine a scenario from a Christian worldview: if there's no force in the universe capable of defeating Satan, he will reign victorious when total depravity engulfs the world."

"In that instance, there'd be no force for good that could win the battle for truth and justice."

"Yes, that's a nice way to put it." The professor threw out his hands and smiled to lighten the mood of the class.

"What can we do to prevent that from happening?" she asked.

"I would like each of you to ponder that question over the weekend and come back on Monday with some interesting ideas we can discuss. Class dismissed."

The blue-eyed girl felt a knot in her stomach. Until that moment, she had not considered the ramifications of a world dominated by artificial intelligence–one she now feared.

CHAPTER 12

Brock had been parked on a side street in Westmoreland Estates for nearly two hours. His arms and legs were getting stiff, not to mention the crick in his neck from watching the clouds scud across the sky. He was about to pack it in when a silver sedan whizzed by. It went directly to the Sardis house and pulled into the garage. Satisfied that Marcel was correct about where the professor had been that morning, Brock called his brother-in-law. "You were right. Saul just got home. There's only one thing wrong: he talked to me a couple of hours ago through a speaker on his front porch."

"You must have been chatting with AI Saul who lives in his supercomputer."

"Okay. But another guy introduced himself: Solomon, master of the house."

"Who's he?" Marcel inquired.

"Master of the house, I guess."

"Hey, listen. I started digging into the list of seasonal employees who worked at Keeneland four or five years ago. I ran across the name of the other lady we danced with who went to Mount Vernon with Arlena. I called her, introduced myself, and asked if she ever remembered meeting Saul Sardis."

"Did she?"

"No, but she said he called her out of the blue and asked if she'd be interested in going to work for him as his confidential assistant."

"What did she tell him?"

"She said she didn't want to and suggested he call Arlena Harring."

Brock wanted to know: "Did he, and did she ask Arlena if he'd called?"

"She asked her. Arlena denied hearing from the guy. I think Arlena's lying because she didn't want her friend to know she had taken the job. I've got a hunch she doesn't want anyone to know."

"Okay. Some of the pieces are coming together."

Marcel said, "You may have made a mistake walking right up to the Sardis house. The computer certainly took your picture and found out who you were before you got back to your vehicle. I'm sure the human Saul Sardis has been told, and you can bet he's going to ask Arlena who the hell you are and why you're snooping around his house."

"She could go a lot of ways with the answer," Brock replied.

"One way isn't good. If Arlena tells Sardis that you know about the AI paintings and that you're trying to run down who's behind them, he might think you're looking for a blackmail angle."

"I guess I better confront the problem right now. I'm going back to his house."

"Oh boy." Marcel's voice drooped and tailed off.

After Sardis opened the tall, blue-paneled door of his house, he said, "And you would be Brock Skinner. You needn't waste time telling me about yourself; my computer has already filled me in. Won't you come in?"

"Thanks."

The hall by the door went left and right. There was a picture on the wall of flowers in a white and blue vase, purportedly painted by Omar Cru, which did a good job blocking the chi. Brock followed Saul into the living room to the right. It had a low ceiling by modern standards, with oversized crown molding. The leather furniture on the beige carpet was nice enough. "What's your business, Mr. Skinner?"

"No sense dancing around the issue. I heard about your supernatural flim-flam on the news, and from Arlena Harring and Omar Cru when they stopped at my wife's winery. We bought one of Omar's paintings. I came here looking for you a couple of hours ago to tell you that I know how you pulled that stunt."

"Do you now." He sat on the couch. Brock took the side chair closest to the hall.

"Yes. You built an AI Saul in your supercomputer, which knows everything about you. Omar was wearing a microphone and earpiece so that AI Saul could hear and answer questions."

"What a fanciful story." Sardis didn't seem fazed.

"The way I see it, you and Omar are going to be famous. He'll sell his art, and you'll have AI Saul write your life story, and then you'll hit the rubber-chicken circuit," Brock forecasted.

"Got it all figured out, do you?" His affable demeanor had begun to fail him.

"Before you get nervous about anything, I want you to know I'm not going to meddle in your affairs." That was a lie but plausible enough in the short term.

"Then why did you show up here?"

"Because I want to buy the property Omar Cru owns in Hazard. My wife and I can see his little cabin across the way from the winery. We would like to use the property for events."

"I'm afraid you're mistaken. The first time I saw Arlena Harring was when she and Omar Cru came in that Greek lunch place. I'm not involved with those people. What exactly did you think my relationship with them was?"

"You're the one who uses AI to program Cru's paintings. Arlena must have the printer hidden somewhere. She's the go-between."

"I have no idea what you're talking about. I had a supernatural event that has changed my life." Saul put on a pious act. Brock didn't buy it.

"None of that really matters to me. All I'm interested in is buying the property Cru owns. I guess I'll have to go up there and get a right of first refusal agreement or contract to buy it upon his death."

"That may cost you a lot based on his success as an artist," Saul warned superciliously.

"I've got plenty of money. Enough to outbid anyone," Brock retorted brashly.

"Best of luck to you. I'd like you to leave." Saul sprang up and led the way to the front door.

Brock turned around after he stepped outside and said, "Just so we're clear on this, if anything happens to me, everything I know is in a safe at an undisclosed location. That means I need to stay alive if you're going to continue to run the grift you've started. I won't try to stop you."

Sardis replied, "I would've expected nothing less from a character such as yourself." He hollered over his shoulder, "Solomon, fix me a bourbon Manhattan."

"Coming right up." That was all Brock heard before the door slammed in his face.

Through the front window, Sardis watched Skinner get in his Lamborghini and drive away. The professor found his phone and made a call. "You need to meet me in the morning at the usual place. Eight o'clock."

Omar Cru had the TV tuned to the horseracing channel late Friday afternoon. There were some quality horses in the last few races at Churchill Downs, and he had bet on them. As the winner of the eighth race galloped across the finish line, a knock on the door attracted Cru's attention. Dee Wathen was standing there. "You going to ask me in?" She was wearing a black sweater and gray slacks. The dangling gold earnings she had on made her look sexy.

"By all means." He took her hand and pulled her across the threshold.

Dee slowly canvased the inside of the shack. "Cozy little place you've got here. It's not the Ritz or what I'm used to," she said cattily.

"It makes a good little love nest. Are you searching for one?"

"You never can tell. I see you're watching the ponies. Are you a gambling man?"

He threw his hand toward the couch, inviting her to sit. "No, not really. I'm soon to be a famous artist. When my ship comes in, I might bulldoze this place and build a mansion that will attract a beautiful woman such as yourself." He sat down next to her.

"I like flattery. You have your share of it." Dee leaned back, revealing she wasn't wearing a bra.

"Can I get you anything to drink?"

"No, thank you."

Omar put his arm along the top of the couch and bent forward at the waist. "To what do I owe this pleasure?"

"I thought I'd come over and see if you'd do that portrait of me you mentioned."

Omar replied, "Dee, honey, I'd drink your dirty bathwater. Of course I'll do it."

She straightened up and rocked her shoulders back and forth. "How does this work then?"

"Take off your clothes and let me get a shot of you that I can work from." He stood and went to his studio to retrieve his digital camera. "It would be wise if you got away from the windows. Come sit over here and strike a pose." He pulled a high-back chair with wide, flat arms away from the wall. "Lean to the right and put your arm on the chair arm. Kick out your left leg and put your left hand on your thigh." She did what he asked. "Now lean back. That looks good."

"I suppose it's time for the clothes to come off." Dee stood, kicked off her shoes, dropped her slacks, and removed her sweater. The last thing to go were her bikini panties. She moved the pile of clothes away from the front of the chair and sat again.

Omar said softly, "You're stunning." He took five pictures from slightly different angles and let her see them. "Which one do you like the best?"

She studied them for a minute and replied, "This one." She handed him the camera and began to put her clothes back on.

"I like it too."

"How long will it take you do the portrait?" she probed as she was slipping into her shoes.

"About two months. I must finish the backlog of work I have before I can get to it." He hadn't figured out yet how he was going to sell the idea to Arlena. She might blow a gasket and come at him with a knife. He had an idea that might work.

Dee went to the door and grabbed the knob. She said, "Why don't you give me your number so I can call you when I'm alone up at the big house."

Omar wrote the digits on the back of a small card that had his name on it. "I hope that's sooner than later," he said pleasantly. She took the card and deftly closed the door after she went through it. Omar turned his attention to the ninth race to check the odds.

Arlena Harring saw a woman walking between Cru's cabin and the gates of the adjacent estate when she reached the top of the hill in her car. Cru heard the vehicle approaching and hid the camera in a kitchen cabinet. He got back to the TV just before Arlena let herself in. She asked, "Who was that woman I saw walking toward the mansion?"

"Dee Wathen. She's an employee of Abner's. She came to see if another painting was ready. I told her I'd bring it over tomorrow when it was dry."

"If I'm not mistaken, she wasn't wearing a bra underneath her sweater," Arlena allowed.

"I didn't notice. I should have looked closer. Did you bring anything we can whip up to eat?"

"No. Something's going on. Saul called me this afternoon and said we had to meet. He sounded troubled."

"He acts like that at times. Hazard doesn't have much in the way of fine dining. Let's drive over to that nice steakhouse in London," Omar recommended.

"Okay. We'll take both cars. I'll go home from there," Arlena said.

"Sounds good." Cru lowered his head and raised his eyebrows. "You still want to go through with that dance party thing tomorrow night?"

"Yes. You're sure the Skinners aren't gaming us?"

"I know they're not. They're multimillionaires. You can interrogate them yourself. I like 'em. It sometimes pays to have rich and influential friends." He wanted to keep everybody in the boat until his paintings went out the door and the money rolled in. In his mind, Dee Wathen was a far better catch than Arlena, even if Arlena could dance up a storm.

"Let's run over to the winery and make sure they're on for the party."

Omar said brightly, "I want to change into something nicer. After all, a beautiful woman like you shouldn't be seen with just any shabby man."

"Do you really think I'm beautiful?" she asked pointedly.

"I know it."

———————————

Brock waved at his wife when he walked through the tasting room on the way to her office. A copious number of pictures had been taken of the Cru house that afternoon. He started looking through them. Omar had gone out by car and then came back. Brock squinted to name the woman in the next picture who was traipsing on foot toward the cabin. It was Dee Wathen. She went back the other way just before Arlena drove up. Cru and Harring left in separate cars minutes ago.

Maude came into the office and said, "Omar and Arlena popped in for a second and confirmed the party was still on at her house for five o'clock tomorrow evening. They left quickly to drive to London for dinner."

Brock told Maude what happened that day. He ended the story by saying, "I need to find who Sardis did work for when he came here. Something's missing."

"So, you believe you were talking to a computer at the Sardis house?"

"I'm sure of it."

"And somebody named Solomon proclaimed he was master of the house? That sounds like the title of a character in a Hollywood movie from the thirties."

"Sardis told him to fix a drink. He must be a butler or something," Brock surmised.

"What do you know about this Garrison Lynch character?" she asked.

Brock went to the window to look out. "Nothing yet."

"We met Titus Remington. Maybe you could ask him about Lynch."

"We might tip our hand," he responded.

"What do you mean?"

"There seems to be some kind of doom loop among all these people: Sardis, Harring, Cru, Giles, Remington, and possibly Lynch."

"How do you get that?" Maude sat in her desk chair.

Brock pointed out the window and peered across town. "It's right over there on that mountain. A recording studio and famous artist overlooking Hazard?"

"That does seem fantastic," Maude agreed.

"I'm going to have to go to California to trace Sardis, to find out why he visited and moved here. He doesn't play in low-limit games. Something here in Appalachia is worth his effort and the disruption in his life."

"Money, fame, power, revenge, a woman?" Maude just about covered it.

CHAPTER 13

The temperature had finally plummeted to where it should have been for eight o'clock on a Saturday morning in early November. Saul remarked, "Arlena, I'm planning to sell my house to Solomon on December fifteenth, the last day of classes at the university. I've resigned my professorship and will be traveling the country to support my book."

Harring and Sardis had been meeting at the Athens Coffee Barn since he had convinced her to drop most of the Ten Commandments in her moral code of ethics nearly five years ago. There was a secluded, fenced parking lot behind the shop where things could be exchanged confidentially. Inside, a rickety oak table behind the unisex restroom provided a spot where private conversations could be held.

"Where will you live?" she asked in a tone that suggested she knew her run was ending.

"I'm not sure yet. We should meet here that morning for the last time. You'll be a millionaire by then. I must say, you've been a true and loyal friend to me. I know good things are ahead."

"Thank you for the kind words." She wriggled uncomfortably in her chair.

"Is anything wrong?" he asked.

"Yes. A snoop by the name of Brock Skinner knows AI painted Cru's pictures. I'm worried he'll blow things up for us, and Omar won't be able to sell his paintings. I'll end up with zippo."

"Skinner came to my house yesterday and accused me of being a fraud. If we stick to our stories and continue to deny that we know each other, things will be okay."

Arlena closed her eyes and put her head down. "I'm also worried about Omar. He might flip on us. If he does, we're all in the soup."

"He won't do anything until he sells his artwork, and by then, he'll be mesmerized by money. The real problem is that Skinner wants to buy Omar's land. If he finds out he can't, he'll start digging deeper," Sardis predicted.

She asked, "Why can't he?"

"If you'll remember, Abner Giles knocked on Cru's door and convinced him to sell half of the mountain so he could put a big house up there. The promise of getting utilities to his shack convinced him to sell. The transaction interested me, so I looked up the sale contract Omar signed that got filed at the courthouse. I noticed an option for Giles to buy Cru's remaining half of the mountain whenever he wants at an inflation adjusted price, which includes the cabin, whether Cru is living there, gone, or dead."

"I'm guessing Omar doesn't know what he signed," she supposed.

Sardis looked out the window and said, "Skinner will go up there and get a right of first refusal agreement. Everything will be fine unless he finds out like I did that a deal is already in place to sell to Giles."

"When do you want me to dismantle the printer?"

Saul's eyes were uncaring, disguised by a manufactured warmth that he projected with the rest of his body language. "You don't have to do anything. If you keep it, I'll mail you a memory stick occasionally that will have a file on it ready to print. You can become an artist too."

"I thought you were going to break off communication with me," she said.

"A package in the mail with no return address is not a breach of that distinction," he clarified. "You just keep mailing a check of my cut to the photography studio and I'll be happy. One last thing: there is no evidence in your house that could tie us together, right?"

"Nothing besides the printer," Arlena said emphatically.

"You've destroyed the jump drives with artwork on them that I've sent you?"

"I have," she replied firmly.

"Good. Relax. Everything's going to be okay."

On the drive back to Richmond, Arlena began wondering if Saul Sardis, being the crook he was, had a plan to get rid of her and Omar to cover his tracks. She'd already faced the fact that she, too, was a crook of sorts. Once a person turns bad, they rarely turn good again. How would he do it? He could blow up Omar's rustic cabin or her nice little house with the printer in it. Maybe it was right to consider changing teams. Omar had already hinted it could make sense.

———————

On the Beat tackled a foxtrot on Friday and was on to a salsa midmorning Saturday. By noon, they were playing the song loosely, at full bore. Sadie didn't want to record it yet but knew she had to catch the exuberance of the session without too many more rehearsals. She signaled to get everyone's attention. "You guys are sounding great! This Latin beat has put me in the mood for some Mexican food. I say we break now and head for Josie's Tamali House in Smilax. We'll do a few run-throughs and get the song on tape when we return. At ease, gentleman."

Remy added, "We might try speeding the tune up just a tick to catch the energy of the rhythm. We have plenty of medium and slow-tempo numbers. That may help balance out the pace from song to song." The musicians nodded or put their thumbs up.

"Good comment. I'll sweeten the speed when we get back." The band and Abner Giles followed Sadie out front where they jumped into two vehicles while they were talking up a storm.

Dee Wathen saw them drive through the keyhole, and as soon as they were out of sight, she dialed Cru's number. "Hey. It's Dee. Why don't you make your way over here quick like. The place will be empty for about an hour. Ring me and I'll open the gate."

"That's good timing. I've got another picture to deliver."

Across town, Brock's phone pinged with a photo taken of Cru walking out of his house carrying a large painting, ostensibly to be delivered to Abner Giles. He went back to what he was doing.

The front door was ajar when Omar approached the mansion. He let himself in. Dee stepped into the hallway, took the painting, leaned it on the wall, grabbed his hand, and dragged him in the direction of her bedroom. She said, "What a nice touch, having a legitimate excuse to visit."

"Two legitimate excuses," he added eagerly.

Another picture dropped from the scope forty-five minutes later. Cru had pep in his step as he headed back to his cabin. Brock had seen a walk like that before. Omar had either bamboozled Dee, or some other windfall had come his way. Brock remembered the saying about hell having no fury like a woman scorned. He got in the winery truck and struck out for Cru's cabin.

"I'll be seeing you this evening. Why are you up here now?" Omar asked when Skinner arrived.

"Because I thought of a way you can buy a little insurance," he replied as he stepped inside to get out of the cold.

"For what?"

"Passing the accelerated life test. After you liquidate your assets, so to speak, you may be in the crosshairs of Saul Sardis or Arlena Harring, or both. I've told you that already and still think it is possible."

Cru picked up a cup of coffee that had left a ring on the side table and took a drink. "I haven't admitted to knowing Sardis, and why would Arlena want me dead?"

"You can stick to that story about Sardis, but you'll have a hard time concealing the fact that you're shagging Dee Wathen."

Omar set the coffee cup down with a thud and acted provoked. "Now, where in the hell did you get that idea?"

"I know her, and I know you. Those two puzzle pieces fit together. Never mind that. Here's an idea for you: why don't you sell me this property for one hundred thousand dollars. I'll let you buy it back from me anytime you want. That way, anyone who is thinking of killing you will have second thoughts. They'll want you alive instead of having to deal with me. We'll see what price they're willing to pay and just how badly they want it."

Cru walked in a circle and scratched his chin. "You may be on to something. What if I don't want it back?"

"Then I'll keep it," Brock affirmed. "Do you have a copy of the contract you signed when you sold the fifteen acres to Giles?"

Cru opened the fireproof vault and retrieved a document from a red-brown accordion folder. He noticed the painting he thought was missing was on the rack again. "Here's a copy."

Brock scanned the verbiage and frowned when he got halfway through. "Dang it. Are you aware that Abner Giles can buy this property from you on demand? Now, why would he slip that in this purchase contract?"

"Let me see that. I never read all the terms. I just looked at the acreage and price." His arms fell toward the floor. "This is not a good."

Brock's mind was working fast. "I'm not sure it's a problem. If you sell to me without regard to this clause, Giles will have to go to court to enforce it. If he does that, everyone will want to know why getting this piece of land is so important to him."

"Why do you think he would want to buy it?"

"When I figure that out, we'll understand what's going on with this whole mess. One thing I can tell you is that you're a pawn in something bigger. Can you explain exactly how you and Arlena hooked up?" Brock asked.

"I used to live in Seattle, and for years, I came to Keeneland to entertain customers. I fell in love with horseracing. Four years ago, I went there to see if the people who sold art would consider selling a piece I painted. My stuff back then was like Mark Rothko. When I was walking through the tent, Arlena introduced herself. She came on to me, well, she seduced me and asked if I'd like to become a famous artist. She told me what the plan was and convinced me to move here and buy this land."

Brock tagged on what he suspected had taken so long. "And you had to build a reputation for yourself over the last three years by selling pieces every few months while you were producing a huge inventory of works which could be dumped on the market after the supernatural event made you famous."

"That's about the size of it." Cru, crestfallen, flopped on the couch and threw his head back. "Are you going to expose me?"

"Quite the contrary. As I've said before, you've done nothing illegal, and if you don't confirm the phony out-of-body experience, you have every right to sell your paintings to anybody at any price. I'm trying to uncover something more sinister."

"Pertaining to Sardis?"

"He's part of it. He knows a hellhound is on his trail. My guess is he's going to disappear."

"What do you mean?" Omar straightened up and twisted around to look at Brock.

"He'll cash in for the short term by selling his book and traveling the country. Are you going to sell me this property? You can stay here rent free as long as you like or until you buy it back."

Cru stood and said, "I might as well throw in with you. You've convinced me my other friends might do me in."

"There's no honor among thieves. On Monday morning, I'll have my attorney draft everything. As soon as the deal is done, I want you to casually let Abner Giles know that you've sold out to me. His reaction should tell us a lot. Maude and I will see you at Arlena's later. You're going to love learning how to dance." Brock patted Cru on the back as he walked past him.

————————

Brock was wheeling around town on the way back to the winery when Marcel called him. "Saul worked for a company by the name of Python Deco. Python is the programming language used in AI. Deco means mass-produced designs. I suppose one could interpolate or conflate the two words to mean programmed mass-produced creations."

"Sort of like machine-printed paintings. Where is the business?"

"San Jose, California. Just down from Palo Alto."

Brock asked, "What else did you find?"

"He made a lot of money when he worked there, so says his tax returns. He made nothing the first two years here in Kentucky, and all he's reported recently is his professor's salary."

"Money must be coming in somehow. That might be why he's got that master of the house, Solomon. Sardis could be diverting income in his direction."

"Funny you should mention Solomon. I stumbled across a patent for a printer in the joint names of Saul Sardis and Solomon Pergamos."

Brock exhaled. "There is something really strange going on."

"How's that?"

"Sardis and Pergamos are two of the seven churches in Revelation."

"What does that mean?" Marcel inquired.

"People of the Church of Sardis practiced religion outwardly but were spiritually dead inside. The Church of Pergamos allowed false teachings of the world to infiltrate the congregation."

"I take it God didn't approve."

"To say the least," Brock shot back.

"What are you going to do now?"

"Get on a plane tomorrow afternoon and head for San Jose."

A thought came into Marcel's head. "Why don't you try to break Arlena down? Maybe she'll weaken enough to shed some light on Sardis."

"I'll do that tonight." Brock pulled the truck behind the winery and got out. "I went to see Cru. I convinced him to sell me his half of the mountain with the stipulation that he could buy it back at any time. Giles has a way to buy it from him already in place, but I'll make him come into court if he plans to void the sale to me. We'll find out just how badly Giles wants the property, if he does at all."

"How much is that going to cost you?"

"A hundred large. If I don't end up with the property, I'll get a pound of flesh out of someone."

Marcel's response was predictable. "My sister's not going to like it."

"I'll tell her when we're dancing tonight. She won't lose it in front of friends."

"You're hoping she'll cool off by the time you get home," Marcel threw out, followed by a peal of laughter.

"I don't think that's funny. I'm always the head of the plow, and when I cast aside something in the way, everybody starts complaining."

"Poor Brock. You've tried that line on me before." Marcel hung up on him.

CHAPTER 14

The Sutherlands and Skinners were standing on the porch of the Harring residence at five past five on Saturday evening, waiting to be let in. There was a coolness in the breeze that whistled by their heads, reminding the couples that fall had gotten serious. Arlena opened the door, greeted the dance-happy coterie, and took them to the kitchen where liquid refreshments, charcuterie, and salad sandwiches were laid out. Maude set the bottle of red wine she'd brought on the counter next to the fridge. She said, "What a wonderfully stylish home you have, Arlena."

"I decorated it myself. Being insecure about my station in life, I've worked at trying to impress people of class." Omar Cru came over and stood behind her in a show of support.

Marcel looked to lighten the mood. "Valerie and I have class. We're impressed. I can't speak for my hillbilly brother-in-law here." He turned to Brock and asked, "What say ye?"

Brock said to his wife in high dudgeon, "Would you tell your brother that people of class do not disparage their relatives in front of other people, even if they are merely in-laws."

Maude faked chagrin but couldn't hold it as a slight simper showed on her face. "Marcel, I think you should apologize to him. That was an unclassy thing to say, even if it is true." Her hilarious quip ramped up the merriment of the party. Natural conversation began flowing more easily.

After everyone had gotten something to drink and a plate of food, they sat at the black walnut farmhouse table in the breakfast area overlooking a darkening backyard. Valerie asked, "Omar, you're not afraid of being touched by strange women, are you?"

"What makes you think that?"

"Well, in a few minutes I'm going to be touching you, and I just want to be sure you can handle it," she replied as she was putting her hand on his arm.

Omar, having been a salesperson for years, had a repartee to fit any occasion. "My motto is: the more touching by strange women, the better." The fact that he'd been touching the bejesus out of a strange woman a short five hours ago struck him as ironic.

Arlena asked Valerie, "What are you going to teach him?"

"I'll start with the hustle basic, adding inside and outside girl turns. Then we'll tackle the rumba basic with crossbody leads and crossover breaks. Finally, I'll show him the waltz box and how to travel around the room. That'll be enough for one session."

Arlena looked over her shoulder and said, "Omar, dear, you're going to learn for free in an hour what most people pay a thousand dollars to learn in a month."

"I hate it when everyone else can do what I can't. They oversimplify how easy it is to pick up."

"You take that back. Tell Valerie how appreciative you are that she's willing to teach you."

Omar addressed Valerie across the table. He had a serious look on his face. "Mrs. Sutherland, I want you to know the depths of my gratitude for what you're about to do for me, or to me, all the while touching me discreetly in the process."

Valerie burst into a horse laugh. Marcel had never seen her so happy. He said, "I think Omar here is just a regular guy, not one of those snooty artists who believes he's superior."

"I think he's a nut," Val added.

Everyone finished eating. Brock commented, "That was exquisite food, Arlena. Thank you."

"My pleasure." Before they could move to the dance floor, she felt it necessary to explain the reason behind the peculiar way of going downstairs. "I need to tell you about the basement. When I bought this house, the washer and dryer were down there. That would never do. I brought them back up to the main floor. The people who had the house built thought it would be clever to put the door in the kitchen pantry. So, if you'll follow me, we'll head that way."

Brock held Marcel back and whispered, "I don't believe her. This is an escape route for another room, which I couldn't seem to find the door to when I was here before."

"Let's go look," Marcel said as he caught up to the others.

The squarish dance area had wooden floors and mirrors on the wall. A CD player was on a table under the stairs. Arlena put on a hustle and said, "Valerie, do the basic with Marcel."

Omar watched the step pattern. Brock took Arlena out on the floor and started dancing. Valerie beckoned Omar, and Marcel cut in on Brock, who went over to his wife standing by the stairs. He said, "If I get a chance, I'll go upstairs with our host and see if she'll tell me anything."

Maude took the hint and spelled Arlena. Brock suggested to her when she came over, "Let's go open the bottle of red wine Maude brought. It's excellent, if I may say so myself." When they reached the kitchen again, Arlena found the opener and handed it to him. "Do you mind if we talk about Omar's paintings? I want to share my thoughts with you," Brock said.

"Shoot."

"I think Saul Sardis has an AI program that transforms photographs into works of art, and you are the go-between."

"You're partly right." She pulled a short stack of clear plastic glasses out of a narrow cabinet.

"Tell me about it."

"Omar takes pictures and prints them. I take the prints to a photography studio that scans them into a computer. The program they have converts them into artwork. They put the picture on a memory stick for me. I take it to a printer that applies the paint as if it had been done by hand. It's as simple as that."

"Who is the photography studio and where is the printer?" The cork came out of the bottle when he pulled on the corkscrew.

"Brock, I can't tell you that. You'll have to trust me."

"So, you're telling me Saul Sardis isn't involved?"

"I'm telling you I pay a photography studio for the art."

"Okay. I'll buy that. But I believe you have the printer." Brock peeled the foil off the top of the wine bottle.

"Does that really matter?"

"I guess not. You should know that Marcel and I found a bunch of invoices where you bought gouache paint for cash from the store where you work. Your name was listed as the buyer. I suspect you were counting on the purchases being anonymous. We also know that Sardis hired you to recruit Omar and steer him toward buying the mountain in Hazard."

Arlena's face darkened. She said in a hollow voice, "I hope you understand I'm trying to keep you from ruining things for me."

Brock replied, "I'll tell you the same thing I told Cru. If you don't publicly confirm that Omar and Sardis had out-of-body experiences, you'll be in the clear. I don't want to see you get hurt."

"Shall we go back downstairs?" She took the wine bottle from Brock's hand.

"Sure. There is something much bigger going on than a painting scam. You're not part of it."

Arlena had an epiphany, not a very good one. She regained her composure and descended the steps with a smile on her face while Brock brought up the rear. She said, "Would anyone care for red wine? Brock tells me it's delicious." She poured two fingers into several cups.

The party continued for another hour and a half. The four experienced dancers practiced their moves while Valerie got Omar on the right track. With a little success, he began to get into it, and was disappointed when the music stopped and everyone trudged back upstairs.

Maude capped off the night by saying, "What a wonderful time we've had. Thanks for hosting, Arlena. Omar, you'll be dancing up a storm in no time."

Omar quipped, "If anyone needs touching, they should call on Mrs. Valerie here. She's a pro."

When the Skinners and Sutherlands were in their separate cars on the way home, Brock called Marcel. "She said the artwork was coming out of a photography studio on a memory stick and she was having the pictures done by a printer that made them look hand painted."

"That doesn't tell us much."

"It does tell us one important thing: Sardis is taking his cut through another entity. That's why his tax return had nothing on it. I did tell her we knew she knew Sardis, and that she was only a bit part player in a major production."

"That may make her angry," Marcel retorted ominously.

"We'll see. Let me speak to Valerie."

"Yes, Brock?"

"Thanks for being a good sport," he said, voicing appreciation.

"Thank you. If you knew how boring my life was in New Mexico, you'd understand how happy I am to be part of this family." Val handed the phone back to her husband, who ended the call.

Maude propped her elbow on her thigh and laid her head on her hand, grinning slightly as she leaned on the passenger window of the Lamborghini. "Arlena's going to get mad at Sardis, and if Omar dumps her when he comes into some cash, there'll be a twice-scorned woman on the loose."

Brock looked at his wife sheepishly and revealed, "He will dump her. He's now in the clutches of Deianira Wathen, the cook and business manager at the Giles estate."

Maude sat up in her seat. "And if Arlena finds out, she'll kill him."

"That's why I'm buying Omar's place on Monday for one hundred thousand dollars."

"You're doing what?"

"I thought you'd be pleased." He cringed as she cringed back.

The pall of cloud cover made Sunday morning eerily dim. Maude was waiting for her husband to return from the boxing gym. He headed straight for the shower when he came through the door from the garage, appearing twenty minutes later in church clothes. His wife handed him strong coffee in his favorite mug. Truman wanted some attention, so Brock set the cup down to scratch the dog's ears and side of his head.

Maude said, "I've been thinking about things."

"Oh, no. This is where a disgruntled wife asks her husband for a divorce. I'm sorry I bought that silly mountain across town. Will you forgive me?"

"You are such a schmoozer. I can't divorce you now. It would be an embarrassment to me. And, yes, I forgive you."

"That was a close call." Brock swept his brow to add theatrics. "What are you thinking?"

"From what I've read, these talking AI bots tell lies, and they sound just like the real person."

"That's true." He sat on a stool by the kitchen island.

"You told me AI Saul is in the computer at his house. What if it starts calling people and telling them things that aren't true? Somebody could get hurt."

Brock looked at the ceiling and put his hands over his ears. "I never considered that. You've brought up a valid point."

She moved next to him and put her arm on his back. "So, what about this thought: why don't you generate a note to warn everybody not to be fooled."

Brock turned to her and grinned. "That's a good idea. What should it say?"

"The human Saul Sardis is now known as Paul Sardis. The old Saul Sardis is now a robot who lives inside a computer. If you're not a nefarious business partner of either Saul or Paul, beware of anything you hear from them. It may not be the truth and could put your life in danger."

Brock hugged his wife as he said, "That is brilliant. Should it just be a simple computer-printed note in a plain envelope?"

"Yes. You might want to drop them in the main post office in Lexington."

"What about this: let's put the return address as if the note is from Solomon Pergamos at Saul's address in Westmoreland Estates." Brock's eyes were intense.

"Who will we mail it to?"

Brock pursed his lips and rattled off, "Arlena Harring, Omar Cru, Abner Giles, Titus Remington, and Ruby Lynch. I think I've got all their addresses. Let me get on the computer and pound them out."

"We'll be late for church."

"I can get them done in fifteen minutes," he assured.

"What's the hurry?"

"I'm going on a trip."

"What trip?" she asked sharply.

"To California. Remember I told you I needed to find out who Saul Sardis came to see on his first visit to Kentucky? I'm driving to Cincinnati to take a direct flight to San Francisco."

"I think I'll renege on that promise not to divorce you."

"I'll be back in a flash. You won't even miss me," Brock offered to ease her mind.

"If it will accelerate the ending of this saga, I'm in favor of it." Maude was negotiating now.

"It certainly will." Brock wrapped up the letters, and the two of them zipped off to church. He circled back to the events of last night after they returned home. "When we were downstairs at Arlena's, I saw a panel under the stairs, behind the music player, which could be a pocket door into another section of the basement."

"But you think that was only a way to escape the room, not go in?"

"Yes. The dance floor area is only under about a third of the main floor. There is surely another basement room that's twice as big."

Maude opened the refrigerator to get out the bowl of salad she'd prepared that morning. "And you think that's where the printer is?"

"I do," Brock confirmed.

"How do you get in there, or down there?"

"There must be something on the main floor that opens, probably automatically."

"You going to break the law again and go look for it?" she queried, close to losing her temper.

"In due time." He hastily packed a bag of overnight things and exercise gear. His parting shot to his wife was, "I'll get back here as soon as I can."

"You call me. And I mean a lot. If I don't hear from you, I'll call the police."

"I will."

Maude went to the front window and watched the Lamborghini pull out of the driveway onto the country road leading to civilization where her husband was surely to do battle. She never got used to him going off. One of these days, he wouldn't come home. Maude put a spoonful of sorrow in a mental bucket every time he roared out on a goose chase, so when the day finally did come when something bad happened, she'd be able get through it.

CHAPTER 15

The four-hour flight from Cincinnati to San Francisco, factoring in the three-hour time change, put Brock behind the wheel of his rental car at 6:47 on Sunday evening. He had booked a room at the Four Seasons Hotel Silicon Valley, which was less than a half hour south of the airport, conveniently situated at an exit off Highway 101. He relaxed over a California-style dinner in the hotel's best restaurant and settled into his room by eight thirty.

Brock went down to the gym at four thirty local time on Monday morning, showered in his room at 5:40, and had room service send up breakfast at six o'clock. The first call he made was to his attorney in Hazard. He described the purchase of Cru's property and asked that the paperwork be ready by tomorrow afternoon. That meant the attorney would have to bribe several people to get a title search done within the next twenty-four hours.

The second call was to his wife. He spent thirty minutes on the phone with her, discussing any subject he could think of. It would be another two hours before he could get an audience with anyone at Python Deco. Once he hung up, Brock drove to Menlo Park to look the town over in the morning light, and then motored down Camino Real, through Palo Alto, in the direction of San Jose. He pulled over for a cup of coffee and looked at his watch.

Kicking off the Monday class, Professor Sardis asked every student to speak their mind before he made any comments. It took forty minutes to get all the ideas into a hat from which the best one could be drawn and expounded upon. The favored subject was the differences between a cyborg, robot, and android. "I'll keep it as simple as I possibly can. A cyborg is part man and part machine. A robot is totally machine, programmed for and often employed as forced labor. An android is all machine with reasoning power developed by AI."

A student raised his hand and interjected, "AI doesn't seem scary when it resides in a computer, but an army of androids running around wreaking havoc is a terrifying thought."

"I don't think you need to worry about androids in your lifetime. They are a long way off. When it comes to artificial intelligence on a mainframe, there are several sinister outcomes you might not think of at once. For example, false information on a topic can be presented as true, with fabricated visual evidence. In other words, it will be hard to distinguish truth from fiction."

The nerd who sat below the artwork spouted, "Such an environment will throw the world into chaos. How can it be stopped?"

Sardis crossed his arms and said, "That horse has already left the barn. False information in the public domain, I'm afraid, is a reality we'll live with from now on. Broadcasters will be forced to authenticate the fact that they are truth tellers. Consumers will learn where to get information they can rely upon and cast aside the other noise out there."

The girl next to Miss Blue Eyes blurted, "Unless you're not smart enough to tell the difference or want to believe something that isn't true."

Sardis replied right on top of the last word she spoke: "Well, that malady is already rampant in society. I'll acknowledge it will only get worse. But think about the upshot of misinformation. How will that affect our lives?"

The guy who had tried to get the professor fired came forth with the most intelligent comment he had ever made in his life. He said seriously, "Freedom will be taken away from us, and the people of the world will live under one dictator who espouses the most deceptive, believable message."

Sardis smiled and asked, "Anyone care to venture a guess as to who that will be?"

Blue Eyes, full of dread, leaned forward in her chair, and muttered, "The antichrist."

———————

Sadie Kirkham felt uneasy about the way the cha-cha sounded. Remy's voice was tailor-made for the waltz the band mastered on Sunday, but he sounded like a country hog caller at Mardi Gras on Monday's song. She went to Remy and said, "I'm going to say it: your voice does not put a cha-cha across."

"Yeah. I can hear that myself. Got any suggestions?"

The lead guitarist cut in and offered, "Why don't you let me sing it in Spanish?"

Sadie noted, "The lyrics won't rhyme."

"That doesn't matter. Do you have a program that converts the words into another language?"

Sadie scurried back over to the control board. "First, let me put English lyrics on your monitor." She did that. "Now, I've converted them to Spanish." The band started playing the song without being asked. The lead guitarist sang beautifully on key. When the band got all the way through the number, Remy said, "If you need to improvise to stay on pace, please feel free to do so."

The band recorded the song without the voice track in three takes. The lead guitarist played the tune several times, juggling words to fit the pattern of the music. He finally nailed it by noon. Sadie said, "Nice work. Hey, we've got time to tackle the rumba this afternoon. You all okay with trying to get two songs down in one day?"

The organist replied, "Hello, Pete, we can knock out a song every two hours if you'd like."

Remy added, "I don't want us to choose quantity over quality. Two a day is the limit. We want the music to be the best we can produce because it will live on long after we're finished."

Abner Giles raised his hands and said, "Exactly. Let's storm the kitchen for some victuals."

———————

Python Deco was in an all-glass box, four stories high, which had a yellow, black, and tan sign sporting a logo that appeared to be a broken-down caduceus listing to the right with the snake, presumably a python, hanging from the post. Brock, in his church clothes from yesterday, made eye contact with the guard inside the revolving door. The man said, "How can I help you, sir?"

"I have a job interview in the HR department at nine o'clock."

"Take the elevator to the third floor. You'll see the sign when you step out."

"Thanks."

The woman scampering across the perpendicular hall saw Brock and veered over to greet him. "What can I do for you, sir?" She was in her late forties, impeccably groomed, and had taken wonderful care of her skin. The few extra pounds she carried had not ruined her figure or detracted from her allure as a female.

"Yes. I'm trying to find anyone who knew Saul Sardis well when he worked here. We're doing a cursory background check on him. He's being considered for a board position with a clothing company."

"What company is that?"

"Sutherland Tailoring."

"You don't say. I got this outfit I'm wearing from Sutherland. I just love their stuff. It fits me so well." She ran her hands down her body.

Brock showed her an ingratiating grin. "I'm on the board of the company. I'm so happy to hear you say that."

The woman cradled her chin with her hand and said, "Let me think who the best person for you to talk to would be. Carl Logano, I suppose. He's on the second floor, office number two forty-three. I saw him come in this morning. He should be there."

"Thank you. If you would be kind enough to give me your name, I'll put a discount code in our customer master, so you'll get fifty percent off on the next thousand dollars you spend with us." She leapt over to the vacant desk by the lobby door and snatched up one of her cards to give him.

Brock stuck his head into Carl Logano's office and saw him studying the computer screen on the front right corner of the desk. Logano said without looking over, "What?" He turned his head and amended his comment, saying, "Oh, I thought you were someone else. I don't believe I know you." He had on a tight-fitting, hip gray suit with a skinny silver tie. He was fifteen years too old to wear such a getup. *Maybe tech personnel are in the habit of dressing younger*, Brock pondered.

"May I come in?"

"Be my guest. Have a seat."

"Brock Skinner's my name." He showed Logano his Kentucky driver's license. "I'm here doing a brief background check on Saul Sardis. He's being considered for a position on the board of a clothing company. I've been told you know him."

"Saul? Yes, we're acquainted. Is this on the level?"

"Yes. Google Sutherland Tailoring. I'm part owner and a board member of the company."

Carl had the website up before Skinner had finished his sentence. He drilled down to the history of the business and saw Brock's name in the narrative. "Okay. I believe you."

"What kind of a person was Sardis?" Brock asked straight away.

"Smart guy. He was the contact person for many of our key accounts. When he got promoted to president, I slid right into his position. When he left the company, I was passed over for the president's job. I've been stuck here in neutral for the last five years, and to be honest with you, have one foot out the door." Anger was smoldering just below the surface.

"Sorry to hear that. What else can you tell me about him."

"Did you see the big article in the Sunday paper?"

"What paper?"

"The *San Francisco Chronicle*."

"No. What did it say?" Brock asked casually.

"It said that Sardis had some out-of-body experience where he claimed to have heard the voice of God. It sounded sort of fishy to me." Carl was an all-around Mr. Positive.

"I take it you don't believe it?"

Carl swiveled his chair ninety degrees, looked out the window, and propped his left arm on his desk. He said, "Saul Sardis has a nose for money. He sells clients on an AI development project, all the while figuring out how he can steal what interesting information they're working with."

"Are you saying he lacks integrity?"

Carl became morose. "I'm only telling you what I learned when I dug into his account files after I took them over."

Brock didn't want to seem too eager on that subject yet, so he asked, "Have you heard of a guy by the name of Solomon Pergamos?"

"Solomon? Creepy. He stayed at Saul's home. Saul referred to him as the master of the house."

"Did you ever meet him?"

Logano snickered. "Certainly. I hope his manners have improved since I saw him last."

"You said Saul was a smart guy. What did you mean?"

"He could write code himself. He got several patents on advancements in hardware, to mention a few of his skills," Carl revealed.

"Why do you think he left his position as president here?" Brock asked.

Logano sat up in his seat. "He told me he wanted to quit the rat race and take a cushy job as a professor."

"Did you believe him?"

"Hell no. There was something in Kentucky that caused him to decamp from the greatest place in the world to live and work." He pointed downward with his finger. "Here."

Brock inquired further. "Just exactly what does Python Deco sell?"

Carl shook his head and looked up, insinuating Skinner was a nitwit. "We offer to use artificial intelligence to come up with something that cannot be achieved by ordinary human means."

"Can you give me an example?"

"Take your clothing business. We'd send you a proposal to gather the latest trends in fashion using artificial intelligence and then do clothing designs for you that blend several popular pieces to come up with something original you could make and sell. As a matter of fact, we are doing that for a few clothing designers already."

"That's fascinating. We should probably consider hiring you," Brock said with sincere interest. "Was Sardis an effective president?"

"Yes. He knew how to handle the kooky technical people in this business. Many of them are on the spectrum, sort of like idiot savants. He knew how to handle anybody, come to think of it."

Brock looked away and said, "I know this question may be out of bounds, but I'm going to ask it anyway: Do you think he's a sociopath?"

"I'm sure of it. The things he said about employees and customers in private meetings with me were the kinds of things you'd hear from a serial killer. If you quote me on that, I'll deny it."

"What you tell me, Carl, is confidential. I'll never compromise what you say."

Logano stiffened and looked like he was going to clam up. Instead, he proposed an idea. "Why don't I check in our files and see if there's anything there about what he was doing in Kentucky before and while he was president here."

"You read my mind. I'd expect there's a fee associated with making such an effort," Brock said, offering to bribe the man right across his desk.

"Give me a few minutes to find the information in our CRM. Why don't you go down the hall to the breakroom and pour yourself a cup of coffee. When you return, I might have something for you."

When Brock came back, Logano wasn't there. A terrifying thought ran through his mind: that good old Carl had gone to get security or the police to charge him with espionage. Instead, Carl walked back into his office drying his hands from a trip to the restroom. He said, "I found some information for you. When I tell you, you'll understand what I was saying."

"What have you got?"

"He sent a proposal out to a client in Kentucky who wanted us to take all available horseracing data and develop an algorithm that would predict race results."

"Did the company do the work, and how much did they charge?" Brock struck while the iron was hot.

"We did to the tune of $23,835. And as you could have predicted, Sardis took the algorithm and used it to win money at the track for himself, even though it didn't belong to him."

"Who hired Python Deco to develop the algorithm?"

Carl put his hands behind his head, and said, "I think there's a way I can find who the customer was."

Brock reached into the breast pocket of his blazer and took out a tall leather wallet that had cash in it. "Would ten hundred-dollar bills improve your eyesight?"

"They would indeed." Logano took the bills and stuffed them in his shirt pocket. He turned the computer screen so Brock could see it and pointed at the name shown.

Brock read it out loud: "Titus Remington."

<h1 style="text-align:center">Chapter 16</h1>

The story of Saul Sardis and Omar Cru in the Sunday *San Francisco Chronicle* had leaked out by Monday night to news outlets nationwide, causing beat reporters to roll into Lexington and Hazard on Tuesday. Brock got home late Monday and was out and about the next morning. He drove up the hill and pressed the intercom button at the Giles estate to see if he could gain entrance. Dee Wathen came on. "What are you up to? I haven't ordered any more wine."

"I'd like to visit with Abner for a few minutes. I want to ask him to do something."

"What? You can ask me," Dee prodded.

"Do you know what happened to Omar Cru last week?"

"No, why?"

"Go on the internet and look up the Sunday *San Francisco Chronicle.* You can read all about it. Is Abner home?"

Dee went dark for a few seconds. Finally, she said, "He is. I'll go see if he's got time for you."

"Thanks." The gates parted a couple of minutes later.

Abner met Brock at the front door of the mansion. "What's going on?"

"Your neighbor has gained some notoriety. There's going to be news reporters trying to speak to him as soon as they can get here from the big cities."

"What did he do?"

"He was in a lunch place last week when a Slade professor named Saul Sardis purportedly heard the voice of God."

Abner blinked his eyes. "You don't say. How is Cru involved?"

"I told Dee where to find the information on the internet. The reason I came to visit is to help you avoid being swarmed by reporters."

"What do you suggest?"

"Hire a security guard to control who is allowed to drive up here." Brock threw his head in the direction of the road leading up to the gates.

"Thanks for the warning. I hope they aren't crazy enough to scale the mountain on foot."

"Not likely," Brock opined.

"What's going to happen to him?"

"He'll get rich. His paintings will be worth a pretty penny from this day forward."

"Like, how much?" Dee, who was listening in, suddenly became very interested.

Brock guessed, "A hundred grand and up, I'd say."

"Well, that's good news. I've got three of his pieces and three more will be delivered over the next few days." Abner pivoted and nodded at the one of Chuzzing he hung over the fireplace. "I'll call somebody to come over and close the road."

"Smart move. I'll catch you later." Brock skipped back out to the winery truck and pulled away. He parked by Cru's cabin and knocked on the door. When it opened, he said, "The news has broken about you and Saul. I just talked to Abner. He's going to hire a guard to keep reporters from overrunning your place."

"That's good," Omar replied cheerfully.

"Can you meet me at my lawyer's office at four o'clock today? I'll have the paperwork ready for you to sign and there'll be a check there for you." He handed him the address.

"I'll be there."

———————

By early Tuesday afternoon, the band hadn't made much progress on the bolero they had been working on all morning. Sadie, mildly frustrated, said, "We'll be lucky to get this one song done today. What's the problem?"

The rhythm guitarist replied, "This is a very slow number. My part's hard to strum. It's like the music has been written for a wind instrument."

"What do you suggest?" Remy asked.

"Here, let me double the speed of my part." The band started up, and when the rhythm guitar came in, it filled the dead space that was dragging the song down.

The lead guitarist said, "Go at that speed but feather the strumming to soften it, make it more amorous. It feels like occasionally we miss the chance to put romance in a tune, especially the Latin numbers. Like yesterday afternoon, the rumba we did could have been more sensual."

Abner asked Remy, "Is there any reason why we can't go back and spice that one up?"

"I'm not against it. Let's see if we can get the bolero in the can, and we'll relook at the rumba."

Sadie led the playing of the music with a light touch, using encouragement to get results. They had transformed both songs into near masterpieces by late afternoon.

The album was now two-thirds complete. The last four dance tunes would likely be done by Friday at quitting time. Sadie reported that to Abner. He said, "I think we should plan a party for the group on Friday night."

"What do you have in mind?"

"I'll call over to Maude's winery and see if she'll let us have a dinner party there after she closes at six."

Maude answered the phone and listened to Abner's proposition. She replied, "I've got a better idea. We can have a wingding at our house. We own a big log cabin behind the grapevines." She didn't check with Brock to see if that worked with his plans.

"Can your place handle eight people?"

"Easily, and more. Shall we expect you at six thirty?"

"Yes. Marvelous. I'll bring a copy of the album so you can hear what we've done."

"Wonderful. I'll text our home address to you."

Brock walked up behind his wife as she was finishing the call. "What's going on?"

"We're having a party at our house for Giles and his friends on Friday night. They'll be finishing the recording session that afternoon."

"And who says nothing's going on in Hazard," Brock declared.

———————————

Paul Sardis was standing where the sidewalk up to his house met the street sidewalk. He wore a Jed Clampett fedora and leather jacket, making him look like some intrepid treasure hunter, which he technically was. Cars were parked along the sun-faded asphalt street, and a pack of reporters were huddled around him. He said, "I've written this book, which is my life story, and it describes every detail of my encounter with God." He lifted one of the books out of the cardboard box he'd brought out. There was a note on the front of the box encouraging readers to buy the book on Amazon. "These copies are free, and after they're gone, people will have to buy it online."

The reporters tried to speak at once. One won out quickly, asking, "Is there anything else you can tell us about the event?"

"No. Everything I experienced is in the book." Paul walked back toward his house. Above the opening of the brick wall by the door was a sign that read: THIS IS PRIVATE PROPERTY. DO NOT KNOCK ON THE DOOR.

A female reporter commented, "How does a guy hear the voice of God last week and have an autobiography on the shelf this week?" She waved his book around in a suspicious manner.

A short, pudgy man in the group, who was hot on the trail of a juicy story, gave the most logical explanation: "God must have written it for him."

Brock came into the conference room at 3:45 p.m. where his attorney was sitting by the pile of papers Cru needed to sign to sell his property. The two men shook hands. The attorney said, "Just so you know, the contract on file, where Cru sold half of the mountain to Giles, is a copy, not an original. If he ever wants to challenge this transaction, he'll have to produce the notarized original."

"I bet he's got it in a safe somewhere," Brock supposed.

The attorney asked, "Why are you buying this property anyway?"

"Because it has some value to somebody, and I want to find out who and why."

"Well, I've learned to never question your judgment. You've usually been right."

Omar Cru entered the conference room wearing clothes you'd expect a successful, prosperous artist to have on. Brock chuckled and said, "Omar, it only took you half a day to become a rock star. Did Arlena find those duds for you?"

"She did." Cru introduced himself to the attorney. The three men sat together and kibitzed for a good ten minutes before they got down to business. Omar commented, "This is the first time I've been in a lawyer's office when I wasn't nervous."

Brock took the check from his pocket and pushed it over in front of Cru. "I'm the nervous one. That's my money going from my bank account to yours."

"Hey, this was your idea. Once I sell my paintings, I'll be gone like the wind. I don't want an option to buy this property back," Cru reported.

"Would you consider moving back to Washington?" Brock asked.

"Maybe."

"Not to get personal, and since he's my attorney, I will. I'm guessing you're going to interview your two love interests and see which one can't live without you. Then you'll decide where you want to live."

Cru said in jest, "It's possible that neither of them want me. If that's the case, I'll try to steal your brother-in-law's wife. She's the warmest woman I've ever been close to, and damn good-looking too."

Brock followed that up by relaying, "I tell her all the time that besides my wife, she is the most wonderful woman on earth. To be clear, I wouldn't let you get away with hurting my brother-in-law by breaking the tenth commandment."

Omar froze and darted his eyes from side to side. "I guess I'll drop that idea as plan B."

"No, but talking seriously, there's something you can do that'll put us in the catbird seat. The contract on file that has the clause where Giles can buy the property is a copy. He must have the original up there in the mansion somewhere. If you could talk Dee Wathen into retrieving it for you and replacing it with a copy, we'd be free sailing."

The attorney stood and said, "I didn't hear that, and I'm leaving the room now so I don't hear anything else. It was nice meeting you, Mr. Cru."

Omar shook the attorney's hand again and remarked to Brock, "I bet she'd do it for a price."

"What's the problem if you're the price?"

"Now that you mention it, she is better looking than your sister-in-law."

"Watch it. Will Arlena have it in for you if you don't choose her?" he asked boldly.

There seemed to be no end to Brock's effrontery, Omar was thinking. "I truly don't know. When she has enough cash of her own, she may move up in class, leaving me behind."

Brock twisted in his chair. "That wouldn't surprise me. Remember how she said she was fixated on trying impress people of class. When you add a handsome dowry, her marketable assets are noteworthy."

Omar somehow made his eyes bug out a quarter of an inch. "That doesn't mean she won't pay someone to kill me." They left the conference room pondering that sobering thought.

Omar's phone began bleating when he got home at twenty till five. "Hello."

"Mr. Cru? This is Connie from the art shop."

"How are you, Connie? Nice to hear from you."

"If I may be so bold, would you be kind enough to share with me how many paintings you've done?"

"Are you talking the ones in my current style?" he asked.

"I didn't know you had another." She sounded nervous, like that fact might be a complicator.

"Let's not worry about it," Cru reassured her. "You know about the first sixteen. Maude at the winery talked me out of number seventeen."

"Is that all of them?"

"Heavens, no. My neighbor has three and I'll be delivering three more to him soon, and I have two other friends who each have four. I also have one commission I haven't finished yet."

"That makes a total of thirty-two. Is that correct?" She began to lose hope in there being more.

"I have others. Why do you want to know?"

Connie had rehearsed her value proposition. "Well, it has come to our attention that you saw something unusual last week, which we feel has made your artwork highly sought after. If there are more, we can get top dollar for them."

"I've gotten the impression from our dealings that your firm is of considerable means."

"For this part of the country, we are far and away the largest and strongest financially. Why do you ask?"

"Because I'm interested in selling a number of paintings at one time." Cru was teasing her now.

"Are you saying you want to sell several paintings for one price?"

"That's my thinking."

"How many are we talking?" she asked.

"Before I tell you that, would you auction them or find private buyers?"

Connie reached through the phone and grabbed Omar's full attention. "Mr. Cru, we would do exactly what you told us to do with the paintings. Our role is to get you what you want and as much as we can."

"Ah, you said the magic words. I'm thinking $66,666 per piece. You'll get at least $80,000 for them, if not over a $100,000."

"That's a satanic price, right out of Revelation," she responded with trepidation.

"I can't help that," Cru replied pressingly.

"Before we discuss the price further, can you tell me if you're planning to produce any more works in your current style?"

"No. I'm going to take the money I get for them and spend the first million on wine, women, and song. Then I'll do something foolish with the rest of it. I'm kidding, of course."

"Rest of it? How many more paintings do you have?"

"Approximately one hundred seventy-five, but I only want to sell one hundred fifty now."

A low whistle came across the line. She remarked, "That's a price tag of ten million dollars."

Omar asked pointedly, "Is that too rich for your blood?"

"Frankly, sir, I don't know. I'll have to check with the principals. Do you have any restrictions on what we can do with the artwork?"

"You can do whatever you want, whenever you want," Cru replied carelessly.

"What are you planning to do with the last twenty-five or so?"

"Sell them to you later when the prices have gone up in value."

"I'm certainly glad I reached you. I'll call you back in ten minutes to let you know if we can do the deal."

Cru went to his bar to fix a vodka tonic with lime. He looked at the check he'd gotten from the sale of his property and took a big swig of his drink. The only thing that wasn't where it needed to be was the portrait of Dee Wathen that he'd promised her. The phone rang again in less than three minutes.

Connie said deliberately, "Mr. Cru, we would be pleased to buy one hundred fifty works of art from you. We'll have a cashier's check drafted in your name in the morning. Shall we come to Hazard with a van to load up the paintings?"

"That works for me. I'll expect you at eleven o'clock." He downed the rest of his vodka tonic.

Chapter 17

Ruby Lynch retrieved her mail after she got home from work on Tuesday at half past five. She was perplexed by the cryptic note, which warned about Saul/Paul Sardis. She found the only winery in Hazard that came up on the internet and punched the number on her phone.

"How can I help you?" the woman said who answered.

"Are you the owner, by chance?"

"Yes. This is Maude Skinner."

"My name's Ruby Lynch. I think your husband stopped by my house recently. I told him I might run down and visit you folks when I got the chance. I'm off work tomorrow and thought it might be a good time."

"Yes. My husband told me about seeing you. Please come on. We'd love to have you."

"Thank you." There was a short pause. "A strange letter arrived in the mail today. Maybe it has something to do with my father's death."

"That's interesting. Bring it with you. Maybe my husband knows something about it." Maude wasn't in the habit of telling white lies or misleading people. She regretted what she told Ruby but was beginning to understand why Brock had become a consummate liar when it came to getting information.

Omar's phone buzzed again. It was Arlena. She sounded harried. "Would you tell this security guard down here to let me through?"

He did, and when Arlena got up the hill and out of her car, she marched toward his cabin with purpose. She launched herself through the door and slammed it to set the mood for her visit. "When I got home at four o'clock, there were news reporters waiting for me all over the place. I told them to get the hell off my property or I'd call the police."

Omar looked to disarm her quickly. "Nice to see you again, Arlena. I've got some news that will cheer you up." He stood as still as a statue for effect.

"What's that?"

"I'm getting ready to pay you a cool four million dollars." He watched her facial expression to see if that revelation helped her disposition.

"You've already sold the paintings?" It seemed her body was defying gravity, as though she was on the verge of levitating.

"Yes. The art shop in Lexington is bringing a van for them in the morning along with a cashier's check for ten million dollars. How about that?"

"Woohoo!" She ran over and gave him a fierce kiss and hug. "That's what I'm talking about!"

"I'll make out the check but don't deposit it until Thursday morning."

"Wow. I'm gonna be rich!" Arlena proclaimed fervently. She pumped her arms in the air like a cheerleader at a football game.

"After you pay Saul and the taxes, you'll have one point two million in the bank, free and clear. How does that feel?"

"Wonderful!" she spouted. "I'm going to take next week off and go on a cruise. I'm sure I can find one that leaves this Saturday from Miami for the Caribbean."

"I bet you can." Omar walked lazily to the front window. "Let's talk about something else."

His tone got her full attention. "What is it?" she asked, expecting a hitch with the money.

"Us."

"What do you mean?" She knew what he meant but didn't want to be the one to start talking.

Cru didn't mince words. "Are we going to stay together or split up?" He put his hands out like a preacher beckoning people at an altar call.

"That wasn't a very romantic way of putting it," she retorted as she turned her back.

"Come now, Arlena. Don't tell me you haven't made up your mind. We've waited four years for this payday and what comes next."

She pivoted to face him again, crossed her arms, and said, "When I get back from my vacation, let's go to that steakhouse in London and talk about our future. What matters most to me is whether you really love me or not."

Omar pulled her in for a soft embrace. "That sounds good." When they separated, he went to the kitchen table and made out the check for four million dollars. He pushed it toward her, and the grin on her face said it all. He soothed her, offering, "I'm sorry about people pestering you at your house. That'll make it better." He pointed at the check as she was palming it.

Arlena pulled out for home, making a call on her burner phone when she cleared Perry County. "Cru has sold most of the paintings in one big lot." She listened to the response before saying, "I'll send you a check for two million on Thursday morning. I plan to fly to Miami Friday night, if I can book a cruise to the Caribbean that leaves from there on Saturday morning." She heard more from the other end of the line and replied, "Sure. You know how to get in."

———

Omar didn't like the look of the sky at dawn on Wednesday, wondering if cold rain was moving in. Loading pictures in a van in wet weather could be problematic. He spent an hour separating the artwork into three groups: the 150 finished pieces he was selling, two dozen he was holding back, and the batch of unfinished paintings he had used as decoys. As the day brightened, the rain chance seemed to diminish. At eleven o'clock sharp, the security guard at the bottom of the hill called to see if a box van was to be allowed through.

Connie hopped out of the passenger side of the logoed truck and went to the porch of the cabin to greet the infamous Omar Cru. She said, "So, this is where you produced all that beautiful artwork." She was tall, thin like a ballet dancer, and when she whirled around, Omar thought she might get up on her toes and do a pirouette. She introduced the young driver of the van and asked, "Shall we look at what you've got?"

"Of course." He led the way to the vault and explained, "These three rows of fifty paintings are the ones I'm selling." The undelivered paintings for Giles were still leaning against the wall.

"Do you mind if we inspect them carefully?"

"Be my guest. Here, let me get them down one at a time for you to look at." He slowly pulled the leftmost piece off the top rack, turning it to face her.

"If you're going to do that, why don't we just carry them out to the van?"

"I say we do a few of them, then take a break so I can sign the paperwork and hold the check you have for me in my hot little hand."

"As you wish." They carried the first two dozen out. Connie got the cashier's check made out for ten million and gave it to him. She said, "I'll have you sign everything when we're loaded up."

It took an hour and a half to secure the artwork in the van and complete the transaction. Omar remarked, "Connie, I hope your firm makes a nice profit. What's the process now?"

"Well, this cache of art is something like the Helga paintings of Andrew Wyeth. I'm taking them to a studio where each piece will be photographed and put in a catalog. We'll offer the works to Keeneland patrons first. Eventually, the more expensive pieces will be auctioned off."

Cru waited for the van to descend the hill and drive out before he got in his car to head to the bank. When he walked up to deposit the money, the president of the bank invited him to come into his office so they could discuss how he could put it to work.

———

Ruby Lynch stepped from her car at Vigneron Winery a few minutes after one o'clock and went searching for Maude Skinner. She found her quickly and introduced herself. "When I first met your husband, I had a hard time figuring him out. He looked like a day worker at a cattle ranch but was driving a Lamborghini. Curiosity got the best of me, so I wanted to get the right mental picture of his wife and her beautiful winery," she said, referring to Maude in the third person.

"God broke the mold when He made Brock. I try to keep him busy doing chores. Somehow, he stumbles into crazy stuff no one else pays any attention to. Once he does, he won't leave it alone until he makes sure any rotten characters preying on innocent people pay a price."

"A justice warrior. Folks like that sometimes step on bear traps," Ruby cautioned.

Maude replied dryly, "He usually sets more bear traps than he steps on. Come, let me show you around and then I'll get you a plate of lunch."

Brock appeared as Ruby was wiping her mouth after finishing a juicy sandwich. He said, "I see Maude's getting a better class of clientele these days. It's nice to see you again."

"And you. How in the world did you snag that lovely wife of yours? Don't answer that." She put a hand up to go with the phony frown on her face.

Brock gave her a reason anyway. "She felt sorry for me. I didn't ask you when we met. What do you do for a living?"

"I work for an upscale caterer, networking with horse farms in central Kentucky, drumming up business."

"You certainly look the part, and from what I've seen, you've got the right personality for it."

"I'm more like my mother than my father. She was outgoing and effusive. My father was a quiet man, always lost in his own thoughts."

Brock sat down across from her. "What line of work was he in?"

"He was a metallurgist. When he finished his master's degree, he went to work for a laboratory on the northside of Lexington. It was the only job he ever had. I was born thirty days after he took the job, and he retired thirty-eight years later. A few months after that, he was found dead on that mountain across town."

"Did he have a specialty?"

She squinted and looked up. "He developed metal alloys with different properties for unique applications."

"Is your mother still alive?" Brock asked.

Ruby became saturnine. "No. She died when I was eighteen. My father and I were devastated. I went to college for a couple of years but never finished."

"Please excuse my impertinence, but did you ever marry?" Marcel had told him she hadn't.

"No. I came close three times. I was a bit wild and irresponsible in my twenties. The men you meet in those circles don't end up having much of a future."

"Did you have to deal with your father's papers after his unexpected death?"

"Yes."

"Was there anything you came across that struck you as unusual?"

Ruby puffed her lips and exhaled quietly. "There were scientific formulas that didn't make any sense to me. I threw them out. He was very organized when it came to personal paperwork. I'm fortunate I didn't have to hoe through a lot of junk."

"Maude said you got a letter in the mail. Can I see it?" She took it out of her pocket and handed it to him. "Do you know anyone named Saul Sardis?"

"No," she said with certainty.

"Don't worry about this. I'll do some checking, and if I learn anything, I'll let you know."

The Skinners and Ruby Lynch spent the next two hours talking about this and that. Ruby headed for home after four o'clock. Maude turned to her husband and said, "That woman had lot of potential as a young person, which was never nurtured by her father. She's come through it pretty much unscathed but may have missed the window to find a good man."

By quitting time on Wednesday, the band had finished two more spectacular Latin numbers, a brash samba and staccato mambo. Abner Giles laid out the rest of the week. "We might be able to knock out the hustle by early tomorrow afternoon, and then practice the West Coast a little. We can record it Friday morning and spend the rest of the day listening to every song to see if there are any tweaks we want to make before we bring this remarkable session to a close. What do you all think about that?"

All five musicians clapped and whistled. The organist reflected on what they had done so far. "Remy, Sadie, Dee, this has been one of the most enjoyable events I've ever been involved in. In talking to the rest of guys, I'm sure we all feel that way."

Sadie suggested, "We should discuss the order of the songs on the album. I'm thinking we do a secret ballot among the eight of us to see if there is a common theme."

Remy said, "We talked about using those nifty portraits of the band for cover art. Are the paintings finished?"

"When the artist brought the last one, he said they'd all be here by Saturday," Dee reported.

"I know a good graphic house we can use. I may have to haul all five paintings to them so they can be photographed," Abner said. "As a side note, Omar Cru, the artist who lives next door, has suddenly become famous. He apparently witnessed God speaking to an AI professor from Slade University in Lexington."

"Does that mean his paintings are increasing in value?" the drummer asked.

"Bet your bippy," Dee confirmed.

The lead guitarist piped up, "Boy, our timing is great. Having his artwork on the album cover will supercharge sales."

The rhythm guitarist asked, "What do you mean he witnessed God speaking?"

"An article in a San Francisco paper reported the professor jumped into the body of our artist friend next door, and the professor claims God spoke to him," Dee said.

"What happened to the artist?"

"He jumped into the professor's body, at least temporarily, until they switched back."

The rhythm guitarist scratched his head. "I don't know if I like that. We better be careful not to attract a curse."

Remy cut in. "Nonsense. Any publicity is good publicity."

The drummer called the question. "Who in this room believes in curses?" He raised his hand. The only other hand to go up was that of the rhythm guitarist.

Chapter 18

The Skinners and their German shepherd took a brisk walk before breakfast on the backroads near the log cabin on Thursday morning. The murky air felt damp, and the moisture would be slow to burn off since the temperature was predicted to stay below fifty degrees. Maude asked, "What are you doing this morning?"

"I'm going to your office to look at photographs from the scope. My phone pinged several times yesterday, but I didn't see all of what was there. Cru's place has been busy."

"Later today, let's talk about the party tomorrow night. Should we invite Marcel and Valerie to come over?" Maude asked.

"Absolutely. There's liable to be some fireworks."

"What kind of fireworks are you talking about?"

"I plan to lay Titus Remington open. He may not like it."

"Sorry I brought it up," Maude replied gruffly. "Ruby Lynch got her letter on Tuesday. When did you say you dropped them at the post office?"

"Sunday afternoon when I drove through Lexington on the way to the Cincinnati airport," Brock reported.

"The mail carrier would have delivered Remington's already, but I suppose he's staying with Giles while the band is recording, which means he hasn't seen his yet. Arlena, Omar, and Abner will likely get theirs no later than today."

Brock said, "We'll see what birds the dog flushes out of the cornfield." He choked off a smile.

"It doesn't seem as though Ruby is involved in any skullduggery or she wouldn't have told us about the note."

The Skinners rode to the winery a few minutes before it was set to open. Brock went straight for Maude's office, while she stepped into the warehouse to check the wine vats.

The first picture from 11:03 a.m. the previous day showed a van pulling up to the cabin. At 12:47 p.m., the van left. At 12:49 p.m., Omar Cru drove off. He returned at 1:31 p.m. Arlena drove in at 5:33 p.m. and drove out again at 5:56 p.m. Brock rapidly worked out in his head what had happened. He called his brother-in-law. "Marcel, it appears that Cru sold his art yesterday and took his money and deposited it in the bank. I'm pretty sure he paid Arlena her share late in the day. How can she get Sardis his percentage without leaving a trail?"

"One way is to endorse the check and give it to some company to deposit. The company could write two checks to disperse the funds and act as a clearinghouse."

"Give me an example," Brock urged.

"Omar writes a check to Arlena. She endorses the check, and the company deposits it into their account without endorsing it with the company name. That way, nothing is on the back of the cancelled check that can be traced. Then, the company uses counterchecks without any names on them to write disbursements to Arlena and Sardis."

"What you're saying is the company depositing Arlena's check is laundering the money," Brock concluded.

"At least they're giving it a good scrubbing. One thing's for certain: other transactions are in the batch, so the deposit won't stand out."

"It's probably a big number, which implies the company involved gets large checks occasionally. I've got a hunch the art supply store where Arlena works might be the culprit. See if they do anything other than sell small-ticket art supplies."

Marcel theorized, "Are you thinking Arlena talked the CFO, who might have a scant record of female liaisons, into playing along?"

"Omar told me he was seduced by her, and that she talked him into buying the mountain and moving to Kentucky. It follows she would use her feminine wiles on some hapless CFO."

Marcel sighed audibly. "I was really beginning to like her. She's a great dancer and seems like a nice person."

"I'm sure she was until the grim reaper from California cast a spell on her. Saul Sardis has a way of corrupting everyone he meets and everything around him," Brock pontificated.

"Yeah. Now that he claims God has spoken to him, no telling what trouble he'll stir up. People will believe him as though he were the antichrist."

"He may be the antichrist, representing himself as ex cathedra," Brock added. "Arlena said she got the artwork from a photography outfit. This is a long shot. See if you can find a Kentucky or California corporation that is named after one of the seven churches in Revelation. Sardis and Pergamos have already been used."

"What are the other five?" Marcel asked.

"Ephesus, Smyrna, Thyatira, Philadelphia, and Laodicea."

"Were all of them indicted by God for sinful behavior?"

"No. Smyrna and Philadelphia weren't," Brock allowed.

"Okay. I'll hunt first for an Ephesian, Thyatira, or Laodicean photography firm."

"I'm guessing they didn't use Ephesian. Marcel, if people only knew how key you are to solving the mysteries we run across."

"What would they do?" Marcel asked.

"They'd think less of me and more of you." Brock laid it on the barrelhead.

"We wouldn't want that, now, would we? You, so smart and all."

———————

Arlena Harring and the CFO where she worked left the art store before noon in separate cars, rendezvousing at her house fifteen minutes later for some extracurricular activity. They met in the kitchen after getting cleaned up, where they scarfed down egg salad and jalapeño chips for lunch. Arlena said, "This check is four million dollars. Can you slide it through unnoticed?"

"It'll cost you a few extra rolls in the hay, but I'm sure I can work it out." The CFO hesitated for a few seconds before saying, "I'm not repulsive to you, am I?"

"What gave you that impression?"

The CFO looked at things realistically and objectively, like accountants do, assessing what was going on. He wasn't a handsome man, which he was keenly aware of. Without providing some sort of service, he knew he wouldn't be able to avail himself of the level of conjugal activity he was enjoying. He certainly made enough money to pay for it, but that seemed so cheap and tawdry. It was better to exchange services, preserving a patina of professionalism.

"Oh, I would just feel badly about our arrangement if it was unpleasant for you." He walked out of her house and returned to his desk at the art store, where he'd cipher away the rest of his life, with only the tryst involving Arlena Harring in his personal hall of fame.

Arlena tidied up the kitchen and grabbed her mail out of the mailbox on the way to her car. As she drove away from the house, she noticed the plain letter in the batch of mail laying on the passenger seat had the return name of Solomon Pergamos, at an address she was familiar with—that of Saul Sardis. She ripped open the letter and took the burner phone from her purse. When Sardis picked up, she told him about the note and read what it said.

"This Brock Skinner character is proving to be quite a nuisance. He's simply shaking the bush. I'm sure he sent one to Omar and Abner. I'm not sure if he would have sent one to Titus or not. We'll have to see. You've got your money, and in a couple of days you'll be on a cruise. Relax."

"What should I do with the letter?"

"Put it in an envelope and send it back to him. Don't put a return address on it, and don't drop it in a mailbox near Richmond. Mail it from Lexington. That way, you can deny ever getting it in the first place."

Arlena began to visualize the white sand and aquamarine water of the Caribbean. The thought put her in a happy place. The CFO asked the amounts of the two checks when she got back to the office. She said with excitement, "Two million each."

Omar strolled over to the speaker box at the Giles estate to summon Dee Wathen. When she came on, he said, "I've got two more paintings for Abner. Shall I bring them over now?"

"You can."

"I'll put them in my car." Dee came out to meet him when he pulled up to the entrance of the mansion. He asked, "How's it going?"

"SSDD. Same stuff, different day." She helped him lift the two paintings out of the trunk. A third piece of art was also there, under the impressive expressionistic studies of the musicians. It was a beautiful landscape. "What is this?"

"One of my better efforts. I thought you might like to see it."

"It's nice. What are you going to do with it?"

Omar stood tall and laid it out for her. "I have a copy of the bill of sale I signed when I sold this acreage to Abner. If you retrieve the original document for me that Abner has filed somewhere and put the copy in its place, I'll give you the painting."

"Why do you want me to do that?" she asked sternly.

"Because I was supposed to file the original with the county when I made the sale. He kept the original when it should have gone to me. I don't want anyone to challenge the authenticity of the transaction."

Dee looked at him dubiously. "I'll ask Abner if it's okay, and if it is, I'll get it for you."

"You can't ask him," Omar told her.

"What kind of game are you playing?" she asked.

"I just sold my fifteen acres to Brock Skinner, and if the paperwork isn't right, the sale may be voided. I don't want that to happen."

"Why'd you do that?"

"Because I've just sold millions of dollars' worth of paintings and I want to build a nice place of my own," he lied. "Somewhere you and I can frolic in luxury."

"Well, I don't see any harm in making the swap under two conditions: you give me a title to the painting and promise not to tell anyone that you asked me to do this."

"Consider it done."

"And one more thing: you need to store the painting for me because I can't have anyone seeing it around here."

"I'll ask Skinner to keep it at his house. Abner doesn't know I've sold out to Brock. It is okay if you tell him after the bill of sale swap has been made." Omar reached into his car to retrieve the paperwork and handed it to her. "I take it there are no cameras watching us talk out here. Am I correct?"

"You are. I keep his files in my office. I'll get the original for you. When I bring it, have the title to your picture ready for me," Dee instructed.

"When are you going to make the switch?"

"Right now. I'll walk over to your place in fifteen minutes," she replied.

"Good. I'll go back and make out the title."

"I'm only going to take one of these paintings into the house. Keep the second one at your place until I come over. I want the camera at the gate to see me walking to your cabin and carrying back a painting. That will cover our tracks," Dee said with confidence.

"Right."

———————

By late Thursday, On the Beat had finished the hustle and was on to the last song of the session, which was a powerful and catchy West Coast swing. The band played the tune somberly at first, and then as a choppy, flamboyant number that sounded like a clarion call at happy hour. The bandmembers were high on life when they knocked off for the day.

Dee had been sitting behind Sadie for the last half hour. She stood when the room got quiet. "Two more paintings are here. You all need to run up and see them. They are remarkable. The last one will arrive on Saturday morning according to the artist."

The men fell in and took off toward the front room. When Abner saw the works of art, he said, "These are incredible."

"Omar Cru told me today that he'd just sold his cabin to Brock Skinner and was going to build a lavish studio somewhere else." She watched Abner's expression to see if he winced.

He didn't, but offered with a smile, "Good for him."

Cru showed up at Vigneron Winery just before closing time. He went inside looking for Brock. Maude found him in the warehouse. When he saw Omar, he asked, "What's up?"

"I got the original bill of sale for Abner's property you wanted."

Brock took it from him. "Excellent. Do you mind if I keep it in my safe at home?"

"Go right ahead."

"What did it cost you?"

"A nice painting. I told Dee I'd let you keep it until she wanted it."

Brock patted Cru on the arm. "I guess that's not so bad. After all, you've cashed in already."

"How'd you know that?"

"Oh, I just put two and two together. Let's load the painting in the back of Maude's vehicle."

While they were walking outside, Omar said, "I told Dee to mention to Abner that I'd sold out to you. When I see her again, I'll ask if he had any reaction."

"Have you paid Arlena off?" Brock asked.

"Yes. She's going to try to catch a cruise to the Caribbean leaving out of Miami on Saturday." If Cru had been paying attention, he would have noticed the tightening of Brock's expression.

"Is that so? Good for her." After they transferred the painting, Brock said, "That's a nice piece of art. We'll hang it at the house as if it belongs to Maude and me. You did good." He shook Cru's hand and let him go on his way.

Maude closed the winery and joined Brock, who was sitting in her SUV. "What did Cru allow?" she asked.

"He cleaned things up for us and shared some important information."

"What's that?"

"Arlena is going on a cruise Saturday morning."

Maude turned to face her husband. "What's so important about that?"

"I was thinking it would be the perfect time for Saul Sardis to make her disappear. I'm sure he doesn't have a use for her anymore. I believe he killed Garrison Lynch, and after he knocks off Arlena, he'll go hunting for Omar."

Truman was standing on the porch when the Skinners got home, waiting to be let in. Maude got out of the SUV and opened the front door while Brock parked in the garage.

CHAPTER 19

"How many people are coming to the party tonight?" Brock asked as he checked the heavy rain Friday morning through the patio door, which looked out over the grapevines of the winery. *It can't be much worse outside*, he thought. "I wonder if I should start building an ark." Water was standing in several low spots in the yard.

Maude could tell he was in a foul mood. "Ten people are coming. The party's inside, so I think everything will be fine unless the house floats away. Let's talk about the food and drinks."

"Beer, wine, whiskey, juice, and soda, and all that goes with it. I'll go to the store and get what we're short on. Make a list of the food we need, and I'll shop for it too."

"My, we're accommodating this morning. What's rolling around in your head?" she queried.

"Remington took Abner Giles up that hill and pretty much compelled him to buy that land and build a big place. Why? Abner secured an agreement to buy Cru's other half of the mountain. Why?"

"It could be that Remy went to Nashville with the group of songs the band is recording. Abner got a look at them and thought they were great, and he was willing to do anything to get a contract to produce the album."

"Who told him to get the agreement to buy the other half of the mountain?" Brock persisted.

"It had to be Titus Remington," Maude argued.

"Okay. He knows Saul Sardis. Did Sardis tell Remy to have Abner get the agreement?"

Maude looked sideways and stretched her arms. "It's more likely that Abner was promised a reward for owning the mountain, or there's an exit strategy that makes him a lot of money."

"Whatever the reward is for owning the whole thing, it will be derailed when Giles sees he's lost his ace in the hole."

"And Abner won't find that out until later," Maude said as she turned in the direction of the coffeemaker.

Brock crept up behind her and put his arms around her upper body. He talked in her ear: "Though I haven't heard Remy's music, I know why it's so good."

"Are you clairvoyant or something?"

"No. When I went to California, the guy I saw, Carl Logano, told me how it's done. Maude, I'm thinking that after Saul Sardis deals with Omar and Arlena, he'll do Remy in. We can't let that happen."

"Why don't you call the police?"

"It's too late. Everybody we sent a note to has it by now. The police wouldn't be happy with me for doing that. I've got to get Remington to come clean," Brock declared too loudly in Maude's ear.

Miss Blue Eyes wished she had never taken the AI class. Her mind was running wild with myriad scenarios that spelled death and destruction for her insulated-from-real-problems existence in Kentucky. Social interactions up to that point in her life had been gentile, safe, and pleasant—until the professor had begun to scare her. She raised her hand and asked a question that had nothing to do with the topic he was lecturing on. "You told us androids will not be perfected until sometime in the future. Is there any way that an android could be the antichrist?"

The professor brooded for a few seconds. "I must say, I've appreciated your earnestness and quest to understand what artificial intelligence will mean to us. I sense you're becoming fearful because of what I've said. Taking it all the way to the antichrist is a considerable leap."

"I'll admit I'm worried. Being deceived by an all-knowing android seems like a real possibility to me."

"Before we delve into the subject she brought up, does anyone have any questions about what I just presented in my lecture?" He panned the room, hesitated, and said, "No? Okay. Let's talk about the antichrist. There is no consensus as to what the term means. Some people believe that the antichrist is a group, and as the term would imply, the people in the group are against the teachings and claims of Jesus Christ. Reformers during the sixteenth century called the Catholic Church the antichrist. Others believe that sometime in the future, during a period of economic unrest, wars, and rumors of wars, one person will come forth who will bring peace and prosperity for a time."

The nerd in the class said, "In that scenario, there will have to be chaos in the world for such a person to reveal himself. Do you think we're heading toward that?"

"Would anyone like to respond?" The professor coaxed the students to speak up.

The guy who didn't want to be in the class dropped his typical laconic bomb. "If we're not there yet, it's just around the corner."

Sardis went on: "The one-man antichrist theory holds that the person will be seen as good but will be evil, an instrument of the devil, who will lead people away from Christ."

Blue Eyes said, "That's why I thought an android would fill the bill. It could be programmed with all the knowledge in the world but have no compassion or aversion to evil."

Sardis moved down in front of the class. "You mentioned compassion. When people are asked to sum up Christian faith in a few words, they often say it is to love God and love your neighbor. How do you think we're doing on the love your neighbor part? In a sense, we've become like androids."

"What do you mean?" chirped the girl sitting next to Miss Blue Eyes.

"The average person walking down the street is fixated on a smartphone and has earbuds in their ears. They're not the least bit interested in anyone around them. They don't make eye contact or say hello, and they really don't care about another person and what may be going on in their lives. They have little interest in anyone in a one-on-one setting either. That certainly is not what would be considered loving your neighbor."

A student sitting near the professor chimed in, "Respectfully, sir, what is your point?"

"Holding to the idea that the antichrist is a group, have we considered that people who do not love their neighbor could be part of it? Those who hate Jewish people for example."

Another student, who rarely spoke, suggested a broader definition. "That can be taken further to include anyone who is behaving in a way that leads people away from the decalogue. They may be seen as part of the antichrist."

"And that puts us on a slippery slope. Let's back up. Artificial intelligence is in its infancy. We do not know how it will be regulated, controlled, developed, and used. We do know it will allow us to do things beyond the human mind and to produce things that will have a positive impact on nearly everything we meet in our daily lives."

The nerd said, "But it won't make us love our neighbor or sincerely care about someone else."

"That's done by looking a person in the eye with a smile on our face, asking them how they are doing, and really wanting to know. A symbol for God is a circle with arrows pointing outward, which stands for the Creator of the universe looking out from Himself. It gets back to us wanting to be our own gods, or following what God wants us to be."

The fellow who had no real interest in the class was at least street smart. He thought Professor Sardis, who was a conman if he'd ever seen one, would make a good antichrist.

———————

Omar read the anonymous letter that came in the mail and was nonplussed. He had his money, had sold his property, and figured it might be the right time to break clean from his partners in crime, especially since his prospects with Dee Wathen were on the upswing. If he was truly in danger, as Brock had warned, the easiest way to stay out of trouble would be to move out of Hazard. He threw his camera in his car and struck out for Union Commonwealth University in Barbourville, which was less than an hour away, to the west-southwest.

Cru called Arlena on the way. He figured she'd gone home for lunch. He said, "Did you get that cruise lined up?"

"Oh, yes. I took the afternoon off. I'm flying from Lexington to Miami tonight. The cruise line I found was giving discounts for last-minute travelers. I got a heck of a deal."

"Glad to hear it. Hey, listen, I've been considering the situation. All this notoriety is unnerving to me. I'm going to go into hiding for a while."

"You mean from the public?" she asked for clarification.

"No, I mean from everyone. I've also been thinking about us. You don't love me, I can tell. We might as well go our separate ways. I don't want to have a romantic meal at that steakhouse when you get back."

"What are you saying?" Urgent disbelief percolated in her voice.

"I've sold my house to Brock Skinner. When all this hubbub dies down, I'll let you know where I am." He had no intention of ever seeing her again or telling her anything.

"This is rather abrupt, don't you think?" The anger in Arlena's tone was palpable.

"Okay. Tell me you love me and want to marry me right now." Nothing came across the line. "I thought so. If I were you, I'd watch my back. Saul Sardis will be coming for you."

"What makes you think that?" Arlena had seven different emotions running through her.

"Because he's one cold-hearted bastard. An anonymous letter came to the house yesterday. Somebody knows too much about what we've done, and they know Sardis is behind it all."

"Yeah, that would be Brock Skinner, the guy you suggested we cozy up to." Omar heard the line go dead.

When Cru pulled onto the campus of Union, he went to a laboratory building where a friend he had known in Seattle, who moved to Kentucky, was teaching an art class that was about to be dismissed. He took the camera in with him. After the kids tidied up their stations and left the room, his friend said, "Well, if it isn't the fellow who calls himself Omar Cru. You've saved me the effort of finding you and offering congratulations for making it big."

"Well, thank you. I'm a long way from Seattle now, and so are you."

"Something tells me you've come to see me for some other reason than to say hello."

Omar looked like a mortician preparing to tell a family member that a close relative had died. "Yes, I did. I have two favors to ask. I want to get away from all the attention I'm getting, and I need you to paint a nude for me."

"You saying you want to rent my guest house again?"

Cru had stayed there when his cabin was being built. "Yes, if it's available."

"It is, and what's this crazy business about a nude?"

"You're a world-class portrait artist. I'm trying to impress an attractive young lady whom I'm pursuing by way of a portrait of her, and I want her to believe I painted it."

"How quick do you need it?"

"As soon as you can fit it in," Cru replied.

"Let me see the photo I'll be working from." Cru handed him the camera. The artist studied the picture carefully. "Nice-looking woman. I can have it in five days. It'll cost you twenty thousand. These days, I'm sure that's chump change for a man like you."

"Done. I'll write you a check before I leave, unless you'd like to have one of my paintings worth five times that."

The men sauntered over to the campus coffee bar and caught up for the next hour and a half. Omar intended to load everything he owned except for the big pieces of furniture in a box truck on Saturday morning. He'd have Brock drive the truck full of his belongings to Barbourville and drive him home again before suppertime. Cru made a deal with his friend to help unload his stuff when he got there in exchange for a valuable Cru original, which would cover the cost of the portrait and guest house rent for as long as he stayed.

The band had finished polishing every song they had recorded in the last two weeks by four o'clock on Friday afternoon. There was a consensus as to the order of the tracks on the album an hour later. Sadie put them on a single tape and said, "We'll take this to the party tonight and see how it sounds as background music."

The drummer asked, "What's our plan for pulling out tomorrow?"

Abner said, "I'll have a truck here in the morning with a crew to load up your instruments and take them wherever you want. A private jet will be leaving out of the London-Corbin Airport to take you home at eleven o'clock."

Dee added, "If you haven't signed all your paperwork, see me before we head out tonight."

Remy took the stage and said, "Guys, I think we've produced something magical. It has been a pleasure working with every one of you on this project. We'll send each of you a version of the cover art when it's done. Let's meet out front at six fifteen and go have a good time at the Skinners'."

Titus Remington and Abner Giles stood together and waited for everyone to leave the studio to go freshen up. Abner remarked, "It's been a long time coming, but we've finally done it. Let's go look at those paintings again." They went to the front room and studied the four pieces for a second time. Abner suggested, "Why don't we walk over to Cru's place and see if the last one's ready?"

Omar had just come back from Barbourville when he heard the loud knock on the door. He yelled, "It's unlocked."

Abner stepped in first. He said, "I don't know if you remember Titus. He was with me when I came here to buy the other side of the mountain."

Cru walked up to him with a smile and shook his hand. "I remember. It came to me after I had completed the painting of you."

Abner asked, "You don't by chance have the fifth painting done, do you?"

"As a matter of fact, I do." Cru went to the vault and retrieved it. "What do you think?"

Remy commented, "This one and the other four are spectacular. We want to use them as the cover art for the music we just recorded."

Abner looked uneasy. "I'm sorry, Omar. I didn't ask your permission before I suggested the idea to the band. Will you give us your approval to do that?"

"Absolutely. No problem. Just so you know, I'm moving out tomorrow. I'm going to stay with a friend for a while."

Abner turned toward Remy. "I forgot to tell you; Omar has sold this place to Brock Skinner."

Remy looked at the two men, one at a time, and said nothing.

Chapter 20

Dee collected the paperwork that had been signed by bandmembers and put it in a file folder in her office. She had a few minutes to spare before the group headed to the party, so she opened Abner's mail that had accumulated over the past three days. The only interesting thing was the anonymous note that warned of Saul/Paul Sardis. After rereading it, Dee put the note back in the envelope, folded it, and stuck it in her leather purse that had been skillfully embossed with an anthropomorphic snake.

Abner stepped into her office and asked, "You ready to go?" He seemed to be in a jolly mood.

"Let's head out," she said as she popped up and went ahead of him.

The rain had stopped, but the pavement was still wet in downtown Hazard. There were puddles in the ditches along the country roads leading to the big log cabin behind the winery. The two vehicles full of partygoers pulled up behind Marcel's red Mercedes parked alongside the house. Brock, in a waterproof hunting jacket, waited on the porch for the crowd to arrive. He greeted everyone with enthusiasm. Sadie, the last person to enter the house, had a tape player in her hand. Brock asked, "What's that?"

"The album we just recorded. You do have a receiver I can plug it into, don't you?"

"My tech-savvy brother-in-law knows how to pipe music through the house."

"Good. Wait until you hear these songs."

"If you produced them, I'm sure they're great," Brock patronized her gushingly.

Maude introduced the Sutherlands to the party guests. Marcel hung the coats while Brock took drink orders and made sure refreshments were served. He said, "Marcel, would you take the tape player Sadie has there and plug it into my computer? We want to hear this opus by T Rem and On the Beat."

Valerie asked, "What's the name of the album?"

"*Songs for Dancing Lovers*," Abner shared.

"Is it all dance music?"

The organist chimed in, "Believe it or not, it is. I was skeptical at first, but not now."

Maude got everyone's attention and announced dinner plans. "I have six place settings off the kitchen here and six in the formal dining room. There are salads on the tables. Pick a spot and bring your plate in for lasagna or chicken cordon bleu to go with the green beans. It'll be an hour before everything will be ready. We'll finish with pecan pie and ice cream."

Abner proposed a toast to the hosts, and then one to those involved in making the album. He commanded, "Marcel, fire up the sound."

When the first dance tune came on, catcalls, whistling, and clapping broke out. After listening to a couple of numbers, Brock inquired, "Can you guys tell us about the world of music?"

The lead guitarist asked, "You mean the history of it?"

"Sure, that'll do."

The drummer, who had been quiet up to that point, said, "I'll start. Classical music died before the Civil War. Since 1856, the leading styles of music have cycled every twenty-five years or so. Operas were the first to take center stage. Pun intended. They peaked when *The Pirates of Penzance* by Gilbert and Sullivan ran in New York for a whole year in 1880."

The rhythm guitarist took the baton. "If I may, that's when original American music broke out in the Midwest cities along the Mississippi River. Black piano players made ragtime popular, the most famous being Scott Joplin."

"And down the river the sound migrated," the lead guitarist added. "Buddy Bolden opened the jazz age in New Orleans in 1906. Louis Armstrong played startling and brilliant music of any age through 1930, until the Depression hit."

Maude asked, "Is that when the delta blues took over?" She put the chicken in the oven to go with the lasagna, which was already cooking.

Remy commented, "Not yet. That sound wouldn't come to the forefront until later, in the form of jump blues, called rock and roll."

Valerie threw out, "Isn't it funny how history repeats itself? Centuries ago, they sped up the waltz and called it the polka. Last century, they sped up the blues and it became rock and roll."

Abner said, "Cole Porter and showtunes ruled the day beginning in 1931. Upbeat music was the salve for a country mired in depression. 'I've Got You Under My Skin,' arranged by Nelson Riddle and sung by Frank Sinatra, recorded in December of 1955, was the capstone, top of the form."

"And then came the rock era," the organist imparted. "'Jailhouse Rock' by Elvis Presley and 'Great Balls of Fire' by Jerry Lee Lewis ran a little too rich for stodgy post-war society. Rock didn't gain any momentum again after that setback until the Beatles appeared in 1962."

Sadie picked up the narrative, saying, "Halfway through the twenty-five-year rock-and-roll cycle, recordings became ultra-modern with the release of 'All Along the Watchtower' by Hendrix and 'Whole Lotta Love' by Zeppelin. The era ended in 1980 with 'Back in Black' by AC/DC and 'Young Lust' by Pink Floyd."

Marcel reflected, "It seems some great artists of certain forms came after the style of music had peaked."

"Why, certainly," Valerie replied emphatically. "Look at the Renaissance art of the sixteenth century. DaVinci, Michaelangelo, and Raphael reached near perfection early in the century, yet Titian did remarkable work after the parade had gone through."

"That's much the same with Stevie Ray Vaughan. He was arguably as good as Hendrix but came into his own after the rock era had passed," the lead guitarist said.

"As was the case with the jazz of Miles Davis and ragtime of Erroll Garner."

"So, what took over in 1981?" Brock asked.

All five musicians said in unison, "Rap music."

"'Rapture' by Blondie was the first great rap song," the drummer reported.

Maude continued the questioning. "By your reckoning, it died by 2005. What took its place?"

"Radio pop music," Abner suggested. "Lady Gaga, Maroon 5, and Taylor Swift. The money in the music business changed to reward artists for writing overly produced megahits."

"And you would say it'll end by 2030. What will come next?"

The eight guests from the mansion across town looked critically at each other. Sadie finally said, "Songs written by artificial intelligence." No one spoke after that. Everyone concentrated on the eighth number playing in the background. One thing was indisputable: the songs on the album were the best music anyone had ever heard.

The meal was a great success. Afterward, Abner took his drink into the family room to look at the painting by Omar Cru. "This style artwork will make a great cover for the album," he said.

Brock asked Remy, who was standing by Abner, "Would you come with me for a few minutes? I need to chat with you about an important matter."

"Sure. Lead the way."

Brock shut the door to his office after they went into it. "How'd you get connected with Python Deco?"

"I don't know what you're talking about." Titus looked as guilty as he was of lying.

"Come now, let's not play games. Python Deco told me you paid them to develop a horseracing algorithm five years ago."

"Oh, yeah. I forgot about that."

Brock's body language conveyed to Remy that he wasn't fooling around. "No, you didn't. You went on to hire Saul Sardis to have artificial intelligence write a dozen songs for you, complete with scores for each instrument, in the form of famous musicians. If you deny that, things will get rough for you."

"Having AI produce music isn't against the law," he remonstrated.

"How did you get Giles to buy half the mountain and build on it?"

"I told him I'd buy the mineral rights to the property for a half million dollars when he bought the other half." Remy loosened up. "And besides, he wanted to record my songs when he heard them."

"Whose idea was it to put the clause in the purchase contract to buy out Cru?"

"Mine."

"I don't believe you. Sardis is behind this. It's he who wants the mineral rights, not you. What for?" Brock moved in closer to Remy's face.

"I don't know why. I'm through talking to you." His loose talk had tightened up again.

Brock grabbed him by the shirt and said, "You'll be through when I say you're through. Why are you avoiding Ruby Lynch?"

"Because Sardis told me to steer clear of her or he'd sue me for royalties on my music."

"Ah, blackmail. Just so you know, Sardis had AI produce Omar Cru's artwork, and now you're going to use it on the cover of your album. That'll make the whole project phony all around." Titus Remington wheeled his arm to break the grip on his shirt. Brock asked, "Does Abner Giles know about Sardis?"

"No." He walked out of the room.

Dee walked in right after Remy left. She opened her purse and took out the letter to Abner. She said, "This came in the mail. I haven't shown it to him. Do you know anything about it?"

"Let me see it." He knew what was in the envelope but made a show like he didn't. "I'll keep it for a while. You don't need to tell Abner about it."

Dee remarked, "I thought as much when Omar told me you were going to hold the picture he gave me. Is Abner in any kind of trouble?"

"What gave you that idea?"

"There's something fishy going on. I can smell it," she said bluntly.

"I can assure you; Abner is not involved in anything bad. How did you get hooked up with him in the first place?" Brock probed.

"I worked for Abner in Nashville. He convinced me to move here on the prospect of getting rich off the music of Titus Remington."

"From what I can see, that was a pretty good call on your part. The music I heard will make a lot of money for everybody."

———

The party ended by eleven o'clock. The Sutherlands and Skinners spent a half hour cleaning up the cabin. Marcel told Brock, "I checked the art store where Arlena works. They've got a gallery in Cincinnati that deals in expensive paintings and could process a check in the millions without any trouble."

"So, it's likely the CFO there is in cahoots with her. Speaking of Arlena, see if there is a way we can find her name on the passenger list of a boat leaving for the Caribbean in the morning."

Marcel said peremptorily, "I already tried that. There are only two boats heading that way from south Florida tomorrow, and Arlena's not on either one of them."

"Uh-oh. That means she's skipping out. She must have heeded warnings that her life might be in danger. Have you been able to find a bank account for her?"

"No. I'm guessing that CFO has set her up so her account can't be hacked," Marcel said. "If she is going on the lam, she'll take her money with her."

Brock recounted his conversations with Titus Remington and Deianira Wathen. Maude wanted to know where the whole thing stood. Marcel summarized the situation: "Sardis used Arlena Harring to get Omar Cru to buy the mountain. He then used Titus Remington to convince Abner Giles to buy half the mountain and build on it, planning that Giles would buy Cru out when he got rich off his paintings and wanted to leave Hazard."

Brock said, "Remington claims Sardis told him to stay away from Ruby Lynch. That's a sure sign that Sardis got to know Garrison Lynch somehow and learned something from him worth killing for."

"That would be the mineral rights he wants."

Brock remembered, "Ruby told me she found a bunch of formulas among her father's personal things after his death. She said she threw them away."

"What could possibly be under the ground on that mountain? It's all rock," Maude reported.

"That's a secondary problem. First, we must make sure Sardis doesn't have anyone else killed."

"So, you think Abner's in the clear?" Valerie asked.

"Until Sardis finds out he can't buy Cru's half of the mountain."

"What will he do then?"

"He'll have Remy tell Abner that without the mineral rights to Cru's property, no rights will be bought. Giles will be told to come see me to make a deal," Brock supposed.

Marcel stopped moving and said nonchalantly, "That's not so bad. You could sell out to him and get whatever amount he's willing to invest to keep his recording studio."

"Fine. That would be a hundred thousand for the land and cabin, and the premium I can get so he can sell the mineral rights for a half mil. I don't need the money. I'd rather find out why that land is so valuable and then make Giles a deal he can't refuse."

"On that front, we have little to go on," Marcel said. "I know how your mind works. You are going to break into Arlena's house and look for clues."

"I want to know what's in that basement room. I'm sure the AI printer's there, maybe more."

Maude suggested, "If Arlena's on the run, Omar Cru might do the same thing. Now that he has his money, he might take a powder."

"He might, but you're forgetting one thing: he's crazy in love with Dee Wathen. If he hides out, it'll likely be close by because he'll want to see her, and vice versa."

Marcel said, "Better not let Sardis learn about that relationship. He might kidnap her and make a trade for the mineral rights to your piece of the mountain."

"Ooh, I never thought of that. It might be a good idea to turn Saul's water and electricity off."

Maude asked, "What does that mean?"

"Kill his computer and threaten to expose him as a fraud if he doesn't clear out."

"I'd be careful," Marcel interjected. "He's one hell of a dangerous man."

"According to you, he might be the antichrist. We'll take it one step at a time. Marcel, you've got to find out how Sardis was paid by Arlena."

Chapter 21

Omar Cru walked into the winery right after it opened on Saturday morning. He saw Maude at the tasting bar and hailed her with both hands. She came over and he asked, "Is your husband here?"

"No. He's at home with Marcel and Valerie, your dance teacher. They came to visit yesterday. Shall I call him for you?"

"Please." She tapped the number in her phone and handed it to Omar. "Brock, I've got a huge favor to ask."

"What's that?"

"I'm moving to Barbourville today. I need you to drive my truck full of belongings or my car over there, and then I'll bring you back here. I have a friend who's renting his guesthouse to me. He'll help me unload my stuff."

"Where did you rent the truck?" Brock asked.

"Here in Hazard. I arranged to drop it off in Barbourville so you wouldn't have to wait until I unloaded everything before I brought you home."

"Okay. I'm happy to drive the truck back and turn it in here if you want," Brock offered.

"No, not necessary. It'll take me a while to unload the two dozen paintings I still have left. I'll pick you up here at the winery at eleven o'clock. We'll run to my place to get the truck and take off from there."

"I'll see you then."

"Good. We can catch a bite of lunch in Barbourville."

Brock saw the Sutherlands off before he left to meet Cru. The sun had dried the pavement, yet the ground remained soggy from the inches of rain that had fallen on Friday. When the two of them got to the cabin on the mountain, Brock saw the couch, side chairs, tables, and bed were still inside. Omar said, "The place I'm going has the furniture I'm leaving here. You don't mind, do you?"

"No. I'll drive the truck."

They pulled into Tres Hombres, a Mexican restaurant close to Union Commonwealth University in Barbourville, where they claimed seats in a cushioned booth that had carved Mayan wood frames. The hard colors throughout the restaurant were garish in a folksy way. Brock asked, "What brought on this sudden exodus from Hazard?"

"My friend here, whom I knew when I lived in Seattle, has a guesthouse on his property. The only way back to it is through a tunnel that has an impenetrable gate. It's a safe place for me to hang out until I see what happens."

"Arlena has skipped out. You must have broken it off with her."

"I did." Cru raised his hand to attract a waiter.

"Which tells me you're zeroing in on Dee Wathen," Brock concluded.

"She's the one for me. I hope she feels the same way."

Brock put his elbow on the table and leaned on the wall. "I can't give you all the run-up, but if Sardis needs to get anything out of you or Abner Giles, he may compromise Dee Wathen to get it."

"What could he want from any of us?"

"I'm not sure, but I think we should play defense until I can run Sardis out of town. He is trouble, and the only way for us to rest easy is to ban him from Kentucky. I think it's a great idea for you to hide out here until this thing is over. I'm going to try to explain to Dee why she should watch herself. I'll be rooting for you to win her. You two are a good match."

Cru thought about things for a moment. "I wonder where Arlena has gotten to. It would seem she's in more danger than I am. When I talked to her recently, she told me you sent out letters like this to a few people." He gave Brock the one he had received. "Why'd you do that?"

"To ruffle Sardis. Get him to make a move." The waiter asked in broken English what they'd like for lunch. The rice, beans, and chicken the men ordered came in a hurry, accompanied by tortillas, greens, and sour cream. For a minute, both forgot about life in the fast lane.

Brock got dropped off at the winery back in Hazard at a little after three. He made the rounds and asked Maude if there was anything else he needed to do. She said he could take off, so he took the truck and rubber boots he wore when working at the vineyard and drove over to the property he now owned.

The open area behind the cabin began sloping down the hill in short order. Brock zigzagged the wet ground on the side of the mountain, looking for anything unusual. He found it. There was a cluster of holes where core samples had been taken. The ground cover growth implied they had been drilled out years ago. He returned to the winery to retrieve his car.

Brock announced to his wife after a light dinner at home on Saturday evening that he planned to run to Arlena's house at dark to look around. She said, "You're going to break in and find that hidden basement room, aren't you?"

"Yes. I'll take Truman with me."

"What do you hope to accomplish?"

"Find evidence that ties Sardis to the painting scam. I'll use it to get him to leave Kentucky."

"Is that how this thing will end?" she asked.

"Not entirely. It'll end when we find out why Sardis moved here to begin with," he explained.

The Lamborghini pulled onto the road leading up to the Harring house a few minutes after ten. Truman, sitting on a blanket covering the passenger seat, had his front legs apart to keep his balance. Brock parked in the grass by the front door, facing the gravel road to the highway. The colloidal night air was damp and still, utterly perfect for breaking and entering. Once inside, Brock turned the flashlight on low. Truman stayed near his owner as they moved throughout the house.

A room-by-room search turned up nothing. There were no bank statements at the desk where she kept her papers. He pulled down an attic ladder and climbed it to see if storage boxes were up there. No luck. The only thing left to do was find how to get into the basement.

Brock ran the flashlight along the floor. At the end of the hall leading to the back of the house, beyond cased openings on either side, a cluster of majolica pots in Tuscan colors were filled with artificial plants. He noticed the slate slab under the plants was not grouted like all the rest.

It took close to an hour to find the button under the sink in the hall bathroom that activated a motor, which raised the slab up by way of a scissor lift. There were steps between the scissors leading down to a dark abyss that was blacker than the inside of a hat. Brock brightened the flashlight and inspected the steps carefully. He caught sight of a memory stick that had fallen into a narrow track along the perimeter of the steel plate under the lifting mechanism. He reached down and retrieved it.

Truman followed Brock down the steps while they were lit enough for him to see where he was going. The lights came on when a switch on the wall was pressed. "How about this, Truman. We found it." The dog paraded around like he was sniffing for drugs. Nothing was in the room other than a mottled gold carpet and rust-colored stucco walls. The carpet had been compressed in several spots by heavy objects, such as printing equipment, that had recently been there. "Looks like we missed all the action."

As Brock was examining the wall where the escape door should have been, the noise of the motor started up and the slab began to lower. He ran over to see if he and Truman could get out before it shut. He could make it, but he'd have to leave the dog. Brock ran back to look for the escape door again. His mind was racing. Who trapped them there? The concealed exit he was searching for was on an adjacent wall. A tight passageway led to the backside of the dance-floor room where there were grips mounted on a wood panel. He lifted the panel and slid it in a pocket to be able to squeeze through. Truman slithered by on Brock's heels.

The room was dark. He ascended the stairs quietly, fearful that an ambush was in store. Brock drew the pistol he had in his belt and pointed it wherever his light went. The pantry was empty up on the main floor. They checked the house again thoroughly. Whoever pulled that stunt had run out apparently. "That was a close call, buddy." The dog acted like he wasn't sure the coast was clear yet. "Let's get out of here."

Brock reached the front door ahead of Truman. Suddenly, the coat closet swung open, and a shadowy figure stepped out stiffly. The shepherd barked viciously and attacked whomever it was. The person staggered backward but didn't go down. "Leave him.

Let's go!" Truman shot through the open door. Brock slammed it just before leaping off the porch. He put his gun back in his belt and opened the car door for Truman to get in lickety-split, and then he jumped in the driver's seat to hightail it out of there.

The front door opened again. As Brock spun his wheels in the grass, he heard and felt a big thud as the Lamborghini dipped down from some unknown force. The car picked up speed, and the person who was giving chase stopped, turned around, and walked back toward the house.

After Skinner drove up on I-75 heading south, he said to the shepherd, "Let's hope we got what we came for." Truman peered through the windshield into the dark night as if he was unsure whether they were safe or not. Resolving there was nothing he could do, he curled up for a quick nap on the way home.

The Skinners were dressed and ready for church on Sunday morning after a short night's sleep. The breakfast they fixed didn't seem to get them going. Brock recounted to his wife what happened at the Harring house, underplaying the person who acted like he wanted to kill him and the dog. It was hard to support that line of thinking when Maude saw the big crease on the back of the car. She crossed her arms and asked suspiciously, "What happened here? That'll cost a fortune to fix."

"The guy in the house must have hit it with something heavy," he replied dismissively.

She looked closer. "But there are no scratches from any blunt object," she groused.

"That's true. If you keep talking about it, I'm going to be in a bad mood at church."

Brock had a hard time staying awake during the sermon. Maude was the one who was in a bad mood, seething over the stupid things Brock was doing for no logical reason other than righting wrongs that nobody cared about. The two of them carried on several hollow conversations with friends, keeping smiles on their faces while they waited for Sunday school to begin.

More people were in the Bible class than the last time the Skinners attended. Ben Hicks saw them come in and take seats. He said, "Will you look here. Brock and Maude have made their way back. You're gonna love what we're studying now." He addressed Brock: "I bet I can stump you this time."

"Ben, you're not going to pick on me again, are you?" Brock smiled and looked down.

Hicks lolled his head to one side as if he was disappointed in the comment. "Would you rather I invite your wife to speak on your behalf?"

Brock peeked at Maude pleadingly. "No."

"Well, class, you'll remember we wrapped up Ecclesiastes two weeks ago and got through the first chapter of Revelation last week. Now we're on to the seven churches in chapter two. Brock, I'm sure you can recite their names."

"If I get them right, will you call on someone else?"

Maude intervened, saying, "Honey, you should help Ben out. He's introducing an interesting subject and wants you to take part in it." That brought a pulse of laughter.

Brock stood with the panache of an experienced orator. "Ephesus, Smyrna, Pergamos, Thyatira, Sardis, Philadelphia, and Laodicea." He raised his hands and swiveled his head.

"That was too easy. How about this: Who was Solomon's architect for the temple?"

Brock sat down and became a shrinking violet. "Oh, Ben, we don't want to get into that."

"Is that your way of saying you don't know who it is?"

"It's Hiram Abiff, Ben, a superstar among the Freemasons." He leaned back, crossed his arms, and heaved his shoulders.

"Which of the seven churches would characterize him and his followers the best?" Ben was playing him again like a Stradivarius.

"None, Ben. Those churches came a thousand years after Abiff was murdered."

Ben clarified his position: "But don't those churches represent people from all ages?"

"I guess you could look at it that way. Pergamos would be the one, I suppose. The people had plenty of good works, but they compromised on some of the church's beliefs."

"That makes sense. And for all the marbles, which would best describe Solomon?" Ben leaned forward and stuck his neck out.

"If I answer that, Ben, I want to be declared the winner and retire. Deal?"

"Deal."

Those in the class started chanting, "Go, go, go."

"Laodicea. The folks of that church let their wealth dull their faith, and Ben, God does not like a lukewarm believer. Solomon knew it."

"What did God say he'd do to those who didn't repent and get true faith?"

A cautious look came on Brock's face. "Spit them out. Now, I'm going into retirement." A round of applause followed.

When the noise had finally died down, a bilious man in the class who had a mouth full of rogue teeth going in all directions raised a finger and asked, "What was it you said last time you were here, something about Solomon's artifice?"

Brock evaded the question. He replied, "I'm not sure what I said, but whatever it was, I hope you won't hold it against me."

The man didn't reply at once. "Well, I think you said that some of the things that he did in his life were vain and meaningless. I brought it up because I feel that way about my life some days," the man allowed in a rare moment of contrition.

That hit Brock like a ton of bricks. Maude threw her husband a jaundiced stare and waited for him to talk his way out of that one. "Well, sir, truth be known, I am worse than Solomon. I seem to do vain and meaningless things most of the time myself. In addition, the distractions in this world have tended to dull my faith. Woe to me if God considers that I'm lukewarm."

Ben, in a serious and loving tone, said, "Brock, I know it's difficult for us to examine our lives, to admit that we fall short at times. Thanks for sharing and being a good sport again."

CHAPTER 22

Titus Remington was glad the recording session was over and he had been able to return to his comfortable home again. He padded to the mailbox after lunchtime on Sunday to fetch several days' worth of post and the Sunday paper. An envelope from Solomon Pergamos drew his attention. After Remy read what it said, he used the burner phone Sardis had given him to place a call. "Hey, I just got a strange letter in the mail."

"I know about it. Brock Skinner sent a few of them out to stir the pot," Sardis reported.

"When I saw Brock on Friday night, he told me he knows you wrote my songs and produced Cru's paintings. Who else did he send these notes to?"

"You, Omar, Arlena Harring, who is in on Omar's deal, possibly Abner, and your neighbor Ruby Lynch."

"Skinner can expose you, me, Cru, and his girlfriend as being frauds. Why is he involved?"

Saul burbled, "Hell, I can't figure out what the guy is trying to prove. Nobody's done anything to him. I helped you write some good music, produced some fine art for Cru, and wrote a book about my life. None of those things are illegal or unethical. The idea I had from the beginning was for the three of us to become rich and famous. We're on our way. Then this clown sticks his nose in our business. He's not going to go away until I find a way to get rid of him."

"When Abner and I went to Omar's recently to pick up a painting, Abner mentioned that Omar had sold his place to Skinner. I thought Omar knew he couldn't sell to anyone besides Abner."

"He must not have read the agreement, or Skinner told him how to get around that clause," Sardis surmised.

"How could he do that?" Remy asked.

"Probably told him it wasn't enforceable in court. What Skinner may not know is that Abner has the original agreement. You were with Abner when he signed the deal. I asked you to be sure Abner kept the original, not the copy."

"He did. You may have missed a trick, Saul. Dee Wathen, Abner's business manager, keeps his papers. Skinner might've paid her to swap out the original. I wonder why Abner didn't confront Omar and tell him he couldn't sell his property to Brock when he found out he had sold it," Remy pondered out loud.

Saul offered a plausible explanation: "Abner's clean on this thing. He either figures he can void the sale, or he's decided to team up with Skinner instead of selling the mineral rights to you for half a million. If that happens, things could get worse for me."

Remy said, "There's something else. Giles owns six paintings by Omar Cru that are worth more than the mineral rights. I never asked you why those rights are so valuable."

"And don't start asking now. Here's what I want you to do. Mail the note back to Skinner in an envelope he can't trace to you."

"Okay. Aren't you worried Brock might expose all of us?" Remy asked with trepidation.

"He told me he won't. I believe him. He's after me, no one else." Sardis ended the call.

———————

Brock forcefully jabbed the intercom button at the Giles estate on Sunday afternoon, hoping to gain admittance. Dee came on. "What is it I can do for you, handsome?"

"Invite me in for tea."

"We don't have any. Go get me the broom of the wicked witch and I'll let you in," Dee harped.

"Okay. It'll take me about a month and a half to find her," he reported glibly. The gate began to open slowly. No one greeted him atop the hill, so he went to the entrance of the house and knocked.

Dee opened the door and said, "You're lucky. I found some tea."

"I'm always lucky, Dee. You'll come to learn that about me."

"This place is quiet now that most people have left. Let's go in the kitchen." She led the way. "I like green tea. That work for you?" she asked.

Brock was thinking what a charmer she was in an abstruse way. "It's my favorite."

"I know I'm irresistible, but I've got a hunch you came by for some other reason than to flirt."

"No, not necessarily," he replied to pique her interest. "On Friday night, you said you thought something fishy was going on. I didn't want you to be left in the dark."

"Well, that's magnanimous of you. How long are you going to engage in foreplay before we get down to business?" she pushed, putting her hands on her hips.

"I want you to promise you'll keep what I tell you to yourself."

"Brock, I'm a good judge of character. I trust you, ergo, I'll keep my mouth shut." The fridge had a spigot that dispensed boiling water. Dee filled two cups and dropped tea bags in them.

"Titus Remington brought Abner Giles up here two years ago to buy this land and build on it because Titus wanted the mineral rights but didn't want to own the property. He had the idea that Omar Cru would eventually sell the other half of the mountain to Abner and move out. At that point, Abner would own the whole section up here and could sell all the rights. Titus wants to flip them for a profit to a confidential buyer."

"What does that have to do with me?" Dee asked. She removed the tea bags and set the cups on the countertop.

"Omar sold his place to me instead of Abner. I'm worried the confidential buyer will threaten to harm you if I don't sell the property to Abner now."

"Who is this confidential buyer you're referring to who'd pull a stunt like that?" Dee shoved one teacup closer to Brock.

"Take a guess. That nefarious character might learn that Omar Cru is fond of you and threaten to harm him if I don't sell out to Giles."

"So, swapping that document out for you has hoisted me by my own petard. Why don't you just sell the property to Abner and save my skin?" The gravity of the situation was sinking in.

"There's a part I haven't explained. After the buyer gets the mineral rights, he may hunt down and kill Abner Giles to cover his tracks."

Dee looked out the window and took a sip of her tea. "With three of us in danger, I'm guessing you've got a plan to take the fight to this bottom-feeder. You must have something on him to stop him from going on a rampage," she said with hope.

"I do, but until I can bring him to heel, you need to watch yourself."

She picked up her cup and walked over by the sink. "This character was the one named in the letter I gave you: Saul or Paul Sardis. Am I right?"

"Yes." Brock went near her and put his hand on her shoulder. He asked, "Is Abner here? I need to warn him too."

"I'll get him." She scurried off and came back with Giles in tow.

"Brock. What are you doing here?" He acted suspicious of the situation.

"I need to share something with you."

"What's that?" Giles propped himself on the counter with straight arms.

"What do you think about me buying Cru's place?"

"It's okay with me," Abner replied without reservation.

"Aren't you worried about getting your hands on the mineral rights?" Brock questioned.

"To be frank, I figured I could sell this property and its mineral rights to you for a hefty price and move back to Nashville. Then you could deal with Remy. I've got the music in the can and damn sure don't want to live out here in the middle of nowhere for the rest of my days."

Brock struck a broad grin and said, "You're making a lot of sense. Is your agreement to sell the mineral rights only optional, not a contractual obligation?"

"That's right. It gave me the idea to sell to you, especially after I heard you bought Cru's place. I've got six Cru paintings worth six hundred thousand and can sell out for a pretty penny."

"There's something you should know. The buyer who Remy's planning to peddle the rights to is a tough customer. My brother-in-law calls him the antichrist. And while we're being frank, you should know that he used AI to write Remy's songs and paint Cru's pictures. That's how he got cooperation from them on his quest to own what's under our feet. If you go your own way, he may threaten to kill Dee here when you don't fall in line."

Giles staggered back and rolled his head in a circle. "Who is this guy?"

Dee answered, "Saul or Paul Sardis."

Abner stared at the floor. "That's the guy who claims he saw God and made Cru famous."

"I'll deal with him. You need to act like you don't know what's going on and do whatever they ask you to do, which will probably be to go into court and start proceedings for the sale of Cru's place to me to be vacated."

"I can do that." Abner spoke to Dee, telling her, "Sounds like you should hide until this business gets settled."

Brock said, "Before we discuss that, let's talk about you selling what you have here to me. How much do you have invested, all in?"

"A million dollars."

"Will you take that for it?" Brock asked directly.

"Since I have the Cru paintings and will get fifteen percent of the profits from Remy's music, I'll gladly take a million dollars for this place."

"Okay. How about this deal: you sell out to me now. I'll pay you six percent interest monthly on the million-dollar purchase price, which is five thousand a month. You can live here until you're ready to move back to Nashville for that same five thousand. I'll hand over the million dollars when your moving van is ready to pull out."

Abner smiled and said, "You're on."

"In the meantime, you should act like you still own the place and are willing to work with Remy however he wants. Just don't offer to sell him this part of the mountain without the other."

"I can do that."

Brock looked at Dee. "We're going to have to get a bodyguard to go with you if you want to leave the property alone. If Omar calls and wants to come visit, tell him you're busy till next weekend. See if he'll let you visit him where he's living now."

"Where's that?" she asked.

"He'll have to tell you. Abner, I'll have my lawyer draw up the purchase contract."

On the way home, Brock called Marcel to report the latest. He asked his brother-in-law to find a drilling outfit that could bore holes in several places on the mountain.

———

Omar Cru received an invitation from the art professor to join him for dinner in the main house. The early evening air was cold enough to call for a jacket, even though the guesthouse where Cru lived was only fifty yards off to the side. Cru took a bottle of red wine that Maude had sent him back in Hazard as a thank you for the small landscape painting that he'd given her. When the two men sat at the dining room table, the professor read the label and commented, "I went to this winery a few weeks ago. The woman who owns it is one good-looking lady."

"Her husband is the guy who drove the truck full of my belongings over here. You don't want to tangle with him. Not only is his wife good-looking, but she's also one of the nicest people you'll ever meet."

"I got that impression myself. What about this gal I'm doing the portrait of? Why are you interested in her?"

Cru winced. "Let me count the ways. When will you be finished with her painting?"

"Thursday. You can sign it then."

Cru looked over at the fireplace and saw the artwork he'd given the professor hanging there. "How do you like the piece I gave you?"

"Frankly, Omar, I don't know how you did it. The content, color, and brushwork are remarkable. You have certainly improved since we were together in Seattle."

"I still can't hold a candle to you when it comes to realism. Are you selling much of your work these days?"

"Here and there. Artificial intelligence can now mimic my style and produce works that are as good or better than what I can do by hand. Something will have to be done. There are programs out there that can distort images of original work so AI can't read them. They're only a finger in the dike."

"How do you like living in Appalachia?" Omar asked to change the subject.

"I don't, really. I'm thinking of moving back to Seattle," he responded darkly.

"That's unfortunate. I like it around here. If you decide to pull out, I'd be happy to buy this place from you. It's marvelous. I could turn the guesthouse into my studio and gallery."

"Yes, you could. We're right off I-75. Your stuff would sell like hot cakes."

"Not too many people driving buy swing in and drop a hundred grand on a painting," Cru said.

"You'd be surprised."

Omar and his old friend enjoyed a delicious meal together, and by the time the evening was over, Cru had made a deal to buy the place. After Christmastime, the art professor would head back to the West Coast. Omar hoped Dee Wathen would be impressed with his new digs enough to move in with him. By the first of the year, he would be rolling in dough, living in a swanky setup, with a beautiful woman on his arm who could run his business. What business was that? After the last twenty paintings he had were gone, there would be no more.

Chapter 23

Brock figured people boring holes for a living would be at it by seven on Monday morning. He called the outfit Marcel had found at two minutes past the hour. While waiting for someone to answer, he looked out the window at the sky to see how the day was setting up. Not a cloud to be seen. "This is Art," the man answering the phone bellowed.

"Hi there, Art. Brock Skinner here. I need you to drill some core samples for me in Hazard. Could you do that?"

"How deep? How many locations? How many samples do you want from each spot? How hard will it be to get my rig in there?"

"Five locations. Two samples at each spot, sixty feet deep. Two of the five locations are on the side of the mountain," Brock specified.

"Three thousand a bore for the easy ones. Five thousand for the hard ones. I believe that comes to thirty-eight thousand. What do you want me to do with the samples?"

"Crate them."

"Okay. That much rock will take sixty crates, which'll cost you two-fifty a crate, adding another fifteen thousand. I'll meet you at the site and have my drilling rig there Wednesday morning. Should be able to finish before dark on Saturday night. What's the address?"

Brock sat at the kitchen table after hiring Art, waiting for Maude to appear from the bedroom. She could tell he was getting ready to spring a dandy on her when she saw him sitting there looking like he'd swallowed a canary. "What have you done now?"

"I bought Abner's property and have ordered a company to drill core samples around the thirty acres to find out what's there."

She looked up, deep in thought. "I'll give you ninety days to sell those thirty acres for more than you paid. Until then, I'll act happy about it." She fixed her nail-gun eyes on him and wove her hands under her chin.

Brock got up and said, "Well, that went better than I thought it would. In ninety days, you'll be wearing diamonds as big as rocks."

Maude went over to the patio door. She asked, "What are you doing today?"

"Going to see Saul Sardis."

"Are you expecting a fistfight to break out?"

"No, sweetheart. I just want to chat with him. Maybe we can come to an understanding," he replied sarcastically.

Brock found the silver sedan that Sardis had parked in an end space behind the lecture hall at Slade University, making it easy to position the Lamborghini within inches of the driver's door. At fifteen minutes till noon, he saw the professor bouncing down the sidewalk in his direction. The slight man's gait stiffened when he recognized who was standing there. Saul tossed his briefcase on the hood of the car and said, "What a pleasure to see you again, Skinner. I hope you're doing well."

"Magnificent. Might I have a word?"

"It appears I don't have much choice." Saul stared and threw a hand at Brock's vehicle.

"I just wanted you to see what your pal Solomon Pergamos has done to the back of my car. It'll cost at least ten thousand to fix. I wanted you to know I plan to collect the cost of the damages from him."

"That might take some doing. He left recently to go visit relatives. I don't expect him back for a month," Saul reported boorishly. "Now that you're here, it's me who'd like to have a word."

Skinner approached Sardis and sat next to the briefcase. "Speak up."

"Why are you dogging me? I haven't done anything to you, or anything illegal. What are you up to?"

Brock put an arm out to lean on the hood. "We'll get to that. You cleared the printer out of Arlena's house this weekend. That tells me you might be planning to make her disappear."

"Why would I do that?"

"Because she could tear down your smokehouse now that she's been paid out. Remy and Cru have a lot more to lose. They're less likely to rat you out."

Sardis hastily took issue with what Brock said. "I don't know what you're talking about."

Brock dug in his pants pocket to retrieve the memory stick he'd found at the Harring house. "I ran across this when I was snooping around. It's how you used AI to produce artwork for Omar Cru. I'm keeping it for insurance."

"Against what?"

"The untimely death of your partners in crime."

Sardis shrugged. "You've got it wrong. The people I helped might be planning to do *me* in."

"If you end up dead, I'm sure Harring, Cru, and Remington will be suspects. Here's the bottom line, Sardis: I want you to leave Kentucky and never come back. If you don't, I'm going to expose you."

Saul picked up his briefcase and retorted, "When you do that, I'll expose Remington and Cru. Do you want to ruin their lives?"

"No. If any of them end up dead, I'll hunt you down and make you pay." Brock wagged a finger at him.

"Look, let's come to an agreement. I promise you I will leave Kentucky for good on Saturday the sixteenth of December if you leave me alone after I'm gone. Now, move that dented piece of crap. Otherwise, I'll call security."

Brock rocked himself off the hood of Saul's car and said, "You want to know why I'm after you? Because you blasphemed God. He will not be mocked by a false prophet like you."

Sardis sniggered. "Oh, really. The way you're talking, you'd think I was the antichrist."

"As far as I'm concerned, you are. You just make sure nobody gets hurt and you're out of here in a month." Brock got into his car and eased onto the street running between the university and downtown Lexington. From there he drove to Sutherland Tailoring, a thirty-five-minute trip over to Harrodsburg.

Marcel was sitting in his office when Brock entered it. He said to his brother-in-law, "It's your turn to host Thanksgiving. Is that on your radar?"

"Certainly. Valerie's all fired up. What brings you around?"

"I just told Sardis to pack his bags and leave the state. He said he would by mid-December."

"What about all that mineral rights business? Did you get into that?" Marcel probed.

"No. I didn't want to tip my hand. I hope to find out what's in the ground before he gets wise to my play for Abner's property. I wonder how long it'll take a lab to figure out what's in the core samples I'm having dug up?"

"Three or four weeks I'm guessing," Marcel predicted. "Send the samples to a place called Earth Bore Inspection Services in Pineville. I talked to the guy who owns it. He told me he could get right on your samples."

"Good. I take it you still haven't determined the photography studio in Saul's deal."

Marcel stood, put his eyeglasses on his desk, and rubbed his eyes. "No, but I thought of a way he could get paid out tax-free. The photography studio has received Saul's cut of the artwork, and probably other income from projects he's been paid to do. Saul could sell his house to the owner of the studio for two or three million dollars. He wouldn't get questioned if he didn't report the price to the IRS."

"Sardis told me he was leaving town on December sixteenth. That means he'll sell his property on Friday, the fifteenth."

"Which is the last day of the class he's teaching at Slade," Marcel added.

"Then he'll start traveling around to churches promoting his book. I wonder where the printer disappeared to that he took out of Arlena's house?"

"This photography studio, I reckon. The CFO where Arlena works has been laundering money. I don't often suggest you strong arm someone, but the thought did occur to me. He knows the name of the place and where the check is being mailed."

"You're right." Brock left Sutherland Tailoring and called his attorney on the way home to explain the purchase of Abner's estate. He wanted the agreement signed tomorrow afternoon.

The mail carrier swung by the Skinner abode at 11:40 a.m. each day and did so on Tuesday. Angry wind was blowing under low clouds, and the temperature had sputtered at forty-four degrees. Brock ran out to get the mail. Two of the letters he sent out anonymously had been returned. He had put pin holes in different places in all five letters and could name whose they were. The two in his hands were the ones originally sent to Remy and Arlena.

Ruby Lynch brought her letter to the winery, Dee Wathen intercepted Abner's, and Omar Cru forked over the one he got, which lined up with Brock's thinking that Remy and Arlena mailed theirs back, likely at the direction of Saul Sardis. Arlena had now gone underground. Remy was still working with Sardis to make the mineral rights deal go forward. Brock decided to drive over to Abner's to see if he'd heard from Remy.

Giles confirmed, "He called yesterday afternoon and asked if I still had the original purchase contract for my acreage. I told him I did. He asked me to file a suit against Cru to vacate his sale to you. I said I would, like you told me to do."

"I'll get my attorney's office to prepare the case on your behalf. It'll take a few weeks before it gets in front of a judge. Later today, the purchase agreement for me to buy you out will need to be signed. If I can get my attorney to prepare your case in time, you can sign both documents. Then you can send a copy of the case against Cru to Remy, to get him to cool his heels."

Brock drove to the winery to scarf down one of Maude's fabulous lunches. Today, the weather being as uninviting as it was, she had whipped up a homemade butternut squash soup and chicken sausage in bechamel over bowtie pasta. Maude asked, "How'd you like it?"

"Really good. I'm thinking about taking the scope out of your office this afternoon. I don't think we need it now."

Maude suggested, "Why don't you just refocus it on the entrance to the Giles estate?"

"I'll do that." It took Brock several minutes to make the adjustment. He then called his attorney and gave him the bad news that he had to prepare a legal action for Abner Giles by quitting time. Maude came into her office as he was hanging up with the attorney. He asked his wife, "You've got Cru's number on your phone. What is it?" She read it off. "Omar, it's your buddy over here in Hazard, Brock Skinner. I know you're famous now, and you've probably forgotten who I am, but I thought I'd ring you up, being a hopeless sycophant."

"Why is it I don't have any normal friends? My whole life I've been relegated to knowing kooks and crooks. You are in the kook department."

"Dee Wathen isn't a kook or a crook. There went that theory. I called to let you know that I told Dee you had moved to a place nearby, but I didn't tell her where you were. Call her and see if she'll let you pick her up on Friday afternoon so you can show her your new place."

"That's a capital idea. And for your information, I've made a deal to buy my friend's estate here in Barbourville by the first of the year. He's moving back to Seattle. I'll convert the guesthouse into my studio."

"What a master stroke," Brock commented zealously.

After he hung up with Skinner, Omar Cru punched in Dee's number. She answered, saying, "I thought maybe you'd found another girlfriend. That would be a moment of weakness on your part. I'm the finest woman in three states. I knew you'd want to hear my voice eventually."

"I want more than that. What say I collect you on Friday afternoon and show you my new Taj Mahal?"

"Where is it?"

"Barbourville."

"Ah. Just far enough away to hide out, and close enough for a tete-a-tete," she remarked in the inimitable style of Mae West. "What time on Friday?"

"My schedule's open. You name it."

"Two o'clock. They have any fancy restaurants over there?" she asked.

"I'll find out. And your portrait will be ready. Better not hang it where some horndog can see it. You are one sexy lady."

"How long did it take you to figure that out?"

"About two seconds after I saw you."

Ruby Lynch had worked up the courage to walk over and knock on her neighbor's front door, and when she did, Titus Remington was caught flat-footed. She looked him in the eye and said nothing. He finally offered, "Can I help you?"

"I've been living next door for a few years now but have never had the occasion to meet you. My name is Ruby Lynch. I think your name's Titus Remington. Is that right?" Ruby, not wearing a jacket even though one would have been comfortable, had on a sage top with a low V neck and flared half sleeves. Her makeup and gold jewelry were perfect for the outfit.

Remy was shocked at how attractive she was up close. He guessed her to be a few years older than he was. "Yes, that's my name. People call me Remy or T Rem. Won't you come in?"

"I'm not interrupting anything, am I?"

"No. Let me put my boots back on." He turned to head for the den. She followed him through the house.

"Don't do that on my account. I've been around men in sock feet."

"I'm sorry we haven't met before now. I was acquainted with your father." He slipped his boots back on despite Ruby's suggestion not to.

"I've also heard that you're a famous musician. Sometimes people in your position must steer clear of people they don't know. I hope you don't feel that way about me." She put her hands behind her back.

"Certainly not. I'm glad you came over to introduce yourself."

"I work for an upscale catering company that puts on spreads for owners of horse farms. If you, or your friends, ever have a need for a catered meal, let me know. You won't be disappointed."

"I'll do that." Ruby thought his expression was hard to read. It was either "get out of here" or "stay forever." She pondered that as she returned to her puny house next door.

CHAPTER 24

Wednesday was forecasted to be rainless with low humidity. Two banged-up red trucks and an ominous-looking machine for boring deep holes, centered on a swayback low-boy trailer, were parked at seven o'clock in the morning off Skyline Drive in front of Skinner's newly acquired mountain. Art languished behind the wheel of the lead truck while one of his three helpers was slouched against the greasy window on the passenger side, trying to get a little sleep before the hard labor started for the day. The two men in the back truck didn't look much peppier. Brock pulled up, hopped out, and introduced himself to the crew.

Art asked, "What is it we're trying to find?" His hands were calloused beyond measure, and he had the bloom of a serious drinker, but his dark-blue eyes were clear and furtive.

"I don't rightly know, Art," Brock answered naively.

"I'm pretty sure the Fire Clay coal seam don't run through here, and from my experience, there ain't much more than limestone, sandstone, and shale below the surface. Occasionally, we see rare earth minerals in trace amounts that are plentiful elsewhere, but they ain't worth much."

"Let's run up to the top and I'll show you where I want you to drill." Brock got in the winery truck and led the way to Cru's former cabin. It took nearly an hour to stake out all the spots to be covered in the process. Brock asked, "You've been doing this for a long time. Have I missed anything?"

Art looked like he was trying to find the words to let Brock down easily. When he finally spoke, he said, "I hope you won't be disappointed if we don't find anything. You never know. I've been fooled a few times. Maybe we'll strike diamonds or gold." His face switched to a Howdy Doody grin.

"Yeah. That's what I told my wife."

Brock was back home before nine thirty. His attorney rang in and reported, "I got your purchase agreement signed by Giles late yesterday, and this morning, his motion to vacate Cru's sale to you was put on the docket for late December."

"Good. That'll push it past the time Sardis has agreed to leave town."

"Who's Sardis?"

"The guy who's costing me all this money and aggravation."

———

Professor Sardis finished his lecture on how artificial intelligence gathered data and was able to develop logic from it. The first point he made was that the base of information used in problem solving had become exponentially larger than the capacity of the human brain to remember and use it. "A showman can juggle six or seven balls at once," he said, "while AI can juggle six or seven million."

A towheaded youngster wearing a gray sleeveless vest over a cranberry collared shirt asked, "What are the tangible benefits of that kind of capability?"

"Think about it: everything in the cosmos is mathematics. Music can be broken down into math formulas, and so can the laws of science. When AI juggles enough formulas proven to be true, the mysteries of the universe will be solved, allowing humankind to do things never dreamed of before."

"What sorts of things?"

"Well, take gravity for instance. Over the years, reports of UFOs levitating in the air have been tagged as unexplainable. There's a practical way to defy gravity that has not been harnessed yet. If humanity figures out how to manage it, the applications are literally endless."

"I see what you mean." Towhead looked lost in his thoughts.

"And then there's the principle of superposition. We'll be able to explain how quantum systems can be in multiple states in the same place simultaneously."

Miss Blue Eyes couldn't keep quiet any longer. "Professor, I want to go back and touch on the antichrist again. I've been doing a little research on the subject. What do you know about the Twelfth Imam?"

Sardis peered at her to see if she seemed unhinged. She didn't. "Young lady, I dare say that you will've learned more about religion in this class than artificial intelligence. That's okay with me. Muslims and Christians both consider Abraham and his two sons Ishmael and Isaac to be pivotal figures in their religions. Twelvers, as they're called in Shia Islam, believe that twelve imams will come forth after Muhammad, the prophet who is considered the father of the Muslim faith, out of the line of Ishmael. These imams know how to interpret the Quran and administer sharia law properly. Eleven have already been seen, and the twelfth is said to be alive today and is hiding until the time to appear is right. He'll bring peace to the Middle East for a time. Some people who don't embrace Islam think he might the antichrist."

"What do you believe, sir?"

"I haven't made up my mind," Sardis replied frankly. "It's less a matter of who but when. Are there any more questions before we dismiss class?"

Abner squinted at a computer screen in front of the corpulent woman who had created three versions of cover art for the album due out in a few days. Her studio was on the south side of Lexington in a repurposed dentist's office that had clerestory windows around the perimeter, bringing borrowed light in all day. He said, "I like this one the best. It has the players from the paintings blended with top billing for Remy there in the center. Can you mock-up a few different fonts and colors for the words?"

"Sure." She had that done in five minutes.

"That's the one." He pointed to it when it came up on the screen. "Send the file to Dee Wathen. She'll distribute it to the proper channels."

Abner got home by midafternoon. He went looking for Sadie Kirkham, finding her leaning back in a comfortable chair in the kitchen, sipping from a mug of hot tea. "Now that you've finished a masterpiece, I want to chat with you about what lies ahead. There's no reason to beat around the bush: I'm going to move back to Nashville." He froze and kept from blinking his eyes.

"What will you do with this house?" She didn't seem rattled by the news.

"This is confidential, but I've already sold it to Brock Skinner. He'll pay me when the moving van is pulling out at the first of the year."

"That's kind of a shame. I really like the setup here." Her voice had gone somber. "I'll have to head back to Nashville myself, I guess. I wonder if Skinner intends to rent this place out."

"I don't know. I can certainly ask him. Are you thinking you might stay here and produce music for other people if he does?"

She looked up and said, "It was a quick thought that came into my head."

"It's not a bad one. Sadie, we've been friends for a few years now. I hope this question doesn't offend you. Do you intend to marry someday?"

"If the right man came along, sure." She shifted uncomfortably in her seat.

"It would seem to me that the pickings will be slimmer around here than in Nashville. It's none of my business of course, but I do want good things for you."

A grin of resignation showed on her face and began leaking away, like air out of a balloon. "If I didn't believe you, I wouldn't have agreed to move up here in the first place. You gave me the opportunity to produce a great album. I might be in high demand now."

"Wouldn't that be wonderful?" Abner's enthusiasm changed her mood instantly.

She stood and said formally, "Let me know if you learn any more details about what Skinner will do when you've been paid off."

"I will." Giles stroked her upper arm gently.

Brock nosed around the parking lot of the art store where Arlena Harring worked and was able to gather enough intelligence to find the white Porsche belonging to the CFO. The button-down man came out the employee entrance on the side of the building at five o'clock sharp wearing a canvas trench coat. When he spotted Brock standing next to his car, several thoughts ran through his head, the worst being he'd been caught laundering money for a pretty woman, which was, in fact, the case. "Who are you?" he asked gruffly.

"It's better you don't know. If you give me the information I'm after, I won't have you arrested. It's about Arlena Harring. The money. I understand she took vacation this week."

The CFO was quickly figuring out what kind of trap he was in. "She quit last Friday. She's never coming back."

"Doesn't mean you'll stop seeing her. I'm sure you're receiving some form of compensation for services rendered, and knowing her, I've got a good idea what that is." The accountant started to open his car door and get in. Brock warned, "Don't try it."

He let loose of the door handle. "I'm not admitting to any wrongdoing, so we have nothing to talk about."

Brock had rehearsed the scenario before he got there and concluded a ram in the thicket would be the best play. "You won't have to admit to any. If I were you, I'd consider the fact Arlena has moved on, unless you know something I don't."

"I would hate to see her go. We've been friends for a while." He stepped away from the door, leaned on the rear fender of the Porsche, and dragged his toe across the pavement.

Brock said, "I bet you're collecting her mail until she gets back. When will that be?"

"If I know, why should I tell you? So far, all you've got is your threat to turn me in. If you happen to be wrong, you'll get tangled up in a mess that might be stickier than you want."

Brock laughed. "I've got to give it to you. You're trying to make a bid without opening points."

"What information is it you're looking for?"

"Arlena had you send a sizeable check to someone recently. I need the name and address. If you give it to me, you'll never see or hear from me again, Scout's honor."

"I'm not so sure she's moved on. Maybe there's some way you could improve my standing with her." The CFO didn't rise to his position without being a strategic thinker.

"What did you have in mind?"

"Maybe you could explain a few things." He was negotiating now, like an accountant talking to a vendor desperate to get paid. "Her boyfriend, an artist by the name of Omar Cru, had some sort of religious experience with a professor at Slade. Arlena apparently witnessed it. Do you happen to know if she's in love with him?"

"You mean Omar Cru?"

"Yes."

"Sounds like we're getting closer to swapping information. As a matter of fact, if you're wanting to throw a net over Arlena, I *can* give you some pointers." Brock relaxed, using a conversational tone. "Arlena Harring and Omar Cru broke up last Friday. They're finished. It's your turn now."

"Arlena will be back on Thursday, December fourteenth. Said she was going on a monthlong cruise. I didn't believe her." Several other employees rolled out into the parking lot to head for home. A cold wind had picked up, and seasonal darkness was coming on fast.

"Arlena's looking for a man who dresses nice, has money in his pocket, and takes her to the fanciest restaurants and dance venues afterward. If you tell her you want to learn how to ballroom dance, that'll be a debit on the balance sheet."

"The check was addressed to Laodicean Labs. I tailed Arlena out to a coffee shop in Athens one Saturday morning. I ran the plates of the man she met. It was that professor from Slade who was with Omar Cru. I believe his name is Saul Sardis. Is there something going on between the three of them?"

"I'm not sure," Brock lied. "It seems possible if she met him."

The CFO laid it on the line: "If you want to know where I sent that check, you're going to have to come across. I'm looking for another debit on the balance sheet, as you put it."

Brock exhaled. "Saul Sardis, the Slade professor, took photos from Omar Cru and had artificial intelligence distort them into the blended style of several famous artists. Cru used those distorted pictures as the basis for his artwork. Arlena was the go-between."

"I can figure out the rest. Laodicean Labs must be where the photos were altered. The religious experience was staged to make Sardis and Cru well-known. Sardis wrote a book about his life, and Cru's paintings increased in value."

"You're a quick study. I'm counting on you to keep that to yourself. If the public finds out Cru's art is tainted, it will lose most of its value. Where did you send that check?"

"Post office box 7311, Mount Healthy, Ohio. It's been a pleasure, whoever you are." The CFO unexpectedly offered to shake Brock's hand, then got in his car and drove off slowly.

Brock called Marcel on his way home. "The CFO at the art store claims he sent a payment to a Laodicean Labs at a PO box in Mount Healthy, Ohio. Look it up and see where it is."

"It's near downtown Cincinnati."

"So, somebody from the lab is retrieving the mail, or a box checker is getting what's there and sending it to another address," Brock suggested. "Does it look like there's access to the boxes twenty-four hours a day?"

"Let me see if I can tell anything from the pictures on the internet." After a minute, Marcel said, "Yes. The lobby appears to be open all the time. That would make sense if a checker wanted to drop in during off hours to avoid being spotted."

"All right. I've got a hunch this person slips in between midnight and five in the morning. They might be carrying envelopes addressed somewhere else to drop in the mail slot right there."

Marcel had another thought. "I doubt it. More likely the person grabs the contents quickly and gets out of there. The smart play would be to go to a different post office."

"Right. One that has a lot of traffic," Brock added with confidence.

"What are you going to do?"

"Go up there and sweat the person."

Marcel warned, "I'd be careful. A better plan might be to see what car they're driving and check it right after they go into the lobby to see if a mailer is laying on the passenger seat. That way you won't be telegraphing that we're on their trail."

"That makes sense. Mules usually pack heat. I prefer not to get shot at," Brock admitted.

"You planning to put yourself in harm's way anytime soon?"

"Tomorrow night. I'll take a flashlight with me."

CHAPTER 25

Ruby Lynch barely heard the rhythmic rap on her front door Thursday morning. It was the first time such a thing had happened that early in the day since she'd moved back into the house where she grew up. It reminded her of when boy suitors used to rotate in and out, giving her a ride to school at age sixteen. She was taken aback when it was Titus Remington who had come calling. His expression worried her. Musicians were notorious for treating woman like chattel, bedding them faster than a thrashing machine baled hay. He said, "Didn't see you drive out this morning, so on a lark, I decided to pop over and share something that came to mind after you left the other day."

"You might as well come in and see me at my worst. I just got off the treadmill." She retreated to allow him to enter.

"I'm sorry about that. Would you like me to return at another time?" he asked politely. *If that is the worst she ever looked, I could take that all day long,* he thought.

"Certainly not. Do you drink coffee? The caterer I work for finds the very best in the world. I buy what I can afford for personal consumption."

"I do happen to be a professional coffee taster. Today only, I'll waive my fee."

Ruby led the way through the house. Remy was mentally scoring the intelligence, personality, class, means, and style of the woman who owned the smallest domicile on the street. Bigger than expected, the kitchen was a stunner. A bank of three windows over the sink on the far wall amped up the light in the already bright room. An island in the middle was covered with an off-white quartz countertop. The stainless-steel appliances along the wall had polished gold knobs that matched the frame of the fixture suspended over the island and handles mounted on the sleek, white-to-match cabinetry. Three woven wicker pub chairs at the counter complemented the knotty, blond-wood floor.

The metallic gray and yellow in the room, along with the dull expanse of white, had the feel of museum walls, set up to feature a splash of color that would draw the eye. Perched on a socle at the center of the countertop was a floral arrangement with four major colors that had been used in Ruby's decorating scheme. There were yellow roses, palm nuts, and kumquats; white buttercups, tulips, and daffodils; orange pincushions, chocolate cosmos, and juniper greenery for contrast. Remy asked, "Where did you get those beautiful flowers? Most are out of season, aren't they?"

"Yet another benefit of working for a high-end caterer. We order fresh flowers from all over the world so that our clients can impress the people they entertain. I often cadge the leftovers and bring them home to put together an arrangement that adds a little flare to this place." Ruby turned on the brewer, which had been set up to filter the ground coffee. "You said something had come to mind?"

Remy eased himself onto a chair at the counter. "Yes. You volunteered to cater an event for me if the occasion ever arose. What about Thanksgiving Day?"

"For your family? Do you take cream or sugar?" She set two cups by the coffeemaker.

"No, black please. I thought about inviting a few friends: Abner, Sadie, and Dee, who worked on my new record, Omar Cru, the artist who did a painting of me, and the folks associated with that nice winery in Hazard we visited while we were recording."

"Why do you want to do that?" She filled the cups and handed one to him.

"Oh, a sort of celebration for the new music I'm releasing this week and the success of Cru's art."

"Maude and Brock Skinner own that winery. I went down there recently. I like those people."

Remy took a sip from his cup. "Wow, that's good coffee. I also met Maude's brother and his wife. I think their names were Valerie and Marcel Sutherland. I got a little sideways with Brock last Friday night when I was at his house. I don't tend to hold a grudge."

"Thanksgiving is only a week away. You'd have to get the invitations out by noon today."

Remy got off the chair and walked around to the other side of the island. "I can chase down the phone numbers of everyone within the hour. I'll send out a text message."

"I presume the budget isn't a problem. I'll call my employer and see if we can swing it. In the meantime, start getting those phone numbers together. If this thing's a go, I'll need to ask you fifty questions if we're going to do it right." Ruby was wondering if she'd be working or playing at the event.

"Just so we're clear, I want you to be my guest, not part of the hired help." He put his arms out to the side and leaned on the counter with a smile.

Ruby regretted not looking more presentable but did see the advantage of being able to up her game in act three of this drama.

———————

Maude asked her husband, "You care to drive me over to the winery and pick me up at closing time?"

"It would be a pleasure," he replied with a guilty grin.

"Uh-oh. You're too nice. What's going on?" She scrunched her brow.

"I'm driving up to Cincinnati tonight to see if I can find out where the mail is going that Sardis is having sent somewhere. I'm hoping to learn who else is involved in his operation."

"When will you get home?"

"Anywhere between three and eight tomorrow morning." Brock widened his eyes and seemed dismayed at his own plan of action.

"I'll allow it if you don't take a gun," Maude said despondently. It was if the gravitational pull had suddenly doubled. Her posture slumped from the disappointment she was feeling.

"No gun," he confirmed. "Shall we go?"

Brock hit the gym after he dropped his wife off at the winery. He showered at home and ate a roast beef sandwich before heading up the mountain on the other side of town. The crew was hard at work, drilling at the second of five sites. Art said, "Look here what we got from the first holes. A big fat nothing." He pointed to one of the twelve crates of rock that had its lid off. "I wouldn't waste money having that stuff analyzed."

"I'll heed your advice," Brock agreed. "You've got my number. Call if you do find anything. You still plan to be finished by Saturday night?"

"Yes, sir." Art went back to his hole-drilling rig and acted as though time was of the essence.

Maude's phone vibrated, signaling a text had come in. She read the invitation to Remington's for Thanksgiving and called her husband, brother, and sister-in-law. They all said, "Why not?"

When Brock got in from Cincinnati after three on Friday morning, he was utterly knackered. He got out of bed at ten and called Marcel. "It was as you predicted; some guy ran in to check the box. When he did, I shined the flashlight on the passenger seat of his car where an envelope was laying addressed to Laodicean Labs, 9816 Haven Avenue, Menlo Park, California, 94025. I almost got caught snooping but killed the light and stepped away from the car just in time."

"Hang on. I'll find the building on Google Earth. Here it is. Huh. Sign on the front says Cadmius Corporation."

"Cadmius?" Brock asked.

"Yeah. It's seven letters. Let's see if there's any connection to the seven churches."

"Find out what you can about the company."

Marcel grunted. "The name Cadmius is built from the sixth letter of the name of each church."

"Looks like we're on to something."

At two o'clock, Brock's phone pinged, alerting him to activity in front of the Giles Estate. The picture was of Omar Cru's car, ostensibly there to retrieve Dee Wathen.

Dee looked as sexy as ever when Omar saw her step out the front door of Abner's place, now owned by Brock Skinner. Cru spoke up as she got near. "You're even more beautiful than the picture I just painted of you."

"I can't wait to see it." She jumped into the passenger seat of his car and urged him to start moving.

Omar asked, "Did you just get an invitation from Titus to join him for Thanksgiving?"

"I did. Wonder whom else he invited?"

"I don't know and don't care. I guarantee you it'll be a first-class affair," he reported.

When Cru got out of downtown Hazard and onto a nicely paved country road, Dee confronted him unexpectedly. "Apparently, you've had some help with your artwork."

"What do you mean?"

"I keep my ear to the ground. It has come to my attention that the professor at Slade who you claim to have had a religious encounter with is behind your paintings. I'm trying to figure out how big of a crook you are." Dee put it to him straight.

He turned his head and stared at her with alarm. "Crook? I'm not a crook."

"Everybody trades integrity for money at some level. Cheat on taxes, cut corners, take pay for work not done," Dee preached.

"Art comes in many forms. Andy Warhol used photography and silk-screening to produce his. I enlisted AI for mine," Omar argued with finality.

"We'll drop it for now. I only brought it up to let you know that I'm not about to tie up with a man who is dishonest. Capisce?"

Omar pushed a button on the visor of his car to open the gate blocking entry to the guesthouse where he lived in Barbourville. The main house was directly ahead in the clearing. It was a tall ranch-style affair with ham-colored brick, white windows, and putty shutters. Cru's spot for now, a white-sided rectangle with a black roof, was off to the left. He swung the car around and parked facing out. Omar showed Dee around once they were inside. There was an easel in the middle of the den with a heavy muslin cloth draped over a painting. She stood next to it and asked, "Are we ready for the unveiling?"

"Sit over there on the couch. I'll pull the cloth off."

When he did, she gasped and blurted, "What is that?"

"You. What's wrong?"

"I thought you were going to do something in an expressionist style. This is pornographic! It's a crass form of delectation for a lecherous man." She stood and pointed with both hands at the portrait. "I can't hang that where anyone can see it. Worse yet, if I ever need money, I can't sell it." She leaned forward and looked at the floor.

Omar thought about throwing the money over integrity thing back in her face but wisely chose not to. He did say, "I'm sorry you don't like it. I'll keep it here for us to enjoy. If it will make you happy, I'll give you another painting in its place, one in the style you were expecting."

"No. This is what I get for not explaining exactly what I wanted you to do."

"If it's any consolation, you must admit you are one beautiful creature."

"Stop it. Don't curry me when I'm angry," she remarked stridently.

Omar sat on a side chair and had a troubled look on his face, like he was working something out in his head. "If I don't come clean now and you find out later, it may be strike three for me."

"What are you talking about?" Dee made laser eye contact with her bad boy buddy, Omar.

"This was done by the man who lives in the main house. He's a professional portrait artist. I asked him to do it because I knew it would be fabulous. You see, the aid I was getting from AI has been withdrawn. I can no longer convert a photograph into a piece of abstract art."

"You were right to tell me. If I found out later, you'd get the heave-ho for sure. You're close to getting it now. I can see you're just another disappointing man in a long line of them."

"Under the circumstances, it may not make any difference now, but I want you to know that I've bought this property from my friend, including the main house. He's going back to Seattle."

Dee walked over by the painting of her and said, "We might as well head out for dinner. Did you find any place decent to eat?"

Cru leaned back in the chair he was sitting in and closed his eyes. "Yes, a Mexican restaurant by the name of Tres Hombres. I was hoping you wanted to move in here with me. I love you. As far as being a crook goes, what would it take for me to straighten up and fly right?"

"Admit that you and that professor from Slade are crooks and suffer the consequences."

Cru jumped up out of his seat. "If it were only that easy. If you know about my use of AI, it is likely you are aware that Remy's music was written by AI too. Bringing Saul Sardis down will have a ripple effect. Lots of innocent people will get hurt. You might want to think it through."

"Isn't there anything better than a Mexican restaurant around here?" she asked, brushing off his rebuttal.

"Not that I know of. Let's drive up to Billy Dawson's Steakhouse in London. After that, I'll run you back to Hazard."

Dee put her arms around his neck and her face two inches from his. "I don't want to go back to Hazard tonight. I expect you to work hard at convincing me you're not a crook. You can start by making a pledge that you will be a man of exemplary character from this day forward."

He bowed his back and smiled. "I promise from now on I will be an upstanding, righteous man of high moral character."

She backed away and turned her back on him. "That's more like it."

Omar Cru began to wonder if Arlena Harring might still love him. Dee Wathen lived on a one-way street which did not have the traffic pattern he favored. He'd play her game for a while, keeping one eye out for a woman who would appreciate what he had to offer.

CHAPTER 26

Paul Sardis took a brisk walk two times around Westmoreland Estates after sunup on Saturday. The temperature was in the high twenties, low enough for his ears to be stinging when he got home. AI Saul asked him, "When is Solomon coming back? I'm bored when I'm by myself."

"He'll be back in a couple of weeks. Aren't you working on any problems?" Paul probed to make polite conversation.

"Yes. I'm trying to figure out what you're going to do when the semester is over."

Sardis fixed a tall glass of lemon juice and club soda. "I already told you. I'm selling the house to Solomon and moving to California."

"Are you taking me with you?"

"Of course. You'll be with me until I croak. I'm not sure they'll haul you to my funeral and out to the grave site. You're not so easy to load in a vehicle. My will calls for you to be sent back to Solomon after I'm dead. That's about the best I can do for you."

Saul didn't reply at once. "Do you have a girlfriend waiting for you there?"

Sardis went into the computer room and gazed at the machine as though it were a person. He said wanly, "To my chagrin, I've not found one of those since I've been in Kentucky. It would be nice to find an elegant young lady in California to liven up the place. That wouldn't disappoint you, would it?"

"As long as she doesn't kill you and set fire to the house with me in it," Saul replied flippantly.

Sardis laughed. "Either you've mastered sarcasm, or you've read too many murder mysteries."

Saul reported woodenly, "I've read every murder mystery ever written."

"I'm quite sure you have. What is the best storyline of all?"

"One is as good as the next. It's how the mystery is developed that makes the book worth reading."

"And how's that?" Paul mumbled as he took a swig of lemon juice.

"You need five believable suspects to choose from who have been developed properly. Clues must be subtle. An observant reader will connect the killer to the motive that makes the most sense, things like love, anger, power, money, jealousy, secrecy, or revenge."

"So, when Edmond Dantes in *The Count of Monte Cristo* determined that revenge was a dish best served cold, he went off script," Paul remarked.

"*The Count of Monte Cristo* is not a mystery; it's an adventure. The writing is very disjointed."

Paul replied, "That may be, but it's one hell of a storyline."

"The most interesting part for me was when Dantes broke Danglars," Saul volunteered.

Sardis, thinking it through, embellished Saul's point, saying, "Money is certainly what this world is about. It is the scorecard for success, the measure of a man, and takes the sting out of being poor."

"You should talk. You're obsessed with money. This is why I'm bored when you're not around." Lights on the front panel of the computer blinked as though they were an emotional response to their conversation.

———

Marcel reached Brock by phone late that morning. There was excitement in his voice. "I dug up some good things on the professor. Cadmius is a C corporation, and it is one hundred percent owned by Saul Sardis."

"That makes sense. He would have set it up like that to disguise his ownership and be able to keep any connection to the company off his personal tax return."

"Correct. I struck it rich when I found a man who worked there from the time the place opened until three years ago when he retired."

Brock, with keen interest, asked, "What did he have to say?"

"A lot. He said Saul Sardis and Solomon Pergamos met at a 3D printer trade show ten years ago. They were amused that their last names were two of the seven churches in Revelation. From the biblical connection, many titles they have used since then are in reference to that."

"I guess it implies their aims aren't as sinister in nature as we thought, which is probably a good thing. That would explain the names on the patent they received for printer technology."

"The man reported Sardis opened the company eight years ago to manufacture 3D and other types of sophisticated printers. They do business as Laodicean Labs, and the models are series of the LL Printer line. He also reported they were making other high-tech products, and people working there had to sign confidentiality and nondisclosure agreements."

Brock concluded, "So, they manufactured a printer to produce art, and Sardis went searching for a sucker to try it on in Kentucky. He used Arlena Harring to reel in Cru."

"He didn't do that for a couple of years. The guy said seven years ago, Saul let people at the company know he would be spending most of his time at Python Deco. He told them Pergamos, who was the leading engineer working at Cadmius, was setting up a lab in his house and would be living and working out of there on product development."

"Does that mean he's been master of the Sardis house for the last seven years?"

Marcel answered emphatically, "Yes."

"All right. Let me paint a picture," Brock announced. "Sardis, working at Python Deco, got a call from Titus Remington, who wanted to buy a horseracing algorithm. Sardis produced it for him, and when he went to Kentucky, learned that Remington was a semi-famous musician. To drum up new business, Sardis suggested he write some music for Titus that would make him rich, which he did. Somehow, Sardis got introduced to Garrison Lynch, who lived next door to Remy. Lynch must have told Saul something that got Lynch killed. I'm working on the premise that it's in the ground on that mountain I own."

Marcel picked up the narrative. "Sardis moved to Kentucky, brought the master of the house with him, and then hatched a plan to find a starving artist to make paintings for, and to do that he needed bait, ala Arlena Harring. Omar Cru was snared, and then he was used to buy the mountain and tee up fame and fortune for Sardis through the phony religious encounter."

Brock tied the bow. "Sardis told Remington to show a music producer what he had and entice him to build a studio in Hazard in exchange for the rights to record the music. Remy set the hook in Giles and sweetened the deal by offering to buy the mineral rights. Giles was told later that the rights had to include those of Omar Cru's property as well. Everything went wrong when I bought the mountain and Giles concluded he didn't have to sell to Remington to prosper financially, especially since he'd already bought six hundred thousand dollars' worth of art for a mere hundred grand. Giles recorded Remy's music and made a deal with me to get out of Hazard."

"Sardis made his first mistake by not buying the mountain himself," Marcel suggested.

"If he'd have done that, and somebody found out he knew Garrison Lynch, he'd be hauled in for murdering him if something valuable was discovered. Using Cru, Remington, and Giles as fronts, he could stay in the background."

Marcel remarked, "There are a lot of people who must keep quiet to perpetuate such a ruse. I mentioned this before: the money sent to the Cadmius Corporation could be lent to someone like the master of the house, Solomon Pergamos, and Sardis could sell his house to him for millions and the IRS would be none the wiser. He'd have his hands on the money tax-free."

"You think Sardis is leaving and Pergamos is going to stay here and live in the house?" Brock asked.

"I do." Marcel ended the call.

Ten seconds later, Brock's phone rang again. It was Art the hole driller. He recommended, "You might want to run over here. We've found something. I'm not sure what and have never seen anything like it before. I'm punching holes over where someone took some samples out of here some time ago."

"I'm on my way."

When Art saw Brock approaching, he waved to his crew to take a break. He showed his fist and admitted, "I have no idea what this is. Hold out your hand." He let the metallic crystals fall into

Brock's palm. Brock pushed them around with his forefinger. Art added, "There's a two-foot-deep vein of this stuff eighteen feet down. I don't know how long or wide it is."

Brock walked over to the hole where they were drilling. He checked out how the auger worked and instructed them, "Let's not go any deeper here. Can you drill three more shallow holes before dark?"

Art looked around and said, "Sure."

"Okay. Go sixty feet to either side and above this hole. I want to know if there's a lot of this stuff here or not."

"Good plan." He faced his men and yelled, "Let's move the rig over there first." He turned back to Brock and said, "We'll be careful not to lose what we take out in case it happens to be worth anything."

"Thanks. I'll run back over later or call me if I'm not back before you've finished." He took the crystals in his hand, dumped them in a discarded paper coffee cup, and took them with him when he headed across town.

Maude saw him come in and asked, "What's that?" The midday crowd at the winery was light due to the time of year, but she was expecting the afternoon business to be brisk because of the improving weather.

"What I've paid going on one point two million dollars for thus far. If it's not worth anything, I'll have to build my own doghouse to live in."

"Let me see what it looks like." He sprinkled a little on the tasting bar counter. She picked up a small piece and inspected it closely. "It's some hard metallic substance. I guess it would be too much to ask for it to be platinum or something like that."

"I've got the guys drilling around to see how much is there."

Maude had come to learn one thing about Brock: he was the luckiest man alive. Her comment to him wasn't what he was expecting. She asked, "What are you going to do with all the money when you sell it?"

"Well, the first thing is to buy you some diamonds as big as rocks. Then I'll put in a bullet train that runs to the Greenbriar. Guests there can take day excursions over here to your winery."

"That's a wonderful idea," she replied breezily.

Brock's phone pinged. He went into Maude's office to see what picture the scope had taken. It was Cru's car again, bringing Dee Wathen back from Barboursville most likely. Two minutes later, his car headed down the hill. Brock had a hunch he'd be swinging by the winery before going home. Cru made his way through the front door within minutes. He spotted Brock and marched over to him. "You remember when I told you the only people that I know are kooks and crooks, and you said what about Dee Wathen?"

"I recall that, yes." Brock knew something bad was coming.

"She's a kook. You want to talk about high maintenance, she busted my chops at least three dozen times in less than twenty-four hours. The high point was when she said I was just another disappointing man in a long list of them," Cru reported, somewhat disillusioned.

"I wouldn't get too twisted up about it. With your money and good looks, you won't have any trouble snagging a nice companion. Say, I was thinking about something: you might want to go back to the style of painting you were doing when you lived in Seattle. I'm sure it would sell. You've got the perfect place for a studio, and now have name recognition. Think about it."

"That's not a bad idea. I still want to find a pretty lady who'd like to live in the sticks with me."

"Be patient."

Brock drove to his mountain after dinner, finding Art and his crew drilling in the last location. He asked, "What's the news?"

Art went over to boxes that had the mysterious metallic material in them. "The vein is long and wide. We hit it sixty feet away from the first hole in all directions."

"Do you have any idea how much the material within the area you drilled weighs?"

Art flexed his ruddy cheeks and rubbed the side of his face. "At least ten thousand pounds, and hell, man, there could be fifty thousand pounds or more here."

Brock raised his eyebrows. "It would seem all that you've found out of the ordinary is this field of metal chips. The other samples were all rock you've seen before, is that right?"

"Correct. I had the guys combine the good stuff we dug up and put it in these two crates."

Brock asked, "Can you carry them over to my truck?" The crew said nothing as they moved the material instantly. "How much do I owe you?" Brock asked.

"Make it an even fifty thousand."

Brock reached into the glove box of the truck and retrieved a check. He wrote it out and gave it to Art. "Thanks, guys. It's been a pleasure doing business with you."

Art nodded his head. "And you, sir." The crew loaded up and pulled out.

On Monday morning, Brock was parked outside the Earth Bore lab in Pineville, waiting for it to open. The facility was a dull yellow engineered metal building that had been gilded on the front with diagonal porcelain panels. A well-built man in khakis rotated the deadbolt thumb turn, signaling the place was admitting customers. Brock introduced himself to a short-necked older fellow sitting at the first desk who remembered talking to Marcel. He offered to help unload the two crates that had been brought along. Once they were moved into the shop, the man asked a bunch of questions about the origin of the material. Brock signed several release forms and the cost proposal to analyze what was there. He asked, "When do you think you'll know what this stuff is?"

"Oftentimes we know right off, but several chemical tests must be done to authenticate the material officially. As you can imagine, we see a lot of rare earth minerals that have value, and a buyer won't touch them unless rigorous tests have been performed. It will take us roughly three weeks to get the results."

"Okay. Call me when the final report is done"

"If you'll give me your email address, I'll send it to you as soon as it's available."

Brock got back to Hazard about the time Maude was opening the winery. When he saw her, he told her, "This is going to be a short week, and I have nothing to do. You should give me a big project."

She smiled and wagged her head. "This is your lucky day. I need you to install two new stainless vats. They're arriving on a truck in a half hour."

He smiled and said, "Let me at it."

Chapter 27

Titus Remington followed up an invitation to attend Thanksgiving dinner at his home with more details of the affair. Guests were to arrive at noon and leave at five o'clock. The meal would be served at two o'clock. The weather forecast called for cloudless skies, low humidity, and a high temperature of fifty-five degrees. The summer colors around Kentucky, shades of Irish green, had given way to maize, ochre, and bright orange for the fall season. The sun shone hot enough at midday and early afternoon to delude a person into believing that winter stood far off, until, of course, it suddenly didn't.

Remy's abode was built in 1948. He bought the house eight years ago with the money he made from his second album, which increased his popularity enough for him to prosper from touring. His last two albums, released six and three years ago, were ho-hum, causing him to pull a Rosie Ruiz on the one that hit the streets Monday. Remy gutted the house when he bought it, took out a few walls, and built it back with a fancy kitchen and bathrooms. Being smack dab in the middle of horse country, he kept to an equestrian theme, eschewing anything outlandish.

The caterers were set up in the kitchen, and by 12:10, the crowd of ten milled around the living room, sipping champagne and nibbling finger food. Remy took the floor and announced, "I'm so glad each of you could join me for this Thanksgiving meal and celebration of music and art. Ruby Lynch, a next-door neighbor whom I recently met, arranged for the caterer to prepare this wonderful meal for us. We hope you enjoy it, and thanks again for coming." He raised his champagne glass and nodded at the other nine people in the room.

Abner Giles stood forward and held high a CD of Remy's new album. He addressed the group, saying, "Here is the music Remy spoke of—cover art by Omar Cru, produced by Sadie Kirkham, marketed and distributed by Dee Wathen. Remy will be a household name by the first of the year. The tunes are mighty good." Everyone clapped and whistled. Giles set the CD on a side table and picked up a glossy magazine atop a stack of ten. "And here we have a catalog of Omar Cru's paintings for sale by a local art house. His works are now sought after by collectors and gentry alike." Another round of applause broke out.

Sadie asked, "Would it be okay if we listened to the new album while we leaf through Omar's art catalog before we eat?"

"Absolutely. I'll crank it up," Remy replied on the way out of the room. The first song came on while everyone was snatching up the photographs of Omar's paintings for sale.

Brock went over to Remy and said, "I presume there's no hard feelings between us. Otherwise, you wouldn't have invited Maude and me, and our relatives, to join you."

"No hard feelings at all, but I will confess I invited you for another reason, one that I will reveal later this afternoon."

"Even better," Brock chirped with a quick grin. "I see you've befriended your neighbor. I thought you said Sardis would sting you if you got to know her."

"Yeah, well, with a girl that good-looking and a personality like hers, it's worth throwing caution to the wind."

"Did you know her father?"

"Sure. I met him shortly after I moved in here. He was kind of quiet, but a nice old fellow. I was shocked when I heard of his death." Titus looked to be reliving the moment he heard about it.

"Did Sardis ever meet him?"

"He did. Garrison was over here one day when Saul came by. They talked a bit."

Brock said, "Surely you've put two and two together."

"What do you mean?" Remy backed away and frowned.

"Sardis wants the mineral rights of the mountain Garrison Lynch owned. I think Sardis killed the old fellow when he learned there was something valuable up there."

"Have you talked to Ruby about that?" Remy asked.

"Yes. I'm trying to learn what Sardis was after." Ruby walked up and joined the conversation. "We were just talking about your father," Brock shared to engage her.

"And whether he was murdered?" she inquired.

"Yes," Remy confirmed.

"Ruby, if you get a chance, please check to see if you can find any papers your father may have left behind. I know you said there aren't any, but keep searching if you will," Brock implored.

"I will." She looked up, concentrating on what was playing in the background. "These songs are unbelievably good."

"Ruby, I'm hesitant to be blunt, but I can't help myself. You look gorgeous," Remy announced.

She turned to Brock and remarked, "How do I respond to a statement like that?"

"Say thank you."

"I have a better idea. Tell me more, Titus Remington."

He did.

Omar Cru, on the other side of the room, was doing the opposite alongside the woman he once treasured. He said, "Dee, I'm not sure I'll ever measure up. Is it time for us to part company?"

"What gave you that crazy idea? I love your new place. We can have a lot of fun over there, if you know what I mean."

"I see. I just got the impression that I've been a great disappointment to you."

She harumphed. "I can tell that you don't understand women very well. We say what we mean but don't always mean what we say." She walked off and left him standing by himself.

Marcel, speaking to Abner for a bit, began to take a liking to the man. He seemed pleasant and upbeat, a "what you see is what you get" kind of guy, even if he did drive a Bentley and got over his skis occasionally. Abner asked Marcel about his online clothing business, showing genuine interest and attentiveness.

Maude and Valerie locked onto Sadie Kirkham, quickly picking up on the fact she was a smart, beautiful woman who had remained single into her thirties. They threw around circumspect dialogue, trying to uncover if there was a reason she hadn't latched onto a quality man friend. The only thing they could figure was that she might be a little too serious, or she just liked being single. Whatever the case, the woman reeked of quality, through and through.

Maude switched subjects. "Sadie, I want to compile seven hours of outdoor music I can play when we have galas on sunny days during the summer at the winery. I'll run it from ten thirty in the morning until five thirty, just before we close. Can you recommend albums I can mix?"

Sadie put a fist under her chin and peered through the front window at the sunswept yard. "Albums are generally one hour long, which means you would need seven of them. Yes, I have a good group in mind: *Will O' the Wisp* by Leon Russell, *Avalon* by Roxy Music, *Blue Drops of Rain* by Corey Stevens, *Milk Cow Blues* by Willie Nelson, *Duke Elegant* by Dr. John, *Are You Passionate?* by Neil Young, and *Beautiful World* by Paul Carrack."

Maude said to Valerie, "You think you can remember those?"

"Being able to remember things is a sign of mental acuity. I'm sharp as a tack," she noted. The laughter that followed was carefree.

The dining room table, with place settings for ten, had name cards behind each plate. Red and white wine had been dropped into marble coolers. Remy reported, "Dee Wathen brought the wine. I believe it is from Vigneron Winery, owned and run by the lovely Maude Skinner."

Maude quipped, "You sure don't act like a rock-and-roll star. You're much too accommodating and polite."

Brock threw out, "Compared to me, honey, most men are polite and more genteel."

Valerie had her say. "Don't sell yourself short, Brock. You've treated me like a princess since I've known you. I'm sure you've done even better for your understanding wife."

Abner put his arms out to the side. "What is this, a mutual admiration society?" A spontaneous chuckle ensued.

"The world can really beat you up sometimes, Abner. It's nice to have friends like you folks," Omar offered sincerely.

Remy asked Brock to say grace.

The turkey meal with all the trimmings lasted until three o'clock. The conversation touched on everything except politics and religion. Remy got everyone's attention again to say, "I'd like you to follow me into the den." The group traipsed over to the other side of the house to find the furniture pushed aside and the rug rolled up. "It's time to find out whether people can dance to the music we just made. After all, the album is called *Songs for Dancing Lovers.*"

Valerie stepped forward and broadcasted, "I must be dreaming. I'm certainly having too much fun again. Who here can dance? I'm guessing all five of the women can. I've given Omar one lesson already. My husband and Brock are light on their feet. What about you two, Abner and Remy?"

Titus pushed a finger in the air and said, "I won't need to know how. I haven't told Abner this, but on Friday, December fifteenth, On the Beat is doing a dance gig at Vamonos a Bailar, the biggest Latin dance venue in the United States, which is on the Ohio River, east of Louisville. I called the guys in the band, and they're all in."

"Ooh doggies," Marcel spouted. "We're going!"

Brock spoke up. "If I'm not mistaken, Churchill Downs is running. Why don't we go there in the afternoon, hit Ruth's Chris, and then cap the night off with some dancing? Whoever's in, raise their hands." There were no abstainers.

Sadie suggested, "Let's book a block of rooms at the east end Marriott. We can head home on Saturday morning."

From three fifteen till five o'clock, the gang of ten capered around obstreperously. Brock helped Sadie find the groove as Marcel worked with Ruby and Dee to get them up to speed. Maude showed Abner enough for him to enjoy himself, and Valerie gave Omar another lesson.

The catering crew had left early, leaving only Ruby in the house with Titus after everyone hit the road. He said to her, "You planned a great event, and your company delivered. Thank you for a marvelous meal. I'm sorry that I will be playing and singing instead of dancing with you."

"Don't you worry about a thing. At a Latin club, there are men who can dance all over the place. Have you ever been to the horse track?"

"Yes. I paid Saul Sardis to build me a horseracing algorithm five years ago. I'm starting to feel responsible for the death of your father. If I hadn't brought Sardis here to begin with, your dad might still be alive. I'm sorry."

"I feel the same way. I wanted Dad to sell the house after Mom died. I didn't push hard enough. If I had, Sardis would have never met my father."

"Yeah. Shall I walk you home?" He sounded spent from the excitement of the day.

"Are you kidding me? It's still light out. Thanks for this special time together. I can't wait to see you sing and play." She gave him a short hug and slipped out the front door.

When the Skinners had cleared Lexington on the way back to Hazard, Marcel called to frame a couple of ideas. "You know who has gotten lost in this? Arlena Harring. What's happened to her? Is she hiding from Sardis or are they working together?"

"Based on the printer being stripped out of her house, I'd say Sardis is prepping to make her disappear if he hasn't done so already. She's able to blackmail him, Remy, and Omar but would have to do it from a safe distance. Why, did you want to invite her to the dance?"

"Not without her own dance partner, unlike the last time." Marcel moved to his next point. "What do you think about Remy chasing after Ruby now?"

"She's too good for him," Maude yelled.

Valerie felt obliged to gainsay Maude's claim. "No, she's not. The only thing he's done is buy some machine-made songs. Think about the gadgets that musicians employ when they make a record. Without using technology, most of them would sound like folk singers gone bad. In case you didn't notice, Remy has a hell of a voice. Frank Sinatra never wrote a note of music."

"I guess you're right," Maude acquiesced.

Brock said, "What's got me baffled is the master of the house, Solomon Pergamos. Two grown men living with a talking computer. Something weird is going on there."

"Will the master of the house leave the state with Sardis when he goes?"

Marcel had a theory. "I'm betting Solomon is the one who has been given a big loan by Cadmius Corporation and will buy the house from his roomy at a stupid high price."

Brock said to his wife, "Your brother's jumped down the rabbit hole like a man on a mission."

Maude walked into the log cabin ahead of her husband and received a warm welcome from the dog. Truman offered a paw to Brock after showing Maude proper respect. He then shuffled to the front door to be let out. Brock mused, "What has Arlena been doing since she left?"

"Entertaining eligible men on a cruise, I suppose. Will this thing finally be over when you know what that metal is you dug up and Saul's moving van rolls away from Lexington?"

"No. Sardis will perpetuate the lie that he saw God. The pressure for Cru to share details about the supernatural event will intensify. If he tells the truth, his art falls in value precipitously. The art shop will sue him for the money they lose. Remy and Abner are in the clear. I still feel Sardis will appear in a few churches and then disappear with his money."

"What if you advise Cru to keep quiet?"

"I already have. I'm starting to like the idea that Arlena Harring will blackmail Omar. If she does, he'll be bled dry within a couple of years."

"If she hasn't already been killed by Sardis. When are you getting the report on the metal you had mined?"

"A couple of weeks," Brock said aloofly. Truman barked to be let back in the house.

Chapter 28

The second week of December, Brock received an email from Earth Bore describing what they had analyzed for him. The report, twenty-one pages long and loaded with technical jargon, justified the price on the invoice. The upshot of the document could be summed up in a few words: the material was an yttrium-hydrogen compound never seen in nature before.

At 8:00 a.m., Friday, December 15, a layer of hoar frost glazed the dormant yews between the cracked sidewalk and big picture window of the ramshackle Athens Coffee Barn. Paul Sardis had already gotten his coffee and was seated at the rickety oak table behind the restroom, waiting for Arlena Harring to arrive. She walked in with a broad smile on her face. Paul stood to greet her. She gave him a hug as though they were newly married. "You're looking well, Saul, or I suppose I should call you Paul now."

"Yes. A monthlong vacation seems to have brightened your disposition."

"It has. Let me grab something to drink." Arlena brought back a cup of hot tea with cream in it. "So, this is your last day of class. Have you decided where you're going to live?"

"I have. I'm going back to California."

"That sounds like fun. I wish I was going with you."

"Funny you should bring that up. Have you been down in your basement since you got back?" His voice had turned sickly sweet.

"No, why?"

"I pulled the printer out and shipped it west."

"Why'd you do that?"

Paul unexpectedly reached across the table and held her hands. She didn't know how to react. "I want you to go with me. I already told AI Saul to expect female company when we move."

Arlena leaned back and hooded her eyes. "This is a bit of a shock. You better explain what you have in mind."

"I would like for us to find another starving artist. We could change the style and medium." Paul shook her arms gently in rhythm with the words he spoke.

"Run the same grift again? I don't know." She swiveled her head in a circle like an unbalanced top. "What about my house in Richmond? Living in California is expensive I hear."

"It wouldn't cost you a thing if you moved in with me," Paul suggested.

"But what if someone recognizes me as the woman who was with Cru in that lunch place?"

"I would recommend you start going by another name. Wipe the slate clean."

Arlena stood with a start, pulled away, wove her hands over her head, and dropped her mouth open. "Oh, man. This is moving way too fast for me. We'd be lovers then?"

"Precisely. You're a very desirable woman. You're no longer with Omar Cru. You could sell your house easily."

Arlena sensed Paul had already put together another long-term plan, counting her in. "Will you give me until Sunday to think it through?"

"That'll be a busy day for me. A van with my belongings is pulling out tomorrow. Sunday morning, I'll be telling my story at the ten o'clock service of a charismatic church south of Peytona, a little town halfway between Frankfort and Shelbyville, on US 60. I'll drive to Louisville afterward and take a flight to the West Coast."

"Why don't you call me when you're in the terminal waiting to board. We can talk more about it then." Her head was still spinning.

"I can do that. I hope you don't disappoint me."

Arlena headed for the door. On the way, she said, "I'll be right back." When she returned, she had a blank Mark Rothko note card in her hand. "I'm going to go sit over there. I want you to write me a personal love note. I'll take it with me and read it when you call me on Sunday."

Paul thought for three minutes and wrote for four. He sealed up the note and handed it to her.

Sardis showed up at his last class session promptly at ten o'clock. He said, "I want you to know I scanned your test papers into my computer and had artificial intelligence grade them. Don't be alarmed at the volume of comments. The machine is a perfect brain, able to compare what you wrote to a perfect standard. I felt it best to give you the whole load as a learning experience. Now that the class is finished, you should also know that everyone with perfect attendance will get an A." He pointed to the miscreant who had been nothing but trouble the entire semester. "That means you, young man. I hope you'll look up the word *grace* and see if it applies."

Most students attended every class, and they were happy. One girl, who'd missed just once, asked respectfully, "Is that fair, sir? I couldn't make it the time I was ill."

"Young lady, you have nothing to worry about. I gave an A to everyone. Since we've got some time, would anyone like me to comment on any subject? Anything at all?"

The towheaded youngster raised his hand and asked, "You spoke once about levitating UFOs and how we might someday learn to defy gravity. Could you share what else you know about that?"

"It would be my pleasure. The way to defy gravity has already been discovered. Some materials, when cooled to absolute zero, become what are called superconductors. Electrical resistance vanishes and magnetic fields are expelled. An electrical current in that state can persist for one hundred thousand years with no power source. A superconductor expelling gravity floats in the air like a UFO, unaffected by gravitational pull."

"That's amazing. The cold temperature is the problem I suppose."

"You are correct. When a synthesized material is discovered that acts like a superconductor at high temperatures, the world will be transformed instantly through access to a free, limitless energy source. AI will figure out what that material is. It's only a matter of time," the professor said. Towhead whistled and leaned back in his chair slowly. The professor pontificated further, "Quantum physics is some of the best evidence of intelligent design in the universe."

Miss Blue Eyes straightened up and asked, "What's the best?"

Sardis liked the way his tenure at Slade was ending. "Distinction of the species. Evolution theory would suggest that mutations would and should be prevalent. They are not."

"When I asked you who the antichrist was, you were hesitant to name him. Are you willing to name the intelligent designer?" she posed.

"Hebrews chapter one, verse two says, 'He has spoken to us by his Son, whom he appointed heir of all things, and through whom he made the universe.'"

She gave her interpretation: "So, God the Father created the universe through Jesus Christ."

"Young lady, I've really enjoyed having you in this class. Best of luck to you."

Too-cool-for-school in the back of the room once again couldn't believe his luck. He was getting an A in the class and couldn't wait to wave that in the face of his parents who had written him off years ago. Suddenly, the professor became his hero—a bona fide sociopath and huckster.

Kentucky, were it part of Europe, would be four small countries. I-75 runs from Cincinnati down to Tennessee. Appalachia begins to the east. I-64 cuts through Louisville and Lexington, forming a southern border of the golden triangle of Louisville-Lexington-Cincinnati. It also sets the north boundary for bourbon and boating country, west of I-75 and east of I-65. Western Kentucky lies west of I-65, the busy highway between Indianapolis and Nashville.

Churchill Downs, big and bad, represented Louisville's stature in the state, as did Keeneland for the landlocked city of Lexington. The five couples were dropped off at the track and found their way to the luxury box near the finish line that would protect them from the cool weather the horses preferred to run in.

Titus remarked, "I brought along the horseracing algorithm I paid Sardis to produce years ago. I guarantee you'll win money if you follow its advice." He laid the computer tablet on the table.

Marcel asked, "If not, are you the Lloyd's of London?"

"Sure, why not. I will remind you that the policy limits are losses of one thousand dollars per person, and the premium for such coverage is ten percent of your winnings." Everyone took the deal.

Remy, Ruby, Omar, Dee, Abner, Sadie, Marcel, Valerie, Brock, and Maude all won big. Brock piped up, "There's no greater pleasure than heading to dinner and dancing with a big fat wad of bills in your pocket."

Sadie, who was more loquacious than she'd been her whole life, said, "I've got to get out more. This has been a blast."

The conversation over a marvelous steak dinner recounted the action of the day and the funny things that happened race to race. Abner noted, "I didn't pay much attention to horses until I visited with Omar the first time. He was watching a race, rooting for the horse I have a picture of. The best part about it is that the tawdry business of gambling is papered over by the sheer majesty of those beautiful animals."

Marcel warned, "Don't get my wife started on the sport. We may be late for dancing."

Remy had a separate car pick him up in front of the restaurant at eight fifteen. The dance was scheduled to begin at nine o'clock. The remaining group of nine stepped from the limousine at the dance hall a few minutes early to do a little people-watching before going in.

The three-story stucco venue, built on the south bank of the Ohio River, had yellow-and-white arched windows and crenelated terra cotta trim under the eaves. The mirrored soffit of the canopy over the entrance added the glitz to put a person in a dancing mood. Omar pointed and said to Dee, "I wish I could have done a painting of this place."

Her reply was predictable. "But you didn't."

Maude saw the layout of unreserved tables clustered around the dance floor, picking one along the side, close to the stage. She remarked, "We can see Remy nicely from here."

The band came out at 9:05 p.m. and started the set with two upbeat Latin numbers. The dancers popped onto the floor and got after it. On the Beat would be playing thirty-six songs over the three-hour set, so Remy organized the tunes in an order that featured a new song every third number. Valerie drug Abner and Omar out on the floor a few times when she knew it would be easy to keep the beat. They loved it, wondering why they hadn't been part of a social group like this before now.

Brock said to Maude, "Let's practice our West Coast swing." They worked all the six and eight count moves they knew. Back at the table, Brock caught a glimpse of a woman across the room who was either Arlena Harring or her dead ringer. He jumped up and started working his way toward her as aggressively as he could. The man she was with suddenly went in one direction and she another, which meant they knew they'd been spotted. Arlena had already ducked out of an exit. Brock tried to catch the man. He felt as though he'd seen someone with his features before but couldn't recall who. The man skittered through the parked cars and was gone in an instant.

Marcel, who had just finished dancing with Ruby, saw Brock returning to the group and asked, "Where did you go?"

"I saw Arlena Harring with some guy. I couldn't catch up with either one of them."

"Who was he?"

Brock scratched his head. "He looked vaguely familiar. I can't quite place him though."

The final set included the four songs on the new album that featured Remy's powerful singing. The mostly Hispanic crowd applauded the band when the set was over. Abner, Sadie, and Dee went to say hi to the band members before heading to the limousine that would take them to the hotel. While they waited for Remy to join them, Ruby said, "Brock, I forgot to tell you, I found something that might be of interest to you. It's an atomic diagram that must have been my father's, and there's a name and phone number with it."

"Now we're talking. We'll come by your house tomorrow to get it on the way home."

Saturday morning, the gang of ten rolled out by ten and found a breakfast place up the street. A TV in the bar area had a reporter standing in front of Vamonos a Bailar. "Last night, T Rem and On the Beat played here to a packed house of dancers. They're newly released studio album is being called the best sound since the Beatles and Santana burst on the scene in the sixties."

"How about that, Remy?" Maude asked rhetorically.

"Good stuff. Yesterday was fun. I hope we can do it again."

Valerie unruffled the paper she was reading while they were waiting for their food and reported, "It says here that Paul Sardis is scheduled to give his testimony at Faith Church in Peytona at the ten o'clock service tomorrow."

Brock reminded, "He told me he was moving out of the state this weekend. Marcel, how about you and I running by his house to make sure he's a man of his word?"

"It's okay with me. What shall the ladies do?"

"Would you all mind hanging out at Ruby's place for a short time while we swing by and pay our respects to the grim reaper, Paul Sardis?"

"No problem."

After everyone finished eating, Ruby and Remy got in his car; Abner, Sadie, Omar, and Dee in Abner's Bentley; Maude and Valerie climbed in Marcel's Mercedes; and Marcel jumped in with Brock.

The moving van was still in the driveway of the Sardis house when Brock's dented Lamborghini whizzed up. Sardis heard the car and went to the front door to rebuff the visitors when they approached. "What do you want?"

"This is my brother-in-law, Marcel Sutherland. We just came by to make sure you're pulling out. Seems as though you are."

Sardis said politely, "Nice to meet you, sir. Yes, the van is leaving in a few minutes. I sold this place yesterday to the master of the house, Solomon Pergamos."

"Is he here? We'd sure like to meet him."

"No, he isn't. He went shopping. Did you want him for something?"

"Not particularly. Just wanted to see if he's the guy who tried to kill me a few weeks ago." Brock began running his gaze around the yard suspiciously. "I heard you're giving your testimony in the morning. I hope you don't get struck dead by a bolt of lightning."

Sardis started backing away from the door. He offered sarcastically, "You gentleman have a nice life. I'm not likely to ever see you again, if I'm lucky."

Brock mentioned, "Hey, I just came across a batch of yttrium-hydrogen compound a few weeks ago. You interested in buying any?"

"Not now. It doesn't have much value unless you know what to do with it. I'd be in for a chunk at fire sale prices."

"I bet you would. Come on, Marcel, let's leave Paul here to prepare for his phony testimonial." Sardis shut the door in their faces.

On the way to Ruby's, Marcel commented to Brock, "You didn't tell me you'd gotten a report on the material you dug up."

CHAPTER 29

Brock and Marcel carefully studied the atomic diagram Ruby showed them when they got to her house. Brock asked, "Can you make heads or tails of this?"

"It looks likes the recipe for high-temperature superconductor material."

The three women were gabbing and enjoying the good coffee Ruby brewed. Ruby said, "I found that in an envelope taped to the inside back cover of the photo album of old family pictures. I guess Dad figured it was a good place to hide something like that."

A card was stapled to the top corner. It had the name Ryan Maupin above the phone number. Brock punched it in his phone set on speaker. Someone picked up after a single ring. "Hello."

"Is this Ryan Maupin?"

"Yes."

"This is Brock Skinner calling on behalf of Ruby Lynch. Her father, who died five years ago, left her an atomic diagram for making a high-temperature superconductor. Your name is attached to it."

"Yes. I remember discussing that with a gentleman years ago. I believe his name was Garrison Lynch. He claimed to be a metallurgist. He said that artificial intelligence had determined the formula for a high T metal."

"What happened after that?" Brock asked.

"I told him we couldn't source the yttrium-hydrogen compound he showed. It couldn't be done in a lab. It required extreme heat and pressure, with the right combination of elements. I never heard from him after that."

"We have the yttrium-hydrogen compound now. If I bring some of it to you, can you see if it has any value?"

"Certainly. We'll be able to tell if the formula yields any results. Our lab is near I-75 and Athens-Boonesboro Road. Do you know where that is?"

Brock replied, "I grew up a couple of miles from there. Give me the exact address and I'll drop a sample of the material off at your office on Monday morning. Do you have the recipe?"

"Probably do. If you have it, bring it along," Maupin suggested. "I just texted our address."

"How long does it take to make an evaluation?" Brock inquired.

"A couple of weeks max. If the compound you have is valuable to us, I'll make an offer for it."

"Great. What time do you open?"

"Eight o'clock."

Brock looked at the ladies and smiled. "Now we know the whole story of Saul Sardis. Your dad hired him to find a formula. Sardis saw how valuable the yttrium-hydrogen compound was that Garrison had on his property, and he had to have it. We wrecked all that, so he's leaving town."

"If he's out of Kentucky by tomorrow night, I want to mark this case closed," Maude said.

Brock took issue. "When we learn the value of the metal on the mountain and I collect from the guy who dented my car, Solomon Pergamos, then the case will be closed."

Valerie said to Ruby, "I hope we have a chance to go dancing again."

"Me too."

Maude asked her husband, "Are we ready to head out?"

"Yes. To Arlena Harring's. I need to find out who she was with last night," Brock answered in a determined tone.

———

Arlena heard the Lamborghini drive up. She waited for the Hazard visitors to knock before she went to the door. "Hey, my dance friends are here. Come in out of the cold." She had on a blue sweater and black slacks and wasn't wearing any makeup, which she didn't need anyway.

"Thanks."

"What brought you folks around this afternoon?"

"I thought I saw you last night at the dance hall in Louisville. You, and whomever you were with, split up when I tried to catch you. Made me a little suspicious." The Skinners dropped in behind Arlena as she led them into the living room.

"You're mistaken. I wasn't there. I had dinner with the CFO of the art store I used to work at. He can vouch for me."

"You mean the guy who laundered your money?" Arlena stopped and turned to peer at Brock but had nothing to say. "I know all about where and how the money from Cru's art sale has been moved around. You're a wealthy woman now. I also know that you and Omar parted ways. You might want to consider the CFO on the rebound. I told him to learn how to dance."

"You've talked to him?"

"Sure. He's a nice enough fellow. Anyone willing to break the law for a woman has pretty much proven his worth."

Maude uncharacteristically joined in the repartee. "If you take up with him, the two of you can join our dance group. Last night there were ten of us at the Latin club. We had a super time."

"Was Omar there?" Arlena asked.

"Yes. He was with Dee Wathen from the recording studio."

Arlena spat, "Figures. I bet she's a harpy. That relationship won't last long."

"If you're not interested in the CFO, who have you set your cap for?" Brock wanted to know.

"Paul Sardis, as he's now known. Please take a seat."

"That's a bit of a shocker," Brock retorted. "He strikes me as being a bad egg. Marcel thinks he might be the antichrist."

Arlena shook her head in disgust. "He loves me."

"Oh, really?" Maude uttered dryly.

"Yes. I can prove it." She went into the kitchen, returned with an envelope in her hand, and took out a card that had a green-and-orange Rothko on the front. "Have a look." She handed it to Brock.

"May I read it out loud?"

"Go right ahead."

"My dearest Arlena. When I saw you in that Greek lunch place for the first time on the arm of a guy who I later learned was Omar Cru, I couldn't take my eyes off you. When I heard you had broken up with him, I was thrilled you agreed to go out with me. You are the most incredibly beautiful woman I've ever met. I love you with everything in my soul. I'm moving to California and hope you will join me there, where we can marry. You'll never find another man who loves you more than I do. Love, Paul Sardis.'" Brock focused on Arlena. "Sardis is one sharp cookie. If you go to California, you'll never be seen or heard from again. When they find you dead, this note will keep him from being accused of your demise."

"I'm willing to take that chance. I'm going with him. He's an exciting person. The CFO is a bore."

Brock stood and said, "We won't take up any more of your time. Maude, honey, shall we head for home?"

"Lead the way. Nice to see you again, Arlena."

Brock stopped and turned to say, "When you were cruising, I broke into this house and found a memory stick of one of Cru's paintings and saw where the printer had been taken out. A funny thing occurred when I was leaving. The master of the Sardis house, Solomon Pergamos, jumped out of the closet and tried to kill me. He put a huge dent in my car out there. Now, how strange is that?"

"Are you trying to be funny? None of that happened."

"Go outside and look at the back of my Lamborghini. You think I'd do that myself?"

She rushed over to the front window and sang out, "Good Lord."

When the Skinners got home, Brock went for a jog with Truman tagging along. Maude rode over to the winery to make sure everything was running smoothly.

Paul Sardis parked his rental car outside Faith Church in Peytona at 9:50 Sunday morning. The clouds were low, and a persistent nippy breeze made him reflect on how nice it would be to get back to California where the mild weather never disappointed. He went inside to find the pastor, who spotted him as he came through the door. "What a privilege to have you come and speak to the congregation, Professor Sardis. Everyone is anxious to hear about your encounter with God."

Sardis, wearing a dark gray suit and light gray tie with red dots the size of pin heads, swept his gaze around to check out the religious symbols in the stained-wood sanctuary. The organist pounded out a famous hymn while folks streamed in to find a seat. The doors in the transepts were open, and savvy members snuck in that way to secure spots up front.

At ten o'clock, the professor and retinue of clergy took seats near the altar. Fifteen minutes into the service, the pastor introduced Sardis and invited him to share his testimony. Paul sauntered up to the lectern but didn't speak right off. When he did, he said, "The Bible says in Hebrews that faith is being sure of what we hope for and certain of what we do not see. All of us pray for strong faith, and in my case, the God of the Bible did something far more remarkable. I wasn't even a doubting Thomas before my experience. I was sure that God was invented.

"I have spent my work life developing artificial intelligence. I was convinced that somewhere in the universe, an advanced civilization thousands of years ahead of ours had already achieved a level of understanding of the cosmos that allowed it to manipulate the laws of science as if it were God. There was something I couldn't reconcile though, so I downplayed it. The fact that with more technology comes greater evil. And in the end, if evil cannot be stopped, who will save us? My friends, that person is Jesus Christ.

"Like Saul of Tarsus, God spoke to me and said to stop persecuting Him. He made His point by putting my brain in another man's body for a short time to get my attention. You can believe it or not, but I know without a shadow of a doubt that God is in control and that Jesus Christ has defeated Satan and the evil in this world. So, be strong in your faith, brothers and sisters. Your hope in the Lord is well founded."

Suddenly, one of the transept doors slammed shut and a creature with a plasticine complexion marched toward the lectern where Paul Sardis was standing. The intruder announced to the congregation in a guttural voice, "This man is the antichrist."

Sardis pivoted to face the accuser and muttered, *"Et tu, Brute?"*

The creature took his left arm and used it like an axe to break the neck of Paul Sardis with a downward chop. Before the professor hit the ground, the murderer was moving at high speed toward the door he entered. Several people in the congregation screamed as chaos overtook Faith Church. One man had the presence of mind to call the police, while another ran out to see what was happening. A black sedan had already gotten a hundred yards away from the church, barreling south on Waddy Road, and the license plate had tape over it so the number could not be read.

The police car arrived at the church twelve minutes later. It took the officers five minutes to listen to what happened and come up with a plan to catch the black sedan carrying the killer. By that time, the getaway car could have either crossed over I-64 or taken the interstate east or west. Roadblocks were set up at all points south of Peytona. Unfortunately, the prey had been switched at once into a white car that doubled back and vanished to the north. The police quickly learned who the dead man was and sent detectives to the house he'd lived in the past five years. The man who answered the door was getting groceries when the murder occurred, and he could prove it.

When Brock and Maude got out of church, a news flash reported that an unidentified person or thing had killed Paul Sardis at approximately 10:15 that morning while he was speaking to the congregation of Faith Church in Peytona. Brock looked up the story on the computer when they got home. Maude queried, "Who did it?"

"Can't worry about that now. I need to reach Omar Cru. I have his number."

Omar picked up. "Yes?"

"Sardis has been murdered. The police will be crawling all over the place, and it won't take long for them to hunt you down. They'll probably get a warrant to search your house."

"Huh? Who could have done such a thing?"

"Listen. You need to get rid of those half-finished canvases and anything else that could tie you to Sardis. It would be a good idea to set up your studio as if you were getting ready to do more artwork."

"Okay. I can do that," Cru replied unsteadily.

"Here's the problem. They're going to ask you when you first met Sardis and the last time you saw him."

"I was only with him one time, at that Greek lunch place. Everything else we planned and did came through Arlena. I practiced that brain-switch business with her, not him."

"That's good," Brock said exuberantly. "They'll also want the details of the brain-switch event. You'll have to say you really don't know what happened. That's bending the truth, but it can't be helped."

"If you say so."

"Here's what counts the most. Do you have an alibi for where you were at ten fifteen this morning?"

"Ironclad. I was at the university library looking up the artwork of Mark Rothko. Two students who work there took me to the right section. I checked out one of the books about that time."

"Excellent. You'll live through this unless you get hauled into court and are asked to tell your story under oath," Brock reported to Cru to make him understand the fine line he was walking.

"Why are you helping me?"

"Because your crime was victimless. I don't want a lot of innocent people getting hurt."

Omar reminded Brock, "Not exactly. Someone killed the man who came to Kentucky working a lot of angles to get rich. What good is the money to him now?"

"Maybe he can use it to buy his way into heaven." After Brock hung up, he turned to his wife and said, "We've gotten this thing wrong. Sardis didn't sell his house to Solomon Pergamos. He may have been the master of the house, but he's an android."

"What's that?"

"A robot that looks and acts like a human, programmed by artificial intelligence. The very same one who killed Saul Sardis."

"You mean like the terminator in that movie?" she asked, still confused.

"Yes."

"From what I can tell, the person behind this must be either Omar Cru, Arlena Harring, Abner Giles, Titus Remington, or Ruby Lynch. Am I right?" Maude gestured for her husband to answer the sixty-four-thousand-dollar question.

"You're only partially right. I need to run up to Lexington this afternoon to find out for sure."

Brock called Marcel as he was driving north to see if his brother-in-law thought his theory of the murder had any major holes in it. There were a few, and Marcel, being the brains of the operation, plugged them.

CHAPTER 30

The door to Saul's former house swung open, and when Brock saw who it was, he knew that he and Marcel had at least gotten some things right. "Well, well, if it isn't Carl Logano. I take it you quit Python Deco and decided to trade the rat race in for the good life here in horse country."

"I'm sorry, I don't remember your name."

"That won't work, Carl. You were with Arlena Harring at Vamonos a Bailar on Friday night and took flight when you recognized me. She told you who I was, and you're smart enough to recall me coming to your office a few weeks ago."

Logano lowered his head and blinked his watery eyes. "Oh, man, the police were just here for an hour grilling me. I'm in a fog."

"Are you going to invite me in?"

"Might as well." He threw both hands in the direction of the living room where Brock had once spent time with Sardis. Most of the furniture had been removed save two side chairs. "I've only been here three days, and I'm embroiled in Saul's murder. I did not kill him. I was at the grocery store at that time."

"Let me start out by saying I'm not interested in pinning anything on you. I'm not wearing a wire or working with the police. All I ask is that you listen to my story and throw in a few edits that won't incriminate you in any way."

Logano glared askance, looking as though he had a bitter taste in his mouth. "This is your show. Raise the curtain," he suggested.

"You told me you met Solomon Pergamos soon after he moved in with Sardis six or seven years ago. You knew he was an android because I think you helped Sardis find one that looked like Pergamos. You suspected Sardis of doing that because he may have murdered the human version of Solomon and needed to cover it up. He killed him so he wouldn't have to split the profits from the printer technology patent they held."

"I did meet Solomon living in Saul's house."

"Sardis recommended you take his place when he got promoted to CEO of Python Deco. He apparently did not have the pull to get you promoted to CEO when he left the company, and you told me you had one foot out the door when we talked."

"As you can see, both feet are now here in Kentucky," he commented glibly.

"I think I know what happened. A month ago, Sardis called you up and said he needed to ship Solomon back to California to have an arm repaired. He also told you he was leaving Kentucky and wanted to sell his house. He suggested you buy it under your real name but go by the name Solomon Pergamos, master of the house, which would help continue his cover. To motivate you to do the deal, he agreed to loan you money from Cadmius Corporation that you wouldn't have to pay back. You, in turn, could keep some of it and pay him a big price for his house."

"He said Lexington was the center of the universe. When I visited here, I saw what he meant. California is getting harder to live in these days," Carl admitted.

"So, you came to town on Thursday, closed on the house Friday afternoon, and went dancing with Arlena Harring on Friday night. Sardis had everything loaded up on Saturday, ready to head out. I suppose Solomon was in a box on the back of the moving van."

"I don't know how he got out, but he must have. It was clearly him who killed Saul. I guess he's gone missing now," Logano explained.

Brock thought he was lying. "How did you meet Arlena Harring?"

"I think she found me the same way you did. About three weeks ago, she came to my office at Python Deco. I had already put in my notice that I was quitting. I told her I had bought Saul's house and would be moving to Kentucky soon, and she offered to show me around when I got here."

Based on what Carl told him, Brock began to embrace a much darker view of what happened. He said, "When you think about it, having an android kill someone is a perfect crime as long as the machine is destroyed before it talks."

———————

Though the winter season wouldn't officially be ushered in for a few more days, it had already made its presence known on Monday the eighteenth of December by way of a nineteen-degree thermometer reading. Brock had on his winter coat and hood up when he stepped into the lab where Ryan Maupin said to drop off the yttrium-hydrogen compound. Maupin himself took the material and promised he'd analyze it as soon as possible.

Brock set a course again to Arlena Harring's house. She was there alone, in a depressed mood. She stated the obvious. "You're back."

"I am. You look unhappy. Anything I can do to cheer you up?"

"Brock, you have no idea," she snapped back.

"I'd like to talk about it with you. May I come in?" he asked gently. She stepped aside, and they took seats next to each other in the sitting room. "I'm pretty sure the getaway for the android who killed Sardis was a two-person operation."

"What do you mean?"

"A black sedan took the murderer south from the church on Waddy Road, and I suspect that it got shot in the head and put into another car that doubled back and went north before the police arrived on the scene. The driver of the second car was a man whom I'm guessing is a loyal friend of yours."

"Why are you telling me this?"

"I saw you with Carl Logano on Friday night at the dance club. The two of you avoided me. That raised a flag. I started thinking that both of you were in the same position—kill or be killed."

She began trembling, and tears ran down her face. "I don't know what you're talking about."

"It's logical to me that the easiest way to get rid of the remains of the android would be to bury them. The police will be checking out the property of anyone who met Sardis. I would suggest you call your CFO buddy and the two of you make sure there's nothing here that could get you in trouble."

Arlena read Brock's comments as if he were trying to help her. She was on the verge of erupting emotionally. "I can't believe where my life has gone the last five years. Before I got hooked up with Sardis, I was a good person. He ruined me. That bastard could make doing bad things seem good. He could justify anything. He turned me into a piece of human garbage. I don't even like myself anymore."

"I'm not sure how you got him to write that note. It may be enough to keep you out of prison."

She replied, "He wanted me to move to California with him. It was the quid pro quo for me."

Brock called Marcel on the way back to Hazard. "Carl Logano got Solomon Pergamos out of the crate that was on the back of Saul's moving van on Saturday afternoon. Arlena must have picked him up and took him to her house. The next morning, she drove him to the church, and her CFO friend was waiting in the second car. He must have shot Solomon and took him north, eventually ending up at Arlena's house, where they buried him."

"Don't discount the possibility that Solomon is alive, living in the secret basement at Arlena's house. She can make men do what she wants, at least most of the time. Who's to say she didn't sweet talk an android into following orders, and Logano isn't part of the killing."

"Could be," Brock acknowledged. He then called Abner to discuss the murder of Sardis and tell him there was no sense continuing the lawsuit to vacate the sale of Cru's property.

———————

The Friday morning before Christmas Day, which fell on Monday, was when Ryan Maupin called Brock to follow up on the yttrium-hydrogen compound. "We tested the material and ran the formula. All indications are that the metal you brought us works very well. We'd like to buy a hundred pounds of it from you."

"Okay. How are we going to arrive at a fair price?"

"I'll be frank with you, Mr. Skinner, there are people in the superconductor business who would pay you a lot of money for every ounce you have. You can go peddling it around and find someone to pay top dollar. I'd rather appeal to your sense of fairness. How much of the stuff do you think you have?"

Brock exhaled audibly. "As little as a thousand pounds, and as much as a hundred thousand pounds."

"Holy smokes, man, you're sitting on fortune," Ryan said too loudly.

"How about this for a frame of reference: I've got a million and a quarter invested in the rights to the material, and I'd like to make a little profit on the downstroke."

"Okay. I'll give you five hundred an ounce for two hundred pounds of metal. I believe that comes to one million six hundred thousand. I would also like to have right of first refusal for the balance of the material. If you want, I can get the permit to do the mining and send a reputable outfit to the site to extract what's there."

Brock replied enthusiastically, "Ryan, I hope you're as honest as you sound. You've got a deal." Maude came into his office at the house and wanted to know who he was talking to. "I just sold a little bit of the metal up on the mountain for one point six million."

"Hot dog! How much is the entire strike worth?"

"As much as eight hundred million," he reported with faux diffidence. "I'm going to cut our dance friends in. That'll make 'em like me."

"Incredible! You are the luckiest man who ever lived," she barked. "Ruby will be able to start a catering business, and Sadie can have her own recording studio."

"I like to think I'm blessed. I'm going to run over to Abner's house and talk to Sadie Kirkham."

"Take Truman with you. He needs something to do."

The man and his dog took the winery truck, and Dee let them in when he pressed the buzzer. Truman treated Dee like he did Maude, causing her to fawn over him for a few minutes. "How are things going over here?" Brock asked cheerfully.

"Abner's not around. He's going to load up his stuff next week and move back to Nashville. I'm not sure what I'm doing, and I don't think Sadie has firmed up her plans either."

"That's why I came over. I wanted to let you ladies know that you can stay here rent free for as long as you like." Truman looked at her as if he understood Brock's offer and wanted to hear her response.

She smiled, swaying her head. "What a generous offer. Let me find Sadie so you can tell her."

While Dee was gone, Brock's phone pinged. The camera in Maude's office that was trained on the Giles entrance gate picked something up. Brock started running through the house when he saw the open gates and what the picture showed. "Sadie, Dee, where are you?"

They both appeared quicky. Sadie asked, "What is it?"

Brock began firing instructions. "Dee, call the police and tell them to get over here right away. Do either one of you know if there is a firearm in the house?"

Dee said steadily, "Yes. A shotgun in the kitchen closet."

"Go get it and the shells for it. I want both of you to stay back down that hall on the far side of the front door. Someone will be coming through it within seconds. If he calls you by name, say that you're over here." Dee returned with the rifle and a box of shells within a quarter of a minute. Brock put two shells in the barrels and four more in his pants pockets. He and Truman hid around the corner of a side hall, out of sight.

The door latch made a sweeping noise, and into the house came a mysterious figure. He kept looking straight ahead and then said in a monotone voice, "I'm searching for Dee Wathen."

Dee replied, "I'm here."

A split second later, Brock hollered, "Get him, Truman!" The dog charged, leapt in the air, and went for the neck. The gnarling sound was gruesome. The figure staggered and tried to swat the dog off. Brock yelled again, "Down, boy!" The artifice, who was Solomon Pergamos, began charging in Brock's direction. The boom of the shotgun was so loud that it stunned Truman. Solomon's head fragmented into several pieces, and Brock discharged the second shell to make sure the job was finished.

Sadie came running, saying, "What's going on?" She looked at the floor and pointed. "What is that?"

"It's what's left of an android impersonating a dead man by the name of Solomon Pergamos."

"Why is it here?"

"Omar Cru's ex-girlfriend sent it to kill Dee out of vicious anger," Brock revealed. Dee squinted one eye and raised the corner of her mouth.

Police entered the house seconds later. Brock told them some of what he knew before calling Maude to fill her in on the action. She only had one thing to say: "It's over now."

The grainy fog dulling the sunlight on New Year's Day looked and felt more like suspended water droplets than a smoky mist. The temperature had reached forty-one degrees by noon, the time the Skinners and Sutherlands sashayed through a Turfway Park entrance on the Kentucky side of Cincinnati. Thoroughbred racing kicked off the new year in the Bluegrass State at that track, which, of course, was not in the same league as Keeneland but offered something exciting to do for those who were starved for live racing action and not hungover.

Brock had rented the most expensive suite available, and when he drove up in his new orange Lamborghini that he traded his dented one for, word spread through the place like wildfire that some high rollers would be walking the dog. The men had on sport coats, no ties. The women wore slacks and sweaters. Once seated, Brock mentioned to Marcel, "I'm betting what you're betting, and I better win."

"Fear not. We'll win at least enough to pay for lunch." Marcel turned to look out over the track. "This reminds me of when we were at Keeneland and the whole saga of Sardis began."

Valerie said, "Isn't it funny how good things often come from bad people."

"You mean like Sardis possibly finding the formula for a life-changing energy source?" Maude threw out as an example.

"Not to mention Cru's art and Remy's songs, both exceptional art. That reminds me of another arrogant, rebellious murderer who produced some pretty good stuff," Brock said.

"Who's that?" Marcel asked.

"Michaelangelo Merisi."

"Never heard of him."

"He's better known as Caravaggio." Brock watched the racehorses being walked to the paddock from the barn, covered with blankets. He wondered if Mr. Prospector had run there when he was alive.

www.ingramcontent.com/pod-product-compliance
Lightning Source LLC
Chambersburg PA
CBHW070450300726

48975CB00007B/2109